DANGER FROM THE DEEP

Haakon slid backward under the weight of the water, struggling frantically to get the golden ax unslung from its sheath. He righted himself, staggering, as something more powerful than an iron band, and smelling foully of ancient evil and decay, wrapped itself around his ribs. It was the *kraken*! Up above him, he could see its eyes glowing with a ghastly phosphorescence as a beak-shaped maw opened and closed.

Haakon swung the ax and felt it bite through the *kraken*'s flesh, but two more arms were entangling him now, and something burned like red-hot iron across his back.

"Thor aid me!" he cried. But life—or death—was in Haakon's hands alone.

D1042979

HAAKON 4

THE WAR GOD

Eric Neilson

TM

Created by the producers of
Wagons West, White Indian, and
Saga of the Southwest.

Chairman of the Board: Lyle Kenyon Engel

BANTAM BOOKS
TORONTO • NEW YORK • LONDON • SYDNEY • AUCKLAND

HAAKON 4: THE WAR GOD
A Bantam Book / December 1984

Produced by Book Creations, Inc.
Chairman of the Board: Lyle Kenyon Engel

ISBN 0-553-24541-4

Published simultaneously in the United States and Canada

Bantam Books are published by Bantam Books, Inc. Its trade-
mark, consisting of the words "Bantam Books" and the por-
trayal of a rooster, is Registered in U.S. Patent and Trademark
Office and in other countries. Marca Registrada. Bantam
Books, Inc., 666 Fifth Avenue, New York, New York 10103.

PRINTED IN THE UNITED STATES OF AMERICA

O   0 9 8 7 6 5 4 3 2 1

Author's Note

Although Haakon Olesson and his ship the *Raven* are my own invention, Viking sea-rovers did indeed land on the eastern shores of North America and found colonies centuries before Columbus. This book is dedicated to that spirit of exploration and adventure, which has left its mark so deeply in the history of America, and to the daring seafarers who were the first to touch America's shores. There is something of the Vikings left in all of us.

Contents

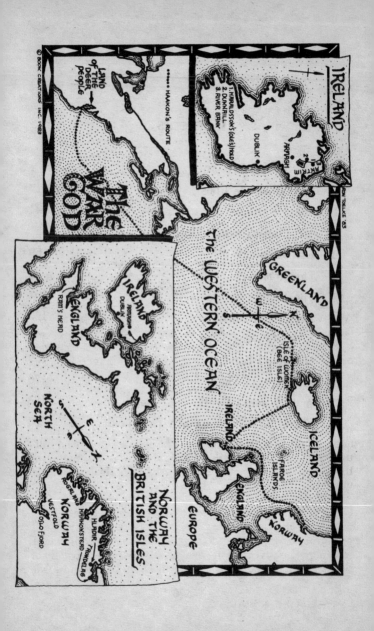

I

The Thing of Hladir

Haakon Olesson ran his hand through his dark beard and frowned to keep the men from Rogaland from interrupting him while he thought. They ringed him silently: hopeful, pale eyes in weather-beaten faces. Their expressions said, *This is a trouble for the jarl to see to. The jarl will find a way out.*

After a time had gone by, the eldest of them said tentatively, "Jarl Haakon?"

Haakon looked up. "Yes, yes, I am considering." He should have expected this, he thought. He had rescued from their parents' murderers the twenty stolen children of a slaughtered Rogaland village. Now it seemed that the children were going hungry and Haakon was not free of the matter after all. He was their savior. The five men from Rogaland looked at him expectantly.

Haakon shifted on his bench in the timber meeting hall that belonged to the Thing, the law court, of Hladir and refrained from glaring at the Thing men who sat, unhelpful, to either side of him. This was no matter of theirs, and they were content to watch Jarl Haakon wrestle with it.

Hladir was a Trondelag town built by old Jarl Haakon Grjotgardsson's family. Now that Haakon Grjotgardsson was dead, Haakon Olesson was rapidly becoming the most powerful jarl in the Trondelag. Hladir was still the center of things, however, so it was to Hladir that the men of Rogaland had come, after a bad winter and while the roads were still barely passable, seeking advice and, unspoken but evident, wanting the jarl to *do* something. That Rogaland was no part of the Trondelag or of Jarl Haakon's responsibility made no difference; Harud Olafsson's murderous men had been in Norway only because Harud was at war with Haakon Olesson. The Rogaland village had got in the way of Harud's black mood. Haakon Olesson had rescued the children and brought them home to Norway from Ireland. He had killed Harud, who had enslaved them—never mind that Haakon had had other reasons for killing him. Now that the children were going hungry because of a lack of food in Rogaland, surely Haakon Olesson would take a hand in the matter again. Even the Thing of Hladir seemed to feel that that was so. They observed him complacently: a dark bear of a man, broad shouldered and square faced, not so tall as most Norse, but strong, with a face that was humorous and stubborn. Haakon Olesson had a reputation for fair dealing, of which Haakon Olesson was now uncomfortably aware.

Haakon fidgeted with the gold cuff on his wrist and the embroidered sleeve of his shirt. He had come dressed in his finest clothes, as befitted a man considering a matter of importance. The men from Rogaland had also worn their best, newly washed and much patched. If Haakon gave them money, which he could afford to do, it would only solve the problem until the money ran out.

"Are there none of the children's family left alive?"

The gray-haired man shook his head. "One or two with uncles or cousins. No more." He spread his hands apologetically; old hands, worn from years at the plow. "Nearly every man and woman over fifteen died when Harud Olafsson's men came, jarl. They spared the children only to take for ransom."

Haakon nodded. The Thing of Hladir looked shocked. The old man didn't want to say that that was Haakon's fault, but Haakon couldn't help feeling that it was. "How have you managed so far?" he asked gently.

"We of the other villages have gone begging," the old man said frankly. "The fields that Harud Olafsson burned have gone to ruin, and we haven't the men to reclaim them. Every village in Rogaland has given its extra stores to make up the difference, but that is gone now, too."

"There wasn't so very much to start with," one of the other men said, and the elder glared at him to be quiet. The younger man twisted his cap in gnarled hands. Even that was patched. Life in the villages could be harsh. They could ill afford extra mouths to feed when there were no laboring hands to go with them.

"We have done our best, jarl. We do not abandon children. But their health is not good, and some of them have troubles in the mind. They wake screaming at night."

Small wonder, Haakon thought, for babes who had seen their mothers slaughtered, and then been crowded on a ship for Ireland. In his mind he saw small Asa, his own daughter, smiling up at him, and he winced.

"And many of them are so young, jarl. While our women are looking to the children, they cannot work in the fields."

The Thing of Hladir tut-tutted. Every hand would be needed at the spring planting. Haakon thought of Asa again. His English wife, Rosamund, spent most of her time just in seeing to Asa, although admittedly Asa took more watching than most. But Rosamund was a jarl's wife with thralls to do her work. The men of Rogaland weren't lying when they said so many extra children kept the women from their labors.

"And what of King Harald Fairhair in Vestfold?" Haakon said. He knew the answer to that, he thought, but it wouldn't hurt the Thing of Hladir to hear it, too. "Harald counts Rogaland under his protection. Have you gone to him?"

"Aye, for all the good it has done us!" the younger man burst out, and there was a chorus of grumbles behind him from the rest.

"King Harald has sent messages," the old man said wearily. "King Harald sympathizes, but King Harald has sent no silver."

Haakon didn't look surprised, and he noted that the Thing of Hladir didn't, either. Harald Fairhair's ambition was to extend his influence over the whole of Norway, including the Trondelag, a point over which the king was currently at odds with Haakon Olesson. He would have little time for orphans in Rogaland.

Haakon tugged his beard again and abruptly hid a grin behind his hand. He was not unsympathetic to the men from Rogaland, but certainly their motherless children were an embarrassment to Harald Fairhair, and one that might earn him an ill name if the word got around. Harald would be grateful—unofficially—to the man who removed that embarrassment. And Haakon had to make some sort of peace with Harald if he was ever going to be able to leave Norway again and keep King Harald from taking over Haakonstead and the Trondelag while he was gone. The last time he had left—to hunt down Harud Olafsson—Haakon had returned to find another Trondelag jarl besieging Haakonstead, with King Harald's acquiescence if not his blessing. Certainly there was a need to put a stop to that.

Haakon stood up, dark bearded and bulky among the tall, fair men from Hladir. "To speak truth, I don't know what is best to be done. But I will send wagonloads of food and some silver in the meantime to buy extra grain, since Harald Fairhair has declined to do so."

The Thing of Hladir nodded approvingly. It wasn't their silver.

"We are grateful, jarl," the old man said. "That will help for a season."

"And no more. Yes, I know. I will think of some other answer by season's end." There was assurance in his voice, and the men from Rogaland nodded, pleased.

The food and money would give him breathing space, Haakon thought, for a season, maybe for two if need be. He would ask Rosamund to think on it; orphaned children would immediately gain his wife's sympathy. Nothing that was motherless went uncared for in Rosamund's domain, from a thrall-child to a lamb whose ewe had died in the bearing. Haakon put his hand on the Rogaland elder's shoulder, a brief touch of reassurance. "It will be seen to." He hoped the "how" of that would come to him. Promises made could not be gone back on, and Haakon had no wish for twenty extra children in Haakonstead.

Behind him the Thing looked grave and beneficent.

They would take credit for any solution he could come to, Haakon thought. He felt his temper starting to slip and bit down on it. The lawspeaker of the Thing of Hladir was a pompous fool, but it would not become the jarl to say so, so he coughed and held his tongue. There was a fire burning in the central hearth, and the room was close and smoky.

The men of Rogaland turned to leave and collided in the doorway with a man on the run.

"Jarl!" Thorfinn Solvisson, who was second helmsman in Haakon's service, burst in. He ignored the men of the Thing, who stared at him in disapproval.

"There is fighting, jarl. And a man dead." Thorfinn was breathing hard, and there was a red gash across his knuckles that was probably from someone's teeth.

"Thor's hammer," Haakon said in disgust. "Can I not turn my back on you for an hour's time? Are you children?"

Thorfinn ignored the jarl's temper, which he was used to. "It's that young fool Donal, jarl," he said grimly. "He has killed a man, and now the man's mates are shouting for the Thing to come and name Donal outlaw. If they don't kill him first," he added. An uproar of voices had begun to swell outside the meeting hall.

Haakon swore and picked up his ax, which he had laid on the floor beside him for the meeting. Behind him the members of the Thing held forth in shocked voices among themselves.

"Where is he?" Haakon said.

"In that alehouse just above the fjord," Thorfinn said. "There was us and the crew of a *knarr* from Jaeren. You had best come, jarl. They're still fighting."

The men from Rogaland ducked out of the way as the jarl strode by furiously, ax in hand. He pushed through the crowd outside, and they eyed the ax respectfully and gave way. The blade had a burnished glow like gold, but it was a businesslike weapon in the jarl's hand. Also it was said to be magic.

Haakon marched down the wet wooden street that ran through the center of Hladir, cursing Donal as he went. A crowd of shouting crewmen from the *knarr*, small

boys, men of Hladir, and the lawspeaker of the Thing
trailed in his wake.

The alehouse was a thatched hall with a tilting sign,
set above the fjord side. The sign bore a sheaf of barley in
fading paint. A man sat in a pile of dirty snow beneath it,
spitting teeth into his hand.

Haakon kicked the door open. A furious stream of
Gaelic directed him to Donal, lying in a corner with two of
the *knarr*'s crew on top of him. A third was pounding his
head against the wooden floor while Donal kicked and
fought. The rest of the men whom Haakon had brought to
Hladir with him were still on their feet, more or less,
brawling among the overturned benches and the shards of
smashed beer horns. A thin man in a dirty apron, who
appeared to be the proprietor, brought a broken bench
down on the head of Haakon's man Hjalmar, then swung it
again at a red-haired crewman from the *knarr*. One body
lay very still in a pool of blood beneath a table.

Haakon swung the flat of his ax blade into the fray to
clear a path and pulled one of the men off Donal. Re-
leased, Donal's fist shot up into the face of the man who
had him by the throat. Haakon flung the first man away
from him and grabbed another. He was relieved to see
that so far no one else had had the stupidity to pull a
knife, but he thought it was only a matter of time. He
slammed the man he had hold of against the side of an ale
barrel, dropped him, and picked up the third. He kicked
Donal. "Get out of here, you fool, before you're killed."

Donal looked up, with fresh blood running from his
nose down over the old scar on his cheek. There was blood
in his dark, curling hair too. He was thin and muscular,
with the wiry strength of a hill pony, and the look of the
Gael about him. His normally cheerful face and blue eyes
were murderous. He stumbled to his feet, knife in hand.

"*Put that away!*"

Donal looked at Haakon and hesitated.

"Thor's hammer, put it *away*! You've done enough."

Donal sheathed the knife. "Yon thief went for me
first." He glowered at the dead man under the table.

A piece of broken board sailed past Haakon's ear, and
he spun around. He swung the flat of the ax again.

"Peace!" he bellowed. The combatants slackened, first his own, then those from the *knarr*. The proprietor was steadily shouting curses at both sides while a river of ale ran over his feet from a broken barrel.

"*Peace!*" Haakon roared.

A man with his hair in two braids, who looked like he might be the captain of the *knarr*, pushed his men out of the way to take stock of the newcomer.

"Call them off," Haakon shouted, "or there'll be another death." He hefted the golden ax.

The captain spat blood into the straw on the floor. "Hold!"

The men began to back away from each other. The dead man lay under the table, a still, silent accusation. Haakon kicked a bench out of his way and glared at both sides in turn.

"Hear me!"

They looked at him sullenly. The alehouse door sagged on one hinge, and interested faces peered around it. The crewmen who had followed Thorfinn to the meeting hall tried to push their way in again, and the townsmen of Hladir pushed them back.

"Now I will hear what has happened," Haakon said. "One at a time. If there is more blood to be shed, I will do it with this." Haakon held the ax up to the face of the captain of the *knarr*.

The captain's eyes were blazing, but Haakon was a jarl as well as a Trondelag man, and the captain was from Jaeren. Town sympathy would not be with him. "He is mad." The captain pointed a finger at Donal, who gave him back a black look.

Haakon looked at Donal consideringly. There was no man who was closer to the jarl than Donal MacRae, but his moods blew from cheer to fury like the wind. This was not the first time that Donal's unbridled temper had made trouble. "What happened?"

Donal shrugged and swayed a little on his feet. Haakon decided he was probably drunk—or it might only be the result of having had his head pounded on the floor. Donal put a hand on a table to steady himself. His blue eyes were as bright as a snake's. And, like a snake, he was quick to strike, Haakon thought, angry with him.

"Well?"

"He drew his knife first," Donal said. "He would have killed me if I hadn't killed him."

A furious babble of protest erupted, and Haakon shouted it into silence. "Why?"

"He could not keep a civil tongue in his head about the Scots, so it may be I said a thing or two about Jaeren," Donal said.

"Aye." Hjalmar Sitricsson pulled himself up off the floor and rubbed the back of his head where the landlord had hit it with a bench. "That one picked the quarrel." He jabbed a finger at the dead man.

"Svein never drew blade until this one had!" the *knarr*'s captain shouted. "He will be outlawed if there is any honor in Hladir! And I claim weregild! For myself and for his brother in Jaeren!"

"Outlaw! *Outlaw!* OUTLAW!" The *knarr*'s crew stamped their feet on the floor, howling for justice.

Haakon took a good grip on the golden ax, holding it in front of him where it could be seen plainly. A movement at his shoulder told him that Thorfinn Solvisson was standing behind him. "You." Haakon pointed at the proprietor. "*You* tell me what happened."

The lean man wiped his hands on his apron, which looked not to have been washed in a twelve-month. "They were drunk." He glared first at Donal and then at the body on the floor.

"I am not needing you to tell me that," Haakon said. "Who drew a blade first?"

The alehouse keeper shrugged. He didn't seem to care greatly. Or maybe the ring of flushed, sullen faces around him made him wary of choosing a side. "I didn't see. But who is going to pay for my ale?" He kicked angrily at the muck of ale and straw on the floor. "And for the breakage? I'll have damages from someone, jarl, I am telling you that!"

Haakon looked at the peeling plaster walls and the listing counter. There were holes in the roof thatch. He didn't think it had looked greatly better before the brawl.

"It may be we have done you a favor," he said sourly. "When was the last time this thieves' den was swept out?"

"I'll have damages, jarl," the alehouse keeper said stubbornly, "or I'll take it to the Thing."

"Weregild." The mutter began to swell again among the *knarr*'s crew in the alehouse and those outside who were trying to push their way through the Hladir men.

"If anyone is owed weregild, it's us," Hjalmar Sitricsson growled. He had no great love for Donal MacRae, but Donal was the jarl's man, and that made it a matter of principle. Hjalmar bunched his heavy hands into fists and stared at the crewman nearest him.

"If there is no justice in Hladir, then we will make some," the *knarr*'s captain said ominously. He put his hand on the sword that hung in a sheath at his belt. Outside, the shouting was growing louder, punctuated by the shrill, protesting voice of the Thing's lawspeaker. Haakon thought that they would be brawling there too in a minute.

"*Silence!*" he roared, and even the yelling outside fell into a surprised quiet. He took stock of the furious faces of the *knarr*'s crewmen and the hard, angry eyes of its captain, and silently cursed Donal again. With no clear-cut right or wrong to be found, he would have to let the matter go before the Thing, or there would be trouble and an ill name for himself—a reputation for high-handed injustice and abuse of power. But the Thing of Hladir had best remember who had sent the most animals to the midsummer sacrifice.

"Go and tell yon graybeards that Jarl Haakon wishes them to hear the case," he said over his shoulder to Thorfinn. "And tell them also that Jarl Haakon wishes it heard *now* and not next autumn." When left to their own devices, the Thing men were not known for their speed.

Thorfinn pushed his way through the sagging door into the babble of voices outside. As he let the door swing behind him, the last hinge pulled out and it dropped in the snow. The interested faces surged inward, and Thorfinn shouted for the lawspeaker.

Haakon looked the *knarr*'s captain in the eye. "In the meantime, you and yours will bide by your ship and stay out of Hladir. My men also," he added as the captain opened his mouth to protest.

Haakon took Donal by the arm, none too gently, and they stamped across the broken door and into the cold sunlight. A great crowd had gathered, and somehow a flock of chickens had been let loose in it. A gaggle of small urchins appeared and trailed the jarl and Donal happily down the street. There hadn't been so much excitement in Hladir since last midsummer market day.

"Look you, Haakon, that one drew his knife first. I have told you." Donal sat by the fire on the fjord side with the looming bulk of Haakon's longship *Red Hawk* for a wind shelter. His blue eyes glittered in the firelight, and his fingers moved restlessly across the embroidered leather of his harp bag, but he didn't take the harp out to play it. Haakon thought that Donal likely knew he was at fault nonetheless.

"So you have. And the *knarr*'s crew have told me something different. So it will have to go to the Thing. And next time curb that black temper of yours."

"It may be that I angered him," Donal said stubbornly, "but he drew a blade first. And, look you, in Scotland a clan chief would not be asking another man to decide a quarrel for him."

"I am only a jarl in my own lands, and not a king in the Trondelag," Haakon said, exasperated. "And the Norse do not take kindly to high-handedness." Donal's face looked flushed and the glittering eyes unnaturally bright. Haakon wondered if the pounding his head had taken was making him ill. Better it should have pounded some sense into his Gaelic skull. "If I make myself a name for unfair dealing, no man that I would want will be willing to follow me." He tried to explain it again.

Donal nodded. His hands still roved across the harp bag, never still. "Haakon, I am sorry," he said, almost inaudibly. "It's a curse from God, likely, a temper like mine. I've never been able to put it away when I should." He thought a moment and brightened. "It goes with being a poet maybe."

Haakon snorted. "Gunnar Thorsten has no such affliction." Gunnar, the jarl's skald, usually looked like a man who had just waked up.

Donal nodded, sorrowful again, changeable as the wind. "Maybe it's in the blood then. My folk are said to have the fairies' blood in them a ways back, though you never know if you can believe a thing like that. But I've fought it all my life. I had fits as a child." The ghost of a smile. "Screaming fits that used to send the maids scurrying around like a flock of wet hens. Very satisfactory."

"Better they should have turned you over someone's knee," Haakon suggested. "Play that thing or put it away before you pick all the stitching out."

Donal looked suddenly at what he was doing and stopped, smoothing the soft green leather. "Aye, Fann wouldn't like it, I expect." Fann was Donal's betrothed wife, handfasted with him when they were children, but not yet wed. She had made the harp bag, laboriously stitching it with scenes from the saints' lives, perhaps with an eye to setting him an example. He put the bag down beside him and drew his knees up, wrapping his arms around them, and began to stare at the fire.

Haakon began to wish he had brought Gunnar Thorsten with him after all, although at the time one poet had seemed to be plenty for a three-day trip, and Gunnar was Haakon's steward, who oversaw Haakonstead in the jarl's absence. Rosamund could have managed it as well, Haakon thought, and Gunnar's poetry would have been welcome, if only to blot out the sound of Hjalmar Sitricsson and Hagar the Simple, who were attempting to make up the lack. Hagar sat with his broad back against *Red Hawk's* hull and wet his voice with swallows of beer between verses, and he and his comrades sang untunefully.

Haakon stood up and unrolled the two-man leather sleeping bag he shared with Donal. Most of the others were already in theirs. With Hladir declared off-limits for the sake of peace, there was very little else to do. A quarter mile down the fjord side he could see the fires of the *knarr's* camp, behind the dark outlines of her hull and the crew's tents. Haakon pulled his boots off and prodded Donal with a bare foot. "Go to bed."

Donal nodded again, maybe in agreement, but he

didn't move. Haakon gave up and dragged the sleeping bag into a tent. He wriggled down into his half and pulled his cloak up over his ears to shut out the unsteady chorus from the fireside.

The next morning the Thing of Hladir, unable to devise a reason for delay that would be likely to meet with Jarl Haakon's approval, met to hear the witnesses for both sides.

The *knarr*'s crew were there with their captain, who gave his name as Sigmund Lambasson. They were considerably more sober than the day before but in no more charitable frame of mind. Donal MacRae was sober also and looking subdued, although those who knew him thought that it was mostly on the surface. Jarl Haakon stood beside him, with the rest of the crew behind them; the jarl's men had come to bear witness for Donal, not much caring whether or not they had actually seen the killing. The alehouse keeper appeared, without his grimy apron but otherwise not greatly changed and still unwashed. He eyed the Thing men warily—his establishment had the reputation in Hladir of being a place where a man was unwise to turn his back on his purse—but his jaw was set in a stubborn line. Somebody owed him damages, and somebody, by Frey, was going to pay them.

The lawspeaker of the Thing of Hladir harrumph'd and took quick stock of the situation. He thumped his staff and said that he would now hear witnesses. There was a clamor from all sides at that, and everyone who had anything to say said it all at once. The lawspeaker thumped his staff again, and Haakon bellowed, "*Quiet!*" The lawspeaker glared at him for speaking out of turn but took advantage of the silence. He waved a hand at the nine Thing men seated on their benches. They were the same men who had gathered the day before to hear the Rogaland farmers: landowners and free men of Hladir.

"Does either side make objection to these nine as jurors?"

"How should we be knowing, since they are all Hladir men and none of Jaeren?" the *knarr*'s captain snapped.

"We are seeking men who will be impartial, not

fellow townsmen," the lawspeaker said. "If you want jurors from Jaeren, bring your case to court in Jaeren."

"Mord Asgrimsson trades in Jaeren," the alehouse keeper said suspiciously.

The lawspeaker leaned toward the juror Mord. "Do you trade with Sigmund Lambasson?"

"No."

"Then you are accepted."

"Magnus Styrkasson is nephew to Jarl Haakon's helmsman!" a townsman of Hladir shouted, eager to put in his pennyworth.

"Magnus's uncle died two years ago!" Haakon snapped. "Magnus is no kin to *me!*"

"Accepted," the lawspeaker said.

"Flosi Borksson is second cousin to Erik Alesson!"

Erik Alesson was married to Haakon's mother, Sigrid, and the lawspeaker balked at that. Haakon fidgeted in irritation while they worked out the kinship at great length, naming grandsires and great-grandsires and descent in the female line, and those who were knowledgeable swore to it all. The lawspeaker disqualified Flosi Borksson and named a substitute, who was accepted after suitable wrangling. A Norse court never felt that it was beginning on the right foot unless there had been a preliminary fight over the jurors.

When no one could think of any further arguments, the lawspeaker solemnly intoned the law as it affected this court: All men should swear to speak truly on whatever gods they held most sacred, and both sides should swear that, having brought this case before the Thing, they would abide by the Thing's decision. The lawspeaker cast a wary eye on them at this pronouncement. Sigmund Lambasson looked grim and Donal MacRae rebellious. Sigmund swore readily, on Odin All-Father and Thor Hammerer and his own hope of a fair death, being the one who had asked for a Thing judgment in the first place. Donal, prodded by Haakon, swore on his honor and his Christian god, and the lawspeaker nearly balked at that too, but the look in Haakon's eye convinced him he had better not.

In the end the lawspeaker had very little more suc-

cess in sorting out the rights and wrongs of it all than
Haakon had had. Donal swore flatly, in accented but fluent
Norse, that the dead man had drawn his knife first, and
Hjalmar Sitricsson backed him up. Thorfinn Solvisson said
honestly that he hadn't seen the fight, but that the dead
man had been drunk and making threats.

Sigmund Lambasson and three of his crewmen said
just as firmly that Donal had gone berserk and that the
dead man, Svein, hadn't drawn a knife until then.

"I claim weregild," Sigmund said again. He pushed
his pale braids back from his face and hitched his beaverskin
cloak more tightly around him. Even with the smoking
fire it was cold in the meeting hall, and his breath stood in
puffs of steam in front of his face. "For myself, for the loss
of a crewman, and for Svein's brother in Jaeren. Also we
demand that this one be outlawed from Norse lands." His
blue eyes rested on Donal. "He is a danger to honest
men."

Donal bridled and started forward, and Haakon's fingers dug into his shoulder.

The alehouse keeper, when called upon, said that he
had a broken door, three broken benches, a dozen smashed
beer horns, the loss of a full keg of ale, and who was going
to pay for the damages?

All of this brought no one any closer to the truth. The
lawspeaker sighed and looked dismally at the witnesses.
He had hoped for one impartial man, but the alehouse
wasn't one that the Hladir shopkeepers favored. There had
been no customers except the *knarr*'s crew and the jarl's
men, seeking ale to warm them and keep out boredom
while the jarl was in the Thing hall. And now the jurors
could come to no judgment that wouldn't anger someone.
Everyone in the meeting hall fixed him with expectant
eyes. "We will talk," he said finally. "Go outside and wait."
He put his hands to the fire and rubbed them as they filed
past. He was old and cold, and he didn't want the jarl's
disfavor, but a man was dead, and honor demanded some
justice more than a statement of no decision. When the
hall was empty, he looked back at the jurors, less pompous
and important than he had been. "Does anyone know who
is lying?" he asked.

"All of them likely," Mord Asgrimsson said.

Magnus Styrkasson looked uncomfortable. "None of them maybe. Or they don't *think* they are. When a man has a skinful of ale, he sees what he wants to see."

"Then how do we find a judgment?" another man said. He gestured with an empty hand. "Out of the air?"

"I don't know," the lawspeaker said unhappily. "But there must *be* a judgment, or there may be blood-feud between the jarl and Jaeren, and that will be bad for all of us."

"I've sailed with the jarl," Magnus said. "And I know the Scotsman a little. Maybe you should have disqualified me."

"By Odin's goat, I need *someone* who knows what he's talking about!" the lawspeaker snapped. "You're accounted an honest man, so speak your mind."

"Well, there is a man dead," Magnus said, "and there's no getting around that. And Donal MacRae needs a lesson taught him. You'll find more men than me who will say that."

There was a grumble of assent. Donal's temper was well known.

"He picks a quarrel as easily as breathing," Mord Asgrimsson said. "This is the third this year, but nobody else died."

Magnus chuckled. "That was pure luck, maybe. But also he is a fine poet."

That counted for something—poetry was much respected—and there was another murmur of agreement. The lawspeaker breathed a sigh of relief. He didn't want to push the jarl too far. "And weregild?"

"Some," Mord said, "but not too much. That Svein was no great loss, I'm thinking."

"Hear now the judgment of the Thing of Hladir."

The combatants had filed dutifully back in, but their gaze was suspicious. The lawspeaker fixed them all with an official eye, took a good grip on his staff, and glanced quickly over his shoulder at the nine jurors behind him. The disqualified Flosi Borksson grinned, leaning against the far wall, and blessed his kinship with Erik Alesson.

This was a jury no man with a brain under his hat would
get pleasure from sitting on.

"In the matter of damages claimed by Ulf Ale-Seller,"
the lawspeaker intoned, "the court finds for Ulf and de-
crees that the cost be paid jointly by Sigmund Lambasson
and Haakon Olesson and such of their men as were
present. The determination of which men are liable, the
court leaves to Sigmund Lambasson and Haakon Olesson,"
he added.

Sigmund and Donal glowered at each other, and
Haakon kept his face expressionless. He had expected
something of the sort on this point of the judgment. If he
were going to get angry, he would save it for important
matters.

"In the matter of weregild in the death of Svein
Sigfusson of Jaeren, the court finds Donal MacRae shall
pay to Sigmund Lambasson silver to the amount of the
price of one cow, and the same amount again to Sigmund
Lambasson in trust for the brother of Svein Sigfusson."

Donal's howl of outrage was drowned out by the
howls of protest from Sigmund Lambasson's crew over the
lowness of the price. Flosi Borksson, still leaning against
the wall, thought that if he were the lawspeaker, he would
go to ground like a badger for the rest of the winter, until a
few tempers had cooled. The worst was yet to come, no
doubt. The jarl wouldn't like losing a spear companion,
and that *knarr* captain from Jaeren didn't look as if he
would be satisfied with anything but permanent outlawry.

"Silence!" the lawspeaker snapped. The old man
wrapped his dignity around him carefully and lifted a
hand. "In the matter of the demand for a judgment of
outlawry against Donal MacRae, brought by Sigmund
Lambasson, hear the decision of the Thing of Hladir—"

Haakon put a hand on Donal's arm, part friendship,
part restraint.

"Donal MacRae is declared outlaw from Hladir and
from the Trondelag for a time of two years—"

"Damn you!"

Haakon's fingers dug hard into Donal's arm. "Keep
quiet," he hissed.

The lawspeaker pounded his staff on the floor angrily.

"For a time of two years, beginning with the first fair sailing weather of this season."

Donal wrenched his arm free. "I am a Scot!" He glared around the room, his temper boiling up like a pot on the fire. "Who are the Norse to tell me where I may have leave to go, and when?"

The lawspeaker swung his staff and caught Donal across the chest with it. The *knarr's* crew began to stamp their feet and mutter. In another second they'd be howling for a longer sentence. "It is only for respect to Jarl Haakon that the term is not made permanent," the lawspeaker snapped at Donal, "so great is your need to mend your temper."

Donal staggered back from the blow and flung up his head, blue eyes blazing.

"These are Norse lands, *our* lands. You have a right in them only so long as we allow. Best you remember that, Scotsman. You will have two years to be thinking it over."

Donal's hand slapped against his belt, in the place where his knife would have been if he had been permitted to carry one to a Thing meeting. The lawspeaker's face exploded into fury.

Haakon's hand shot out and caught Donal by the wrist. He twisted it hard and pushed Donal toward the hall door with his other hand. The lawspeaker's respect for a jarl wasn't strong enough to brook an open insult. Thorfinn Solvisson, looking scandalized, wrenched the hall door open and half dragged Donal through it.

II

"See How She Flies"

"You fool, one more sound and they'll make it permanent, and I'll have a blood-feud with every man in Jaeren!"

Donal opened his mouth to protest again, but one

look at Haakon's face told him he had better not. Haakon and Thorfinn hustled Donal down the track, slippery with melting snow, that led from Hladir to the fjord side, with the rest of the jarl's men behind them.

Hagar the Simple heaved himself up off *Red Hawk*'s deck, his bulk rising like a bear's, and shouted at the shipguard to launch her. Tents, sleeping gear, and cook pots were already stowed aboard. Hagar couldn't imagine the jarl going against a Thing decree, but these were chancy, unpredictable times. The shipguard heaved *Red Hawk* off the gravel of the fjord side and into the shallows.

"Get on board!" Haakon snapped, and Donal clambered over the stern, silent for once. Haakon waded into the icy fjord water with the rest and pushed *Red Hawk* past the shallows. Above them, the whole population of Hladir seemed to be lining the slope. Haakon scrambled up on deck and shook himself like a dog as *Red Hawk* slid into the current.

"The silver will be sent from Haakonstead!" he shouted at Sigmund Lambasson. "In three days' time!"

On the hillside, the *knarr*'s captain nodded sourly. He thought the jarl probably had that much silver with him here in Hladir, but there was no way to prove it without an accusation that would amount to insult. He had a feeling that insulting Jarl Haakon would be a very poor idea just now. The lawspeaker appeared to think so, too. They had come so close to open war that the old lawspeaker looked ready to faint like a maid. A blood-feud was no joke.

"Also the damages for that hovel Ulf Ale-Seller calls a tavern!" Haakon's voice boomed in the fjord channel, and there was a roar of laughter from the Hladir men. Ulf Ale-Seller would nail his broken benches back together and pocket the silver. Ulf never made repairs unless the alehouse actually fell down.

Ulf shrugged. The jarl would pay. It might be harder prying his silver from Sigmund Lambasson. He would wait until the jarl sent the weregild, he thought, and then demand his damages while Lambasson couldn't deny he had it.

The air above the fjord was as icy cold on wet skin as

the water had been, and the deck and shield edges were white and crackling with rime. Hagar took the helm and held the ship steady while the jarl, Thorfinn Solvisson, and the others who had waded through the water stripped off sodden boots and breeches and put on dry ones. He would have a hot bath in Haakonstead, Haakon thought, dancing on the cold deck while he pulled on dry breeches. Rosamund would thank him for it too, no doubt. In a week's time of sleeping by the ship with no one but Donal MacRae for a bedmate, he had seen little use in washing.

There was a fair wind, and when Thorfinn Solvisson took the helm, Haakon called out to raise sail. It billowed above them, striped red and green, a cheerful splotch of color against the black, bare trees and late snow to either side of the Trondheimsfjord. They put out oars as well and bent willingly to them for warmth. *Red Hawk* had been Haakon's first longship; there was a pleasure in sailing her and in her fierce, graceful lines that not even the sight of Donal MacRae, sulking at his oar, could dim. It would be sailing weather again soon, Haakon thought. Viking weather. It had been fine to spend a winter in Haakonstead in his wife's warm arms, going over the farm accounts and helping the herdsmen with the lambing all through a month's cold, pitch-black mornings. But Haakon Olesson was no farmer. It was time to go viking again. Certainly there was a need for Donal to go somewhere. And Haakon had made a vow to a god. He could feel the golden ax in its sheath across his back, as warm as a hand on his shoulder. A man didn't make a promise to Thor Hammerer that he didn't mean to keep. Haakon bent his back to the oar, pulled, lifted his face into the cold wind, and chuckled. He didn't think his men had really believed him when, around the hearth fire, he had talked of this spring's sailing. They would learn.

"Ship in the fjord!" The voice sang out from the far end of the courtyard where a footpath plunged down the hillside to the water. Lady Rosamund shook the last of the grain out of her apron for the gaggle of ducks that quacked around her feet, and listened for the voice to call again.

"It's *Red Hawk*! The jarl's come home!"

Rosamund picked her way through the ducks and geese, being careful not to step on the flock of goslings that skittered back and forth across the dirt like wooden toys on wheels. An old goose honked indignantly at her, resentful at sharing her grain with ducks. Rosamund flapped her apron at the goose and honked back. She was in a fine mood, with Haakon coming home. For two days now she had worn the blue gown with the scarlet hem and the wheat-colored apron over it. They were old and worn, but the ones he liked best on her. The purple-blue of the wool matched her eyes as if both had been dyed together in the same vat. Her long pale hair was freshly washed in the rain vat that the women kept just for that—the tendrils that escaped the white kerchief made a misty aureole about her forehead, over strong, wheat-colored brows, a straight nose with no tilt to it, and a generous mouth. Rosamund was aware that most men found her fair, and Haakon, somewhat more than that, but privately she considered her nose and mouth, and indeed her height, to be too great—she could look her husband in the eye. But since there was no way of changing, and Haakon liked her well enough as she was, there was also no point in wishing.

Beyond the cattle byre, she could see the folk of Haakonstead spilling out into the courtyard to welcome the jarl home. The sun had come out—a fair day at last—and the green sward of the courtyard and the turf roofs of the great hall and the outbuildings showed emerald in the pale light that shimmered off the snow-covered mountains. Even the gray weathered wood of hall and byre had a silver sheen to it. *Spring,* Rosamund thought. All winter in Norway, she longed for spring. England had been cold, but Norway—Mother of God—Norway was as cold as the giants' ice halls in Jotunheim. If she hadn't felt the need to set the servingwomen an example, Rosamund thought that she could cheerfully spend a Norse winter in her bed, huddled under the furs, hibernating like a she-bear.

There was much shouting and a bark of laughter from the footpath as *Red Hawk*'s men spilled over the ship's sides and scrambled upward, toward ale and a hot fire.

Rosamund saw Haakon's dark, broad-shouldered figure head-to-head with the tall, lean one of Gunnar Thorsten, his steward. It was beneath her dignity to run like a hoyden for her husband after no more than a week's absence, but she quickened her pace a little. Guthrun, Gunnar's wife, emerged from their small house beside the hall, hands across her belly and looking green, but determined to give the jarl welcome. Guthrun was with child and unexpectedly was sick in the mornings, which was a source of great indignation to her, who had never had a day's illness in her life. Beside Guthrun's gold head, Rosamund could see Fann's red one, her plain face and pale eyes anxiously searching the milling throng of men for Donal. What Fann thought could have happened to Donal on a peaceful sailing to Hladir, Rosamund didn't know, but Fann had a terror of the viking folk, even Jarl Haakon's, that had never left her, and she had not lost her fear of being alone among them. As Donal came striding up the path Fann put out her hands to him. Rosamund blinked in surprise as Donal brushed past the girl with no more than a word. He stalked into the hall, leaving Fann behind him, bereft.

From across the courtyard Haakon caught Rosamund's eye. His face broke into a grin, and he galloped over the grass like a spring lamb, caught her up, whirled her around, and kissed her. So much for her dignity, she thought wryly.

"What has Donal done?" she demanded when he had set her down again. That Donal had done something, she never questioned. Those black and surly moods came on him when he knew he was at fault.

"Killed a man in Hladir," Haakon said shortly.

"Mother of God."

"And earned himself a weregild debt, which I am going to take out of his hide, and a two-year outlawry."

From the buzz of talk in the courtyard, the tale appeared to be spreading fast. Rosamund leaned against Haakon for a moment, sadly. Donal had always been a wild, unruly man, but lately his rages had come on him more often. Rosamund had tried to think why and could find no answer. Haakon thought that Donal's betrothal was chafing him, but Rosamund could see no truth in that, either. Haakon didn't like Fann, but Donal guarded her with the care of a cat with a kit.

"He is swearing he has no mind to go," Haakon said now, "and he would have told the Thing of Hladir so to its face if Thorfinn and I hadn't dragged him out. Maybe you can talk to him. You were always the peacemaker." He kissed her again on the nose, affectionately, then stooped down and held out his arms for Asa, escaped from her nurse and toddling unsteadily across the grass to him. She sat down suddenly with a bump a yard away, and Haakon scooped her up.

"I'll try," Rosamund said doubtfully. Haakon didn't seem unduly upset, she thought. No doubt if Donal didn't change his mind, Haakon would simply knock him on the head and put him aboard ship. It would no doubt be much pleasanter if matters didn't come to that.

When three days had passed, Rosamund was thinking longingly of knocking Donal on the head herself. He appeared for meals at the long table in the great hall where everyone but the thralls ate at Haakonstead, and afterward he either rolled himself into his cloak in his place on the wide sleeping bench that ran the length of the hall or disappeared entirely, ignoring requests that he should take his harp and play for them or make up rhyming games around the fires that burned in the long hall hearth.

Gunnar Thorsten, who was the jarl's skald as well as his steward, took a dim view of this. He and Donal had eyed each other warily at first, with their pride sticking up like hackles, each measuring the other's skill, but it soon became obvious that their songs and their way of singing them were as different as the folk they came from, and there were no comparisons to be made. Gunnar's talent was words and the way he could give them life, so that they strode through the verse like dragon ships along the whale-roads or warriors into battles; with words he made men see these things. Donal's gift was in the music, although he was a poet also and had learned to translate into Norse in his head. But it was his music, the wild harp song of the Gaels, that called up old gods and kings and made his listeners hear them in the wind. The Norsemen had been suspicious at first, as they were of any new thing, but English Rosamund, who had heard the music before among her father's Welsh and Scottish thralls, would sit for hours, entranced, and gradually her husband's carls and warriors had come to the fireside with her. A story was a story after all, and for these unlettered men, their only key to the doings of the world. Donal MacRae had a wealth of new gods and battles to sing of. And Gunnar Thorsten had found it useful, when he wished to go to bed with his wife, to have Donal MacRae still sitting cross-legged by the fire, with an ale horn propped in the crook of his knee and his harp across his lap, keeping bored men from plucking at Gunnar's sleeve. There was very little for an unwed man to do on a winter night but tell lies about old battles and listen to a tale.

On the third night, when Donal had eaten, wiped his mouth with the back of his hand, and stalked from the hall, Gunnar followed him with his eyes, with a grim set to his mouth that belied the sleepy expression on his face, and Rosamund looked plainly exasperated. Gunnar Thorsten was steward of Haakonstead. He should not be at these men's beck and call like a traveling skald. But if the men didn't have something to do, they would pick fights with each other or start to chase the women instead, and when seventy men began hunting in the women's house at once, it always led to trouble. Tempers were never too even at the end of a long winter. Haakon, at the high table beside Rosamund, was slewed around in his chair, talking to Snorri Longfoot, the carpenter. Rosamund sighed. Haakon had already said that Donal wouldn't talk to him—he never would when he knew he was in the wrong. Rosamund got up and pulled her fur cloak off the back of her chair. She shooed her maid Tordis away with a little wave of her hand. If Rosamund came like the jarl's lady, with a retinue, Donal would no doubt grow more rebellious than he was.

It was already black as a dead fire and bitterly cold in the courtyard. Sputtering torches sent Rosamund's shadow leaping wildly across the grass before her. She stopped, listening, and caught the faint note of harp song. So he would play to soothe his own sulks and not in the hall, she thought. She pulled the sable cloak around her and marched across the yard.

From the cow byre came the warm, steamy scent of cattle and manure, and, unexpectedly, the sound of voices. Rosamund halted.

"This is what I have prayed to the Holy Mother for." Fann's voice sounding weepy. "To go home, Donal, home to Scotland."

Donal growled something unintelligible. There was a sharp burst of sound from the harp strings, angry notes like bees. Rosamund scolded herself mentally for eavesdropping, but she didn't move. She had seen Fann slip out of the hall, but she had thought Fann had gone back to the women's house to cry, which was how she had mainly been occupying her time lately. If Fann had gathered her courage to come hunting Donal when he was in this mood, it was important. Rosamund huddled inside her sables and stayed with a hand on the byre door.

"I would not have had it so—" Fann's voice quavered "—to kill a man to make you go home, but since it is done. . . ."

"Home!" Donal's voice snapped like a broken harp string. "Home to what, Fann? Your father is *dead*, look you—you *saw* him dead, killed by the Danes that came raiding. And mine also by now. He was dying of a growth in his belly when the Danes came, and I had no mind to go home again to watch it happen. And what do you think there will be left there for us to find? We were never at peace with our neighbors, any of us in the valley, our whole lives long. My father took his manor with an army, and with an army he kept it. And I've no army to take it back again."

"You don't want it!" Fann snapped. "You *want* to stay here, among these people. *Godless* people"—she was hiccuping with tears and fury—"that give *men* to their pagan idols! Don't deny it, Donal, I know how they worship! You think you owe Jarl Haakon service because he freed us from the Danes, but Jarl Haakon is the *same*!

They are *all* the same, and I dream of them at night. They have *blood* on their hands."

"I gave Jarl Haakon an oath," Donal said angrily. "I am the jarl's man—and a soldier, not a priest to bring heathen to the fold."

"You imperil your soul!" She crouched in the straw, desperate, and tried to take his hand. He pushed her away.

"Jesu! I do not! If Lady Rosamund can live among them, we can!"

"They have made you *outlaw!*"

"I don't *care!*"

Fann drew back a fist and hit him, then stumbled to her feet, sobbing, hands across her mouth. "You are going to go and *leave* me here!" she wailed.

She stumbled to the door, and Rosamund dived around the corner of the byre. Neither one would thank her for hearing that. Fann ran past her, arms wrapped around her thin chest, weeping.

"Get up." Haakon prodded Donal with his foot. Donal rolled over in the straw and opened an eye. Haakon stood over him, hands on hips. "Rosamund said you were here and very likely too surly to talk to, but I have come anyway."

Donal sat up with a grunt. He brushed the straw out of his hair.

"If you really want a fine misery, you should sleep with the pigs," Haakon commented.

"I only wanted solitude," Donal said. "I didn't get it."

Haakon lounged against the wall, grinning under his dark mustache. The cows looked at him curiously for a moment, then went back to their cud.

"I have done trying to talk sense into your head, which is thick enough not to need a helmet," Haakon said. "So now I am telling you. Swallow your pride. We are sailing this season anyway, so what matter?"

"West to look for Tir-na-nOg?" Donal snorted. "Or whatever it is this god of yours has promised?"

"West," Haakon said simply. "West to . . . whatever.

Thor Odinsson has said a new land is there, and Thor Odinsson does not lie."

Donal looked dubious. He had never known any save a few ancient monks who had claimed to speak with God. And from a Christian point of view the gods of Asgard were superstition, thin and insubstantial, a snare for unbelievers. But Donal had held the golden ax in his hand and felt a fierce and ancient power in it. If Haakon claimed to speak with a god through it, Donal could not disbelieve him. Fann would say that it was no god but Satan in another guise, Donal thought, and the golden ax a trap for souls. But Donal had felt no evil in it, only a dreadful power. And Haakon Olesson was close to being a brother. Donal gave it up. He was no priest to sort out these matters.

"You are so sure of this land?" he said. "Hjalmar Sitricsson says we will sail off the edge of the world."

"Hjalmar Sitricsson wouldn't believe in his own existence if he couldn't see his face in a rain barrel in the morning," Haakon said.

"What will we do there?"

Haakon was silent. A new world was coming, that was what Thor Odinsson had said. A new way of things, stronger even than the gods of Asgard, and the gods would fade away before it because everything must have its ending. But not in Haakon's lifetime. Thor had said that, too. In the western land, Haakon and Thor Odinsson both would leave a mark to be remembered by. "We will *see* it," he said finally, his eyes dancing. "And make a settlement there, but the great thing is just to go to it. Think, Donal—a land that no one has seen yet. That is word-fame to make a man remembered always!"

Donal's eyes brightened a little, and his fingers, which had been clenched in his lap as if to hold his anger, began to uncurl. "Aye, an adventure to be sung of in kings' halls," he said softly.

"Good!" Haakon sat down in the straw beside him. He clapped him on the shoulder, pressing the advantage while he could. "We'll sail for Ireland first, and claim my father's land-take again."

Donal's eyebrows rose. "Harud Olafsson's steading?"

"Which Harud's father stole from my father. I want it," Haakon said flatly. "It is the last thing needed to let my father's spirit lie quiet."

"I saw you when you killed Harud," Donal said. "Are you sure you are wanting to touch aught that he has touched?"

"I've a mind to wash it clean of him," Haakon said. "And as for touching what Harud has touched, I've twenty Rogaland brats in my keeping. A piece of Irish land is less trouble than that."

"I wouldn't be being so sure," Donal said. "You don't know the Irish."

"I am half-Irish." Haakon shrugged. "Men are men."

Donal smiled, lazily amused. "Think on your mother, jarl, and say that again."

Lady Sigrid had been born to an Irish house, although she took a Norse name when she wed a Norseman. An old spaewife had told her to do that and also to let her Christianity slide away with the old, forgotten name. Unlike Rosamund, who had come to terms with Haakon's gods only by making a careful balance in which neither she nor her husband reviled the other's worship nor sought to change it, Sigrid had set herself to be of her husband's people entirely. No one had ever made the mistake of seeing that as a sign of weak will. Even now, with swan's wings of gray in her black hair and the winter ache in her bones, she was a wind that very few could stand against—the same wind that blew from Jarl Haakon, Donal thought. Haakon's father, Ole, had been a good man, from what Donal had heard of him, but the strength of the family had been Sigrid's, and the strength of the son was Sigrid's, too.

Haakon chuckled, thinking, as Donal had bid him. "All the same, I will take back my land."

Donal considered. It would be a fine thing to see Ireland and the new country in the west that Haakon seemed so certain of, but the look of the thing galled Donal's pride. "It will seem as if I have given in to the old men in Hladir."

"It is supposed to," Haakon said.

* * *

"So that is settled," Haakon announced to Rosamund. "And when I have seen to the land in Ireland and left some men to hold it, I will take the fool west with me until the Thing's decree runs out and Odin All-Father has sent him some sense maybe."

Rosamund looked up from her stitchery, a rent in the silk hangings that surrounded their bed. The scarlet cloth pooled at her feet like a river, gay against the fjord-blue wool of her gown. Her pale hair was tucked under a clean white kerchief, and her purple-blue eyes were shrewd as they gazed at him. She had come into their bedchamber for a brief space of silence with no voices telling her there were mice in the granary or a smashed crock in the dairy or too few onions for the supper, so she had said. And also, Haakon thought now, seeing her eyes and suddenly growing wary, to speak alone with him.

"Sit down, Husband."

Haakon sat, suspicious, on the edge of the bed.

"You will be gone—how long this time?"

"I don't know. How long is long? How far is west?"

"And how strong is the itch in your foot?" Rosamund said.

"We have had this talk before. I never promised to turn farmer."

"And I never promised to be content with having a husband for five months in the year—if I am lucky and you have not wintered elsewhere. So I have thought about it. Gunnar Thorsten and Guthrun can see to Haakonstead well enough if you make your peace with King Harald. We are going with you, Asa and I."

Haakon gave a yelp of protest, and Rosamund put her needle very carefully into the red silk and folded her hands in her lap. She looked him in the eye. "I do not like wondering if you are dead or not, in some place I have never been. I will not do it again, Haakon."

"No!"

She sat and looked at him.

He flung out his hands, understanding why she wished it, unable to grant it. "It is dangerous. It would be dangerous if we were only going viking. But this—Rosamund, no man knows what is beyond Iceland."

"But *you* must find out."

"Yes."

"Why?"

"Because it is there, and I want to see it." He looked uncomfortable.

"There is more to it than that."

"That is my business!"

She started to answer, bit it back, and closed her mouth. He was right. Never once had he tried to pull *her* away from her Christian god, even when her faith had made a scandal among their neighbors. Folk were used to it now, but once there had been talk of witchcraft. She saw that Haakon was looking pointedly at the silver cross around her throat, and she knew that she had no right to try to come between her husband and his god. In Norway, *she* was the heathen, not he.

Rosamund sighed. "You are right. I'm sorry. But take us with you."

"No. Thor's hammer, you stubborn woman, are you mad? You, maybe, although it would not be safe, and one woman among seventy men is madness—but a year-old child? And what if you have another child on the voyage?"

"That is as God sends. Maybe you are right, but Haakon, I want to see things. You will never know how I wanted to see Constantinople."

Haakon chuckled. "You saw Cadiz."

"Thanks to Harud Olafsson. May my father live to regret the day he betrothed me to that man. I had a most fine view of the inside of a slave ship and the wali's harem until you were kind enough to come and fetch me. Haakon, that is not funny."

He was contrite. "No, I know it isn't. But all the same, I can't take you. No other woman would even think of it."

She glared at him. "We all think of it. It is only that most never say it because some man has said we mustn't. My whole life is bounded by this steading, and when you are here, that is none so bad, but when you are gone, it is a cage."

"And you pace through it like a penned wolf, so Gunnar Thorsten says."

"Gunnar Thorsten should know. He has lived with me for more months than you have. You will not be tied to this steading, Haakon, why are you thinking that I should like it better?"

"I am not a woman."

"You should be for a month or so," she snapped. "It would give you another viewpoint."

They looked at each other unhappily, both of them hating the squabbling and unable to find a way to halt it. Finally Haakon gingerly offered compromise.

"Ireland? Rosamund, would Ireland content you? I am leaving men there to reclaim the land-take, and there is a hall to be put in order. I could leave you and Asa in Ireland with an easy mind, I think."

"Ireland." She turned it over in her mind. She could find no further honest argument for sailing into unknown waters with him. Herself, yes, but Asa, no. He was right about that. And she had never been to Ireland. Now that she didn't have to go there to wed Harud Olafsson, the name enticed her. She put out a hand to make peace. "I suppose I must take Ireland if I can get no more."

He kissed her and stood up, relieved.

She brightened, brisk now, planning. "I must take some of the women with me, Haakon."

"Trolls take it, now you fill up my ship with women!"

"I will need them if I am to put your hall in order," she said soothingly. "And you said yourself—one woman alone, that is not good. Besides, Fann will have to go."

"Fann! I would as soon have a swamp troll on board. They are better company."

"She's afraid of you," Rosamund said.

"She's afraid of her shadow. Do I have fangs?"

"No, but you are no Christian, and Fann is closer to her God than most. She thinks Norse are the devil's kin, and she hasn't learned to think otherwise in two years, so she had best come with me for her sanity's sake if you are taking Donal away."

Haakon scowled. "Donal needs that woman like he needs leprosy. There's no life in her. She won't even bed with him."

"They aren't wed."

"She's afraid to."

"Haakon, that is something they must work out between them. But it doesn't change it that I must take her to Ireland."

"Aaah!" He also looked around him for another argument, exasperated and beginning to grow suspicious. She had planned to burden him with that wet, dreary woman all along. The matter had come too neatly into her talk.

"If I can content myself with Ireland," Rosamund said, "you can have patience that far with Fann."

"She will be seasick," he growled.

"How do you know?"

"I know Fann. She wouldn't miss the opportunity."

Rosamund burst out laughing. "You are probably right, but we must take her anyway. Haakon, you know we must."

"I don't, but I suppose I will do it. For you, sweet." He put his arms around her and pulled her up against him, kicking the silk out of the way. He kissed her ear. "I don't like quarreling with you. You may come with me and bring that dreary woman with you. But only so far as Ireland, mind you."

It was a season of compromise: Donal, complaining loudly, was to leave Norway, and Rosamund, no more than half-content, was to stay in Ireland. Haakon sailed south two days later to talk to King Harald. Donal stayed fuming in Haakonstead—to bring an outlawed man into the king's court would not set matters off on the right foot—but Haakon took a full retinue as befitted a jarl's stature: Gunnar Thorsten, his skald; Knut One-Eye, his chief helmsman; a ship's crew of forty; thralls to do their menial work for them; and horses and grooms for himself and Gunnar. There was a fat gift for King Harald in the hold, and for further show he whistled up Wulf, the great Irish wolfhound who, like Haakon's stolen English wife, had come to him out of the keep of Earl Edmund of the Ram's Head on the Wessex coast. Wulf was the size of a calf and had once bitten a man's hand clean off. King Harald had one of his pups at his hall in Vestfold on the Oslofjord.

Harald Fairhair, who called himself king in Vestfold and who had gained much ground in becoming king in Norway, greeted the most powerful jarl of the Trondelag with lords of state, poets, trumpeters, heralds, and hangers-on until the high hall overflowed with them. His wife, a thin, mousy woman who had been old Jarl Haakon Grjotgardsson's daughter, greeted Haakon shyly and asked with a plaintive wistfulness how things were in the Trondelag this season. Haakon said politely that the land was well, and he didn't see her again after that. Harald had married her for Haakon Grjotgardsson's alliance in the Trondelag and took it poorly that the old jarl had seen fit to die soon after and leave Harald with a plain wife who was now of very little use.

Now Harald surrounded himself with prettier women, and Haakon saw that the current favorite seemed to be the honey-skinned Arab girl Riziya, who had once been Gunnar Thorsten's thrall. Gunnar had seen her too, he noted, and the look in Gunnar's gold-flecked eyes was wary. Riziya's attentions to Gunnar had been close to embarrassing, and Guthrun had stormily refused to wed Gunnar until Riziya went. Then Guthrun had countered by letting Haakon's Alexandrian shipwright, Yazid, pay court to her until there had very nearly been open war. Haakon had been in Constantinople on the trail of Harud Olafsson at the time, and Rosamund and Gunnar had solved his problem with Guthrun, as well as the more pressing problem of bribing Harald Fairhair to leave them in peace while the jarl was absent: They had given Harald the services of the jarl's shipwright for a year and a wolfhound puppy and Riziya to keep. If Yazid hadn't cared to go, he had made no complaint; maybe he knew that Guthrun loved only Gunnar. Now he salaamed gracefully to both the king and Haakon and made a polite sound in Gunnar's direction. Gunnar nodded, mumbled something in reply, and then they carefully didn't look at each other. At least neither looked inclined to stick a knife in the other, Haakon thought, which was all to the good. It was his shipwright as well as peace with Harald that Haakon had come to fetch home again.

It was not possible to come to business at once. That was not the way that things were done. Haakon chafed through an interminable day of games between his men and the king's, of ale and feasting, of poems in praise of both, and finally an exchange of gifts in which each man tried by generosity to gain the upper hand in the coming talk. Haakon presented Harald with an ivory chest of spices that were worth more than gold and a bolt of purple silk from the state silk house at Constantinople, which the Norsemen called Mikligard, the Great City.

King Harald gave to Haakon three casks of Frankish wine and a belt of gold links. Gunnar and two of King Harald's tame poets declaimed a shameless trio of verses in praise of both men, which, as Haakon said afterward, would have led a listener to think that both were mightier than Thor, purer than Balder, and altogether above the race of men. Gunnar smiled when he saw his chieftain fidgeting in embarrassment in his place of honor beside the high seat and feeding spiced mutton to Wulf under the table. But afterward Gunnar grew more subtle. The king's court and Haakon's crew had settled in to feasting at the long tables that filled the hall. Harald sat back in his chair, his gold hair burning in the torchlight against the tapestried walls, his handsome face amused, pleased, and only a little drunk. He *was* a king, Gunnar thought suddenly, and it might be that he, out of them all in this hall, might be the one to be remembered. But that did not mean that Jarl Haakon should go tamely to his hand. He began to weave a new poem. When a thrall passed by with a ewer of ale, he waved a hand to have his horn refilled, relieved that Riziya showed no inclination to leave the king's side to serve him. He took a long drink and stood up, arms outstretched for the hall's attention.

"West."

The word danced in the torchlight.

> "Ocean-guarded, mist-enshrouded,
> Gift of god to viking men.
> Dragon ships, ocean-spanning,
> First to touch on alien land.
> Gull-following, storm-riding,
> Where the sun sets—*West*."

The hard-muscled men in the hall stilled their talk, drained their beer horns, and laid them down. The words ensnared them, compelling them to a vision beyond their knowing, past the western edge of knowledge where the sun dropped down and the gods' realms might lie. They were sailors all, seafarers, rovers, even King Harald's court, and Gunnar's vision turned every eye toward him and then toward the dark-haired jarl who sat beside the king.

Harald had expected treaty talk, maybe even another bribe, possibly a war. Not this. He knew the jarl's skald wasn't merely spinning words. There was purpose to his song. He lowered his ale horn and handed it over his shoulder to Riziya without looking at her. "Is this a skald's vision out of an ale pot, or your own?" he asked Haakon softly.

"Oh, it is mine," Haakon said. He took a plum from a silver bowl and turned it in his fingers. "Some men say that the world is round, like this. If that is so, there are things on the other side that men have never seen. Would you like to know, King?"

"A king must always seek knowledge," Harald said noncommittally. "As Father Odin did." But the word had caught itself in his brain. *West*. He would sleep on it, he thought, in case a dream should come to him, but in the morning he would hear Haakon Olesson out. The unexpected should always be given a hearing.

The peregrine ruffled her feathers and shifted her talons on the king's fist so that the gold bells on her jesses chimed a faint, sweet note above the rustle of hounds and huntsmen through the tall grass.

"I have always thought that this is the best time in a day," Harald said. The dawn breeze rippled the blue silk of his shirt, so that Haakon could see the pattern of mail rings under it. The king took no chances, he thought, grinning.

Haakon put his knee to his horse, and they moved out through the meadow behind the hounds. Haakon heard Wulf's deep bark and a shout from the huntsmen. Harald twitched the peregrine's hood off by its feather crest. She snapped her head around, yellow eyes riveted on the movement in the grass. She rose in a swooping circle, seemed frozen for an instant in midair, and dived. There was an explosion of beating feathers above the grass and a scream that cut off sharply as she snapped the pheasant's neck. It fell in a flurry of limp plumage. The peregrine shook her feathers into place and with a shriek of triumph tore at the pheasant.

The king swung the lure, and she screamed at him, too, but she beat her wings upward again and settled sulkily on his fist. He fed her with his other hand, a piece of flesh cut from her kill. "That is my fine lady, that is a princess," he crooned to her, then dropped the red leather hood over her head again, and turned to Haakon, smiling. "The best bird I have ever flown, I think. In some ways she reminds me of your Englishwoman. She stood me off finely last season."

"I am not so sure," Haakon said. "The king has a fine new ship in his ship house, and I have a bare keel in mine."

"True," Harald said. He stroked the back of one finger down the peregrine's spotted feathers. "Your Yazid proved to be all that was claimed, and I have always a need of ships. What can *you* offer, jarl?"

The king seemed in a mood to speak frankly, with his lords and his retinue out of his hearing. Haakon chuckled. He would prefer to be blunt. It saved time. "To keep you out of Haakonstead while I am gone? Word-fame, Harald Halfdansson. Word-fame such as no king ever had before.

To go west over seas under the king's banner and give the land the king's name. *That* is what I offer."

Harald looked thoughtful. That was true fame and worth having. Worth more than taking Haakonstead and getting an ill name out of it if Haakon Olesson came home a hero. And if he never came home, of course, then Haakonstead would still be there for the taking. A king should learn to bide his time. Harald smiled, charming and careful, and cocked his fair head to one side. "And are you so sure of this land? What if there *is* an edge to the world, and you sail—*whish*—right off it?" He made a plummeting motion with his free hand.

"I am as sure as I can be," Haakon said. "No man knows what the Norns know. But Thor Hammerer has never done me an ill yet, and it was in a dream of Thor that I saw the land." That would have to content the king. Haakon had no mind to say that he had spoken with the god and could even summon Thor sometimes with the golden ax—if the god had a mind to come.

King Harald looked impressed. The gods of the Aesir were real to these Norsemen, as tangible as a man's ship or his sword if they so wished it. Harald had heard that Haakon Olesson had become Thor's servant. And if that were so, it might be ill-advised to be unfriends with him. Harald Fairhair was a king because he had learned when to take friendship over a fight.

"I saw a—a commission of the men of Rogaland this month past," Haakon said, seemingly changing the subject to give the king a space to think in. "They came before the Thing of Hladir to ask help for the children that Harud Olafsson stole. Since it seemed to me that that was in part my fault, I have given a promise to see them cared for. With your permission, of course." He inclined his head gravely. "I have no wish to take on myself a matter that the king wishes to make his own."

Harald's blue eyes narrowed shrewdly. "I have a care for all in my domain," he said. He made much of studying the question. "But if you feel that your honor requires this pledge, certainly I would not stand in the way of it." That was very useful of Jarl Haakon. Harald thought that the jarl knew exactly *how* useful, and that decided Harald.

The jarl knew too many ways to give the king an ill name if he should choose.

"Touching on the other matter—I will give you a letter to say that Haakon Olesson sails in the king's name. And the safety of your land will be my first concern in your absence." His blue eyes smiled at Haakon, friendly now, but with a watchfulness behind them that was like the peregrine's.

Haakon held his hand out on the bargain, and the king clasped it. Haakonstead would be safe in the jarl's absence. After that the king might try to put a foot in the Trondelag again, but that was as it should be. Harald Fairhair was not a man to keep still any more than was Haakon Olesson.

Haakon sailed home with his shipwright and the king's pledge of peace, with the king's sponsorship of the voyage cut with a sharp hammer into a rune-stone for all men to see. He was tired of talking and persuading and tiptoeing through negotiations with Harald Fairhair. He wanted to see the building of his ship begun, the wondrous ship that Yazid had always claimed his god had told him to build. Why Yazid's Allah should wish a ship built to sail for Thor Hammerer, Haakon hadn't tried to understand. Perhaps in some ways the gods were all one force and all men were swept along by it. He didn't know. He only itched to feel the new ship under his feet and be gone.

Yazid leaned against the sternpost, looking back as *Red Hawk* made her way down Oslofjord to the open sea. The red-and-white checkered cloth of his head scarf fluttered in the cold wind, incongruous above a beaver-fur cloak and Norse boots. His dark eyes were slightly amused as he watched King Harald's hall grow smaller in the distance.

Haakon came to stand beside him. "I am grateful for the service you gave to Harald Fairhair." Yazid was a free man. He needn't have done it.

"More grateful than the king will be," Yazid said.

"He seemed pleased enough."

Yazid chuckled. "And so he will be, unless he decides to take his ship against yours by and by. There are one or two things about the king's ship that I will show you if that happens. It is awkward if the mast unsteps suddenly, you know."

Haakon studied Yazid's hawklike profile and burst out laughing. He wouldn't put it past the Alexandrian to have laid a trap or two aboard the king's ship. "I think," he said, grinning broadly to make it a compliment, "that the Arabs are a race more devious than the trolls and considerably subtler than the poets."

Yazid shrugged, but there was a flicker of amusement in his eyes. "I am a shipwright. There are many things that can be done with a ship."

"Have a care what you do with *my* ship."

"Ah, *your* ship!" Yazid was serious now. "I can see how she flies even now, inside my head. I built King Harald a fine ship, but there has never *been* a ship like the one I will build you!"

That proved to be the opinion expressed by Knut One-Eye and the crowd of inquisitive Norsemen who daily went to peer through the ship house door at Yazid, Snorri Longfoot, and the work gang that the pair of them drove ruthlessly from dawn to dusk. When Yazid had departed for the king's court in Vestfold, the ship had been only a bare keel; all the green timber had had to be stored in water and the troughs wrapped in blankets through the winter to keep them from freezing. Now she began to rise above the blocks on which her keel was braced, neither warship nor *knarr* but something quite unlike either. She was heavier than *Red Hawk* and the other warships of the viking folk, with a higher freeboard and more hold space, solid and stable enough to weather a rough sea, but no one would ever take her for a fat trading *knarr*. Her lines were long and clean, and Haakon could see the speed in her, even as she sat on the keel blocks. She was armed like a fortress, with unexpected devices from Yazid's vast store of knowledge. Knut One-Eye glared at the unfamiliar lines of the hull like a man whose horse has just sprouted wings, but Haakon found her beautiful.

"What is that?" He jabbed a finger at a wooden cradle

bolted to the foredeck. It enclosed two skeins of sinew and
a leather sling.

"It is a catapult," Yazid said, "such as the old Romans
used to build. Stones go here"—he put his hand in the
sling—"or pieces of chain, and it is wound so—" Yazid put
his weight on a lever, and a series of wooden teeth clicked
past a ratchet. The twisted sinew hummed as it grew taut.

Haakon jumped up on the newly laid decking and
squatted down to peer at the teeth as they turned. His
eyes were bright and interested.

"A large stone will hole a ship's hull," Yazid said.
"Chain fouls a sail and oars."

A snort behind them came from Knut. "Lose a hand
in that, I reckon."

Haakon ignored him. "Does King Harald's ship have
this?"

"I am not mad," Yazid said. "And I am the only one
who can build a catapult for a ship's deck, I think. But I
warn you, it takes practice to fire properly." He jerked his
head at Knut, who stood scowling at the alien device. "He
is right about that much."

"Then we will practice," Haakon said cheerfully. "What
else does this ship of mine do?"

Yazid nodded at the freshly trimmed mast being
stepped into place by Snorri Longfoot and Hjalmar Sitricsson.
"There will be a net of thin cord, tightly baled so it won't
catch the wind. And a spring to make it fly outward."

Haakon grinned as the usefulness of that hit him.
"Over another ship?" He stood up, hands on hips, head
tilted back. There was a slot cut in the mast top, where he
supposed the spring would be set. Whether the net was
also ancient knowledge rescued or some inspiration out of
Yazid's head, he didn't know, but truly this was a ship such
as no man had ever owned—an explorer, to go out and
bring home a new world. "*Raven!*" Haakon said suddenly.
He had been trying for weeks to think of a name for the
ship. It should be *Raven*, for the birds that flew each
morning from Odin's shoulders and returned at night with
the world's knowledge. He jumped down from the deck
and pushed his way past Knut, slapping him cheerily on

the back. Behind him Hjalmar looked at the slot cut in the mast as if a snake might come out of it.

"Rosamund!" Haakon headed for the hall, shouting for his wife. He knew now what he wanted the women to sew on the sail.

After that Haakon spent every spare minute he could find in the ship house, gloating over his ship, Rosamund said, as if it were a woman. As for Yazid, he worked like a man with demons leaning over his shoulder, and if that was done partly so as not to see Guthrun and regret the might-have-been, still the results were very fine to look at. In two weeks *Raven* was complete. She was painted red and black, with scarlet oars. At her prow, instead of a dragon's head, was her namesake, beak open and wings furled behind her down the forestem. Snorri Longfoot had carved her, and every feather was in place. The sail was scarlet with a great black bird across it, wings lifted in flight and talons outstretched. As she stitched, Rosamund found that in spite of herself she too had been seduced by the ship and by Haakon's excitement. Never had there been a ship like *Raven*. The day they pulled her from the ship house into the sun, she seemed to sail on the air.

Yazid had built her, Haakon had dreamed of her, and Snorri Longfoot was more than half in love with her himself, but to the rest of the jarl's men she was a strange, almost monstrous creature. Knut said he doubted that she'd steer properly with all that extra bulk. Hjalmar said likely the net would come down of its own accord and drown them all. The rest stood around like a herd of nervous horses, eyeing *Raven* warily and shifting their feet. At any moment, Rosamund thought, they would throw up their hands, whinny, and stampede.

Haakon ignored them. No one had yet had the nerve to say he wouldn't sail on her, and Haakon had spent all his arguments long ago, arguing all winter just to convince them that he wasn't mad and that there really would be something to find in the west besides a sea-road into eternity. They had a right to be wary; this was risky business. And nearly as important to the Norse, if they did find Haakon's new land, there might be nothing in it to raid—or gold beyond imagining. They were half-enticed by the prospect, half-convinced that they would all go down to dine with Ran. Ran was the sea goddess, a robber by name and nature.

Haakon rocked back on his heels, whistling cheerily, and every corner of his heart not already occupied by Rosamund and Asa went out to *Raven*. They would come round when they had sailed in her, he thought. "See how she flies," he said softly, echoing Yazid. "See how she flies."

III

Abbot Cormac

"—*and* it's ill luck to have women on board." Hjalmar Sitricsson went about his work muttering while Thorfinn Solvisson eyed him with some amusement. Hjalmar was one of the best of the jarl's men: a good fighter and an honest comrade. But Hjalmar viewed the established order of his world as a very fine thing indeed and saw no need to make changes in it. He greeted new ideas with grave suspicion and the ears-laid-back look of a stubborn horse.

To Hjalmar, *Raven* was suspect in herself: a new kind of ship that was neither fish nor fowl, and very probably dangerous, loaded with foreign devices—and now with women. Hjalmar liked the jarl's lady—all the men did—but it was the addition of that shrill, tiresome wench of Donal MacRae's—and Freya knew how many thrall-women and nurserymaids—that provoked him to grumbling. No way to go viking, loaded down with nurserymaids.

"It is only until Ireland," Thorfinn said cheerfully, but he thought it was likely to be a lively voyage.

Raven was nearly loaded, with ninety men and ten women, counting the jarl's lady, Fann, and Asa, who was everywhere—"Underfoot like a rat," as Hjalmar said—with old Bergthora, her nurse, lumbering after her. Asa inspected the bilges and nearly fell in, climbed into the hold and opened a meal sack, and appeared at the knee of anyone who was eating anything, blue-purple eyes fixed hungrily on his. She would have to be under someone's care every minute of the voyage, Rosamund thought. It might be just as well that they were only sailing as far as Ireland.

Haakon's mother, Sigrid, and her husband, Erik Alesson, came downfjord from their own steading to see them off on the day of sailing. Haakon put his arm around his mother and kissed her forehead. She looked a little sad, he thought. Sigrid had not been back to her girlhood home since the day that Harud Olafsson's father, Olaf Haraldsson, had driven them from Ireland more than fifteen years ago. She was happy in Norway, happy with Erik Alesson, but Erik said that sometimes she spoke the Gaelic in her sleep, and lately those dreams had come more often. Now that her son had achieved a fine red revenge on Olaf Haraldsson and his house, Haakon thought that Sigrid's thoughts were turning more and more to happier times.

He smiled at her. "What shall I bring you from Ireland, Mother?"

Sigrid sighed and laid her head against her son's chest. "Peace with your kin," she said seriously. "Don't fight them, Haakon, if you can help it. Except for Kilian, they were all kind to your father and me." Her brother Kilian was a priest, and he had never spoken her name again after she had married a Norseman. "I am a Norse woman now. I have been since I married Ole. But I wouldn't have you at war with your kin."

"I've no mind to make war on anyone," Haakon said cheerfully. "We are explorers, *Raven* and I." His gaze lingered affectionately on the black and scarlet ship.

Sigrid snorted. "You are as peaceable as a whirlwind. But you are leaving your wife and babe there, so go gently."

"Certainly." He grinned. "Anyone who has had Olaf Haraldsson as a neighbor should thank his gods to get me."

He whistled up Wulf, and even when he reached

Raven a hundred yards down the fjord side, Sigrid could still see the bounce in his step. Haakon was a rover. Never was he happier than when he was setting out for somewhere. Sigrid put her arm around Erik Alesson, standing solid and comfortable at her side. She was glad that Erik had no taste for roving and was content these days to manage their farm and let other men go viking. *I must be getting old*, she thought. *Too old to go back to Ireland and see if Kilian still hates me. Let Haakon go.*

Raven made her way out of the Trondheimsfjord into the open sea with her scarlet wings spread. Thor Hammerer had sent them a fine wind to sail on for his quest. He ought to have, Haakon thought. Haakon had given Thor six of the best goats on the steading for that wind, and a roan horse for good measure. Rosamund hadn't liked that, but she and Haakon had an agreement: He sacrificed to his gods as he saw fit, and she didn't watch. One didn't slight Thor Odinsson. Now she sat comfortably on a sea chest on the deck, smiling into the wind and sun and determined to get the most from her short share of the adventure. Bergthora was beside her, keeping a good grip on Asa, and Wulf sprawled at her feet, tongue lolling out cheerfully. Wulf liked to sail. He had parted from his homely, good-natured mate, Gerd, and their latest litter of pups without a backward glance. Fann, as predicted, was seasick.

Haakon stood with his feet braced against the swell of the open sea and let Knut One-Eye take the helm. If ever there was a ship that nearly steered herself, it was *Raven*, and from Knut's closemouthed expression as he leaned on the tiller, Haakon thought that he was thinking things over. The two other helmsmen on board, Thorfinn Solvisson and Kalki Estridsson, were also changing their tune, although at the moment they were still peering with deep distrust at the catapult, bolted to the foredeck, and Yazid's net, carefully balanced and lashed to the mast top.

"Yazid!" Haakon cupped his hands and shouted. The shipwright scrambled down off the overturned hull of the ship's boat, where he and Snorri Longfoot had been tightening the lashings.

He salaamed, a habit that had ceased to make Haakon

uncomfortable and had instead become merely a part of Yazid. "Jarl?"

Haakon let out an excited breath. His eyes danced. "I want to try the net, Yazid. Now, while the wind is fair." Later, into the Orkney Islands and the Hebrides, it would likely be stormy.

Yazid looked at the men lounging on the oar benches in the sun. "And stir things up?"

Haakon laughed. "Certainly. They will find a way to annoy me if they aren't busy. Also," he whispered confidentially, "I wish to show off for my wife."

"As the jarl commands. They will cease to think there are demons in my net when they have used it once."

Haakon hooked his thumbs into his belt and tilted his head back, ready to watch the show. "Proceed."

Yazid nodded solemnly, but there was a wicked light in his dark eyes. He went and tapped Hjalmar Sitricsson on the shoulder.

"*Hai*, Hjalmar, don't launch yourself by mistake now!" A crowd of cheering, hooting Norsemen offered jovial advice as Hjalmar climbed the rigging to the perch Yazid had constructed at the mast top. Even Donal MacRae, who still felt that the Thing of Hladir had made a fool of him and whose mood had been none too sunny since they sailed, was laughing. Hjalmar glowered at them over his shoulder, caught a good hold on the rigging, and lifted the other hand in a rude sign as he clambered skyward.

"Now," Yazid called as Hjalmar reached the perch. "Find the pin, and stay to one side so you are not in the way!"

A cloud of gulls circled overhead, eyeing the commotion curiously. Hjalmar shook his fist at them. He jabbed his hand at the bronze pin protruding from the mast and swore as it skinned his knuckles.

"Move to the side!" Yazid called.

Hjalmar cursed again and wrenched at the pin, scrabbling at the mechanism with both hands. It seemed to him to have a malevolent life of its own. He was directly in front of the baled net, deaf to Yazid's shouts. The Arab danced up and down on the deck in a fury. Hjalmar got a grip on the pin and pulled it. The net leaped out at him like a dark cloud. It dropped over the foredeck with Hjalmar and two startled sea gulls in its grip.

Haakon clawed at the net, cursing too now, trying to fight his way from under it. Rosamund, on her sea chest, just beyond the edge of disaster, rocked back and forth mirthfully. The foredeck was a heaving confusion of men and net. A steady stream of Arabic curses flowed from Yazid, punctuated by squawking gulls. "Allah give me strength, you cannot sit in *front* of it!"

The edge of the net writhed, and Haakon rolled clear of it. He stopped cursing and lay on the deck panting while Wulf licked his face. Somewhere in the depths of the net, Hjalmar's voice said dolefully, "I *told* you it wouldn't work."

An hour later, the net had been baled up and put away again, this time by Yazid. Hjalmar had been shaken out and dusted off, and his bruises rubbed with salve by a giggling Rosamund. If she hadn't been the jarl's lady, she thought, Hjalmar would have cursed her, too. He had cursed everything else on the jarl's ship, primarily Yazid. Yazid was unrepentant. Hjalmar had nearly ruined his net and the spring that fired it. Hjalmar had the brains of a camel, from whom he was no doubt descended.

Raven beat her way through contrary winds past the Orkneys while tempers mended. Donal MacRae came out of his sulks enough to sing by the fireside at night when they found a suitable stretch of coast to beach the ship and camp. *Raven* was big enough to be lived aboard for weeks at a time in the open ocean, but there was no point in doing it if they didn't have to. The jarl of the Orkneys had no quarrel with Haakon Olesson, and when it became plain that they hadn't come raiding, he came down to the fireside one night and argued with Haakon until dawn over whether the world was round, flat, or bowl shaped. The jarl of the Orkneys didn't particularly care, but Haakon had good ale on board, and the voyage of the *Raven* was high adventure. It would be fine to say that he had talked with Haakon Olesson first and given him sage advice.

From the Orkneys they worked their way west past the Hebrides and then south to Antrim, the lands around Larne on the northeast coast of Ireland. Haakon's old steading lay in the river valley of the Bann below Lough Neagh. Haakon kept a sharp watch as they sailed up the river, but he wasn't expecting trouble. *Raven* didn't look like a warship, although it couldn't be said that she looked like a *knarr*, either. Still raiders didn't come in broad daylight with a deck full of women. The last time Haakon had sailed this way, to burn Harud Olafsson out of his hole, he had brought two longships in by night, slipping silently through a fog as thick as wool. Today it was sunny, and the green riverbank and the hills above the valley were inviting.

Rosamund watched the shore with interest. She would have come this way for a bridal if she had been forced by her father to marry Harud Olafsson, a dreadful prospect. But now, to take the ruined steading and make it her own, with Haakon for a husband—that would be pleasure. A beautiful green land, Ireland, she thought. Greener even than England. She put Asa on her hip and went to lean over the bow to watch the riverbank slide by. A cloud of starlings swarmed overhead, flickering black bits of birds against the sunlight.

"There," Haakon said, pointing. "There it is, on that rise."

He narrowed his eyes suddenly, just as Kalki Estridsson shouted, "There are men in the fields, jarl!"

Haakon pulled Asa out of Rosamund's arms and pushed her at Bergthora. "Get in the hold!" He looked at Rosamund. "You, too."

Rosamund shook her head, but Haakon had already turned his eyes back to the fields above the riverbank. They should have been lying idle, overgrown with spring weeds, but the land was neat as a counterpane, tilled and orderly with the first growth of new grain. The apple orchard was in bloom, and there was a tidiness about it, too, that spoke of recent pruning. The men who weren't at the oar benches began to pluck up their weapons.

Haakon squinted at the tilled land as *Raven* nosed her way up the river. The folk in the fields had seen them, also, and were picking up their skirts to run. At first he had thought they were all women, but they didn't run like women.

"Beach her!" Knut One-Eye shouted. "We'll give them something to run from," he growled to Haakon.

"Not till I give the word, Knut," Haakon said. "That is an order."

Rosamund put a hand on his arm. "Haakon, those are monks."

"Yes, I think so too."

"What matter?" Knut said.

Hagar the Simple was gauging the distance and nocking an arrow to his bow.

"Hold, I said!" Hagar lowered his bow, and they ran *Raven* onto the sandy beach below the cleared land while Haakon thought it over. The monks were running away from the fields like ants. They would be easy prey, but he wished to keep the peace here because the Bann valley was on the very edge of the Norse holdings around Larne, and all too close to his Irish neighbors. The best way to start a feud with the Irish would be to slaughter monks. "Take battle order, but keep your weapons sheathed," he said. His own ax was another matter. He hefted it in his hand. "Any man who starts a fight before I say, can fight me afterward." He stared at each man in turn, and they put their weapons away, grumbling. He noticed Rosamund at his elbow. "I said to get below."

"It looks to me as if the danger is all on their side," she said wryly. "It may be I can help you talk to them."

He thought about that. "Then stay at the rear." He shouted for Donal. "Keep an eye on my wife."

They left a shipguard to watch *Raven* and the little hide boat, probably the monks', that bobbed on a tether in the shallows close by the dirt track that ran from the river up to the old steading. The fields were empty now. A hoe and sickle lay in the road, mute testimony to their owners' flight. As he and his men marched four abreast up the track Haakon saw that a small stone building had been begun in the meadow below the old hall. A ring of domed huts like bee skeps encircled it, and what appeared to be a kitchen garden had been planted between them: cabbages, leeks, onions, and the feathery tops of carrots.

Haakon inspected the gardens and the stone building and snorted. The structure had the look of a church about it, and men who built a church intended to stay. They would learn it would be otherwise. His men were muttering behind him, and he turned around and glared them into silence. The ground was littered with tools and scaffolding. Haakon kicked a sawhorse out of the way and planted himself in front of the half-finished stonework. He thought that most of the men had run into that. The steading appeared to be still in ruins.

"We mean you no harm!" he bellowed in Gaelic. A wail of fright rose from inside the stonework. "Where is the leader of the men who have stolen my land?" It was not a conciliating beginning, but Haakon had no wish for the monks to think that because he had not slaughtered them on sight, he would suffer them to stay.

A low, anxious murmur of voices came from inside the church. A tall man stepped across the threshold with two or three others behind his skirts like chicks behind a hen. Haakon took stock of him in mild surprise: a mountain of a man with dark red hair shaved into a monk's tonsure on the top, and a beard just beginning to go gray. He was dressed in the same rough, brown monk's robes that the others wore, and there was a hammer in his hand, but Haakon also noted that he carried a mace in the other.

"I am Cormac," the tall man said. "And we have stolen nothing. If there is a thief here, it would seem to be yourself." He looked pointedly at the armed band behind Haakon, most of whom could speak no Gaelic, which was fortunate.

"I am Haakon Olesson," Haakon said, "and I am jarl of these men *and* this land, and no thief. The land was my father's before Olaf Haraldsson stole it. Now that Olaf and his son are dead by my hand, I am come back to claim it. Whence comes *your* right?"

"The land was left to go to ruin," Cormac said, "after God sent Olaf Haraldsson punishment for his sins."

"Your god had very little to do with it," Haakon said.

"We are all God's instruments," Cormac said blandly. He seemed to think Haakon as good a tool as any for God to use in weeding out the wicked. "I asked God, in faith, for a place to take my flock and build His church, and He sent me to this one."

"Your god was very free with *my* land," Haakon said.

"Is not the land being put to better purpose than when you left it?"

Cormac still had the mace in his hand. His flock, men and a few women, whispered fearfully behind him. Haakon's warriors stared at them, hostile eyes under conical iron helmets. They had no love for Christians. Lady Rosamund was forgiven because they loved *her*; Donal MacRae, because he could sing and fight and because his religion sat but lightly on him anyway. As for any other Christians, they were for killing, and monasteries were for raiding. Cormac seemed to realize this, but there was no fear in his face. He looked more fit to wear mail than a monk's robes. The abbot and the jarl stood sizing each other up.

Haakon had raided a monastery or two in England in his day, and until now it had been his experience that, unlike the Norse, Christian priests did not fight. The only one with whom Haakon had had any friendly dealings had been Brother Gregory in Bulgaria, a gentle soul who wanted only the cloister and the contemplative life, although a brave old man in his way. Abbot Cormac was plainly another sort and looked as if he had old acquaintance with that mace.

"The point is not the purpose but the ownership," Haakon said. "Also, your purpose offends my gods."

"All the same, it is meant to be," Abbot Cormac said gently. "I do assure you."

Haakon felt a gentle touch on his arm and ground his teeth. These days Rosamund seemed singularly disinclined to stay where he had told her to, and he had no wish to slaughter unarmed monks in front of his Christian wife. Abbot Cormac was armed, of course, but he was one against ninety. Slaughter was the only word for it, and it would shock Rosamund down to the bone.

"I am Rosamund Edmundsdaughter, Father, the jarl's wife," Rosamund said gently in the halting Gaelic she had been practicing with Haakon and Sigrid. "Perhaps it would be as well if you did not argue with my husband any more than you can help."

"God be with you, lady," Cormac said, taking in the Norse dress and the silver Christian cross she wore over it. "No doubt it would." But he showed no sign of giving ground.

Behind them, Haakon's men were beginning to mutter and stamp their feet, the itch to fight running through them like a spreading ripple. "The jarl is talking when he should be looting," Hjalmar said succinctly. "That is dishonor."

"That is also the jarl's land," Donal said. "It may be he has no mind to wreck it by fighting over it." He fervently hoped not. Even as a lapsed Christian, Donal couldn't make himself take part in raising a sword against a community of God. He waved a hand at the rough clothes of the abbot's flock and the rude beehive huts. "And are you seeing anything there worth the looting?" he asked Hjalmar scornfully. "Best we wait and see what the jarl does."

The jarl stood glowering from Cormac to Rosamund. He didn't like the killing of unarmed folk himself, but it was no way to keep a vow to Thor Hammerer to let the White Christ's priests settle in on his land. He looked at the golden ax in his hand. The god had made his wishes known through the ax upon occasion, in most unmistakable fashion. It was still now. Faintly warm with the presence that slept in it, as always, but otherwise unspeaking. Thor himself seemed to be taking no offense, which was another mystery.

Rosamund turned to Haakon. "They want only a little of the land, enough to build their church on."

Haakon snorted. "Like King Harald wants only a little of the Trondelag. This is *my* land, Rosamund. Give me a reason why I should let these monks put their foot through the door." *And give me a way to get rid of them with no blood spilled*, he thought. Abbot Cormac seemed to be as unmoving as a mountain.

Abbot Cormac watched the jarl think. Then he stuck the mace through his belt and dusted his hands on his robe. "There is no need that we settle the matter today," he announced. "Your men will be tired, and they have frightened mine halfway to God already." Haakon thought the abbot was mildly amused, even with ninety glowering Norsemen ready to kill him. Cormac pointed up the hill at the empty hall behind its gateless palisade. "We have

taken no part of the hall yonder; there is room for all.
Bring your men to share a meal with mine, and we will
talk after."

Haakon considered this offer, startled.

"It will be simple fare," Cormac said in kindly expla-
nation, "but we are simple folk."

"And thieves," Haakon growled. But he turned to
his men and shouted in Norse, "We will eat with these
monks before they leave here, and you will mind your
manners!"

IV

"... Cousins with a Norseman"

Four days later Cormac's flock were still there. They
hadn't received the jarl's permission to stay, but he hadn't
given them the toe of his boot yet, either. The jarl was
thinking it over.

As for the other Norsemen, after the first constrained
politeness of a communal meal of stew and porridge, they
had retreated to the empty hall on the hill and kept to
themselves. When that was more than they could bear,
they circled Cormac's encampment gloomily, like hounds
on a short leash, but no one wished to risk the jarl's wrath
by starting trouble, especially since Lady Rosamund had
taken to praying in the half-built chapel when Abbot
Cormac said his mass. She was unobtrusive about it, but it
was common knowledge anyway. Donal MacRae went
once, at Fann's prodding, but seemed to feel that that
would last him awhile and didn't reappear.

Fann had emerged weepily from *Raven*'s hold after
Haakon had made his first temporary truce with Cormac,
and now, Donal thought, she didn't look like the same
person. There were a few women among the abbot's flock,
and Fann attached herself to them and to the little com-

munity of Christ with the passionate intensity of the
starving. They were her own kind, and she felt at home
among them for the first time since the Danes, the fearful
pagan men who looked to her so much like Jarl Haakon's,
had taken her. The Danes and the Norsemen were all the
same to Fann. They ran together into her dreams at night.
They had put their bloody hands up under her gown to
amuse themselves, but they had left her virginity to be
taken by the man they had sold her to. That was eternal
shame and sin, and *never* would she be washed clean of it,
although she prayed every day to God's Holy Mother for
release from it. She couldn't bear to think of another man
invading her that way, not even Donal. But here among
Abbot Cormac's folk Fann had begun to think that there
might be a way to be clean again, a way to banish the
nightmares, a way out.

Gradually her face had begun to lose its taut look, and
Donal thought he could see the girl he had known in
Scotland look out through it again. Maybe Ireland would
be what she needed, he thought, cheered. He had hated
to see her miserable and bitter in Norway. A year or two
in Ireland might set her right.

Haakon put his men to repairing the fallen-in roof
beams in the great hall and outbuildings, and to cutting
new turf for them. Rosamund rolled up her sleeves and
scrubbed walls and floors along with her maids, while Asa
explored every inch of the buildings on the hill and the
beehive dwellings below. Bergthora scuttled after her,
scowling when Abbot Cormac set the child on his shoulder
to show her a wren's nest in the chapel roof.

"We will build around her until she has hatched her
family," he assured Asa.

Asa didn't understand Gaelic, but she peered at the
wren's eggs and clapped her hands. She liked Cormac. He
made her think of her father, a comparison to which the
jarl no doubt would not have taken kindly.

Even Wulf took to Cormac, much to Haakon's annoy-
ance. He went to the chapel with Rosamund, and Cormac
gave him bones. Haakon had let Cormac's monks bide
here for two weeks now. The longer they stayed, Haakon
thought sourly, glaring down at Cormac's village, the

harder it was going to be to shift them. The outer palisade was nearly repaired, with only the gates left to be built, and the hall was reroofed now, its turf gay with spring wildflowers that gave the steading a kinder air than the dark keep it had been in Olaf Haraldsson's time. More and more it became the home of Haakon's childhood, and fresh memories came back with every outbuilding shaken into order.

Abbot Cormac was still in Haakon's meadow, the only fly in the ointment.

News of new folk at Olaf Haraldsson's steading traveled fast. The Irish of Ulster had no more liking for Norsemen than had any of their race—especially those on the far side of the valley of the Bann, who had had Olaf Haraldsson for a neighbor. Cormac's settlement in the meadow they had ignored. Cormac was a man of God, and a monastery there might do much to hallow the land that Olaf Haraldsson had laid his black hand on. Also, no one really knew whom else the land should belong to now, although Conor MacLorne had made a possibly valid claim to it on the grounds that it had once belonged to Ole Ketilsson, who had been husband to Conor's great-aunt Deirdre. Conor was the grandson of Deirdre's brother Brendan. Since Fergus MacAidan was the son of her sister Dechtire, one generation closer to Deirdre, that claim was loudly disputed—as was every other matter between Fergus and Conor—so very little had been done about it. In any case Abbot Cormac was a strong-minded man, who had been known to back up God's viewpoint with a mace. No one saw any need to quarrel with him as long as Fergus and Conor were still quarreling with each other.

But when word came that there were Norsemen on the land, that was another matter altogether. There had begun to be talk lately among the Irish *tuaths*, the old tribal territories that each constituted a separate kingdom in itself, that the Irish should band together and drive all the Norse from the land. A second faction held that it was wiser to ignore the Norse and hope that in return the Norse would continue to ignore them. And yet a third had made open alliance with some of the Norse around Dublin

and Larne, a foolishness that both Fergus MacAidan and
Conor MacLorne regarded as being akin to bedding down
with a wolf just because it did not happen to be hungry at
the moment. It was the only thing on which they had
managed to agree since they had been old enough to be
rivals for the kingship of the Dal Crimthann, the *tuath*
over which their family held sway. The king, Dungal, who
ruled at Dunnaill, was old, and a successor might be
chosen from anywhere within the *fine,* the five generations of brothers, uncles, sons, and cousins that constituted the legal family. It was generally accepted among the
Dal Crimthann that the new king would be either Conor
or Fergus, and each pressed his claim daily. Dungal, after
all, was nearly eighty and slow in his mind. Conor and
Fergus effectively shared the rule between them now.

The O'Neill who ruled at Aileach as overking of all
Ulster did not care greatly who led the Dal Crimthann so
long as whoever it was stuck to that and kept his ambitions
away from Aileach. Similarly, he was reluctant to try to
oust the Norse so long as they kept to their pocket of land
east of the Bann. The O'Neill had enough work merely
keeping a large and unmanageable dynasty in hand. The
rulers of the Dal Crimthann were also of the Ui Neill,
traditional overlords of the north, but of a younger line
that had been barred from the succession by the ruling
branch. This was often a necessity because within two
generations a ruling dynasty became unwieldy with poten-
tial heirs. Often whole segments of them were set aside in
order to make a choice possible at all. The spurned
segments frequently dedicated their lives to working their
way back into the succession by any means that came to
hand: maiming the legitimate heir to render him inelig-
ble, calling their neighbors to rebellion, or even seceding
from the kingdom to form a neighboring rival one. The
result was a constant state of war and political upheaval
that left the country vulnerable to invasion. Even the
invaders on occasion had been turned to ousting a rival—
the O'Neill at Aileach found the Norse in Antrim useful in
keeping the Dal Crimthann looking that way and their
eyes off the high kingship.

Norse at Olaf Haraldsson's steading were unpleasantly

close to Dal Crimthann lands. Conor MacLorne came storming into the king's hall at Dunnaill to find old King Dungal playing *fidhchell* with Fergus. Fergus looked up from the game board and raised one black eyebrow at Conor. They were nearly of the same age despite being one generation removed in their descent.

"There are Norse at Haraldsson's Hold!" Conor snapped. His expression was wolfish and truculent.

"Truly?" Fergus's handsome face looked polite and interested, but his wide mouth held a twitch of suppressed amusement.

"Can't be," Dungal grunted. "The old thief died two years ago. Provoked some of his own kind into a war. I remember." He went back to his game board.

Fergus and Conor ignored him. "You'd be knowing if you paid more mind to the *tuath*, Fergus, and less to cheating an old man at *fidhchell*!" Conor gave Fergus a look of contempt.

"Now that's where you're wrong," Fergus said. He made much show of finding Conor's wrath amusing. Conor MacLorne had a temper as red as his hair, and it gave Fergus much pleasure to provoke it. "I've known since sunup, my spies being better than yours, but I've no mind to fight Norsemen singlehanded—I'm not the hero Cuchulain. I sent the word out this morning. I expect my men will be ready to ride by tomorrow sunup. You can come too if you like." He turned away from a seething Conor to study the *fidhchell* board. "If you think you can keep up," he added over his shoulder.

The Dal Crimthann lords and their followers rode into Dunnaill all night long, men, horses, and dogs, crowding the streets between the thatch-roofed houses. Olaf Haraldsson had been a bad neighbor indeed, and the two years since his hold had fallen to ruin had seen more peace on the Dal Crimthann's borders than at any other time since Olaf had stolen it from Ole Ketilsson. The Dal Crimthann had no mind to let another Norseman take root there. That Ole Ketilsson had been a Norseman was conveniently forgotten; Father Kilian, whose sister Dierdre had been Ole's wife, had forbidden either of their names to be mentioned, and in any case it had been over fifteen years ago. Most of the young lords who champed at the bit to wipe Haraldsson's Hold clean of Norsemen had been children when Ole held the land. All they had seen of the Norse was Olaf Haraldsson, and it had not left them with a kindly opinion.

With righteous indignation to unite them, Conor's supporters and Fergus's forgot their quarrel with each other and went together at dawn to hear Father Kilian say mass. When they rode out eastward through the gray-green light, the king's hold of Dunnaill looked as if a whirlwind had passed through it. The streets were strewn with spilled grain, the ashes of doused cookfires drifted in the air, and a piece of the fence around the kitchen garden had been broken and a path churned through, leaving the garlic and young onions trampled into the mud. The air was sharp with the scent of them.

King Dungal looked at the chaos with disgust and stumped back to his bed. Conor and Fergus would drive the Norsemen out of Haraldsson's Hold—if there were any Norsemen there, which Dungal took leave to doubt. Olaf Haraldsson had only held that land, so close to Dal Crimthann lands, by being a blackhearted villain. Other Norsemen were not so determined, whatever the priests said about them. Mostly they kept closer to the cities that their own kind had built along the coast. Or if there *were* Norse, and they were too much for Fergus and Conor, Fergus and Conor would come back slung across their horses, and Dungal would be free to train up an heir to his liking. Neither Fergus nor Conor was the man he would have chosen, but as Dungal grew older, he was losing the strength to argue with them. The king pulled the thick woolen blankets and the soft deerskin coverlet over his ears and bade his chamberlain to post some extra guards. With eighty men gone out of their numbers to fight the Norse, the Dal Crimthann would have reason to watch their Irish neighbors as well. The O'Neill at Aileach, for instance, would like fine to root out a troublesome growth from his family tree.

"Men in the woods, jarl!" Thorfinn Solvisson burst

into the hall where Haakon was enjoying a leisurely breakfast with his family, listening to Rosamund tell him yet
again why Abbot Cormac should be allowed to steal still
more of his meadow and letting Asa dabble her fingers in
his ale pot and lick them off. In the next chamber, where
the weapons were kept, Haakon could hear men pulling
shields and axes from the wall.

He dumped Asa unceremoniously in her mother's
lap. "Norse or Irish?" He lifted his mail shirt from the
floor and began to wriggle his head and shoulders through
the hem of it.

"Irish, we think," Thorfinn said. "They're on horse-
back, all of them, and there's a cross on their banner. I
don't see any armor, either. But they must have forded the
river downstream and come up again through the woods."

"Thor Hammerer blast them!" Haakon, doubled over,
said through the folds of his mail. His head emerged
through the neck opening, and he looked at Rosamund.
"Tell me again how innocent your precious monk is!"

"Whoever's out there, I don't think they're friends to
these monks," Thorfinn said grudgingly. "That lot's running like rabbits for the hold." A babble of voices, Norse
and Irish, proclaimed the truth of that.

Haakon grabbed the golden ax in its sheath from a
table and shrugged his shoulder through the carrying
strap. He pushed his way into the courtyard through a
terrified rabble of Irish, who seemed unable to decide
whether they were more likely to be killed inside by the
Norse or outside by their fellow countrymen. When he got
to the palisade, cursing himself for not having had the
gates rehung, he saw that his men were already fighting.
Wulf followed at his heel, looking interested, and let out a
deep bellow of a bark when he saw that there were dogs
with the invaders—big dogs, who looked uncannily like
Wulf. He gave another menacing bark and launched himself into the fray. Haakon's men opened up the rear of
their lines to let the jarl through, but they were in a
perfect fighting line already. They were well trained.

The invaders outnumbered Haakon's men only slightly,
but they were all mounted and had the advantage of a
gateless defense to greet them. To their disfavor, they

fought unarmored in no more than helmets and linen
shirts, and with only swords and light spears for weapons.
They swarmed around the Norse while the Norse raised a
shield wall against them and hacked from behind it at the
horses and the riders' legs.

"Pull back!" Fergus shouted as the weight of the
charge began to break. "And try to come behind them!"
His own men wheeled to follow him, but Conor's men
appeared to hear no order that didn't come from Conor.
Conor, his flaming hair flying out behind him, was slashing
with a reddened sword at the Norse shield wall from atop
a white horse and had no wish to take his commands from
Fergus.

Haakon, in a foul temper by this time, lashed out
with the golden ax and brought a horse and rider down in
a heap in front of him. Donal was fighting and cursing
steadily in Gaelic at his side. Hagar the Simple was up on
the half-repaired rotting catwalk that ringed the inside of
the palisade, sending arrows into the Irish to good effect
The rest were an orderly formation when viewed from
afar, and a seething, snarling chaos at the center. Haakon
was aware of Yazid on his other side and Yazid's wicked
curved sword swinging with a fatal accuracy. Yazid wore
the pointed helmet and fine riveted mail that his countrymen
made, each separate link stamped with a verse from the
Koran to give Allah's blessing to the slaughter.

A tangle of snarling dogs exploded from the Irish
ranks, and Haakon saw a hamstrung horse go down. A
moment later Wulf was at his heel, his jaws dripping
blood.

Haakon swung his ax again as the rider whose horse
he had killed struggled from the saddle and came at him
As always, the golden ax seemed to take on a life of its own
in battle, shining and unstoppable. The warmth that came
from the golden blade ran up his arm and into his shoulder muscles with a strength that was somewhat more than
mortal. With the golden ax in his hand, he could fight all
day, but he knew that when he stopped he would be weak,
nearly drained, and would eat ravenously for two days
afterward.

Haakon slammed his shield up as the Irishman's

sword slashed at him. He swung the ax, and it bit into the man's side above the ribs. The man fell, openmouthed, with blood sheeting down over his torso. But another man, also dismounted now, swung his sword at Haakon before the jarl could raise his shield again. Something heavy crunched into bone, and the man dropped his sword, howling, with a useless arm dangling.

Haakon blinked in surprise when he recognized the mountainous form looming beside him as Cormac. Cormac swung his mace again. There was the same sickening crunch of bone as the iron head connected with someone's bare kneecap. Haakon, struggling to keep his shield locked into place in the shield wall, saw that the abbot was breaking arms and legs but seemed careful to break no heads.

The Irish charge had lost its momentum, whirling in a confusion of men and downed horses around the Norse lines, and the Norse were beginning to make headway.

"You'll start off wrong in the valley if you kill them!" Cormac shouted. "Then you'll have wars ever after!"

"They are trying to kill *me*!" Haakon shouted back. But truly it was not the way he had wished to begin in Ireland.

"That's Fergus MacAidan and Conor MacLorne of the Dal Crimthann," Cormac said grimly. "They are hotheads, but not fools, not altogether. Offer them surrender, and I will talk to them for you."

The Dal Crimthann. Oh, very fine. He could go back to Norway and tell his mother he had made war with her kin. Haakon shot Cormac a disgusted look and began to push his way back through the press of his own men into the courtyard. He had fought in this hold twice before, he thought, and a sudden sick feeling of nausea swept over him. The first time, the summer he had been fifteen, he had fought Olaf Haraldsson's men and watched them kill his brother and his baby sister.

An Irishman who had somehow got into the courtyard leaped at him, and Haakon swung the ax savagely and caught him just above the collarbone. The man dropped down in a spray of blood. Haakon stood over him, looking down at sightless blue eyes in an oval Irish face, brown

hair soaked with blood. These were not Olaf Haraldsson's
men. And what was more, they were not winning. They
were no threat to Rosamund and Asa. He turned and
sprinted for the catwalk. He wished furiously that he
hadn't killed that man.

Hagar the Simple gave him a friendly nod as Haakon
scrambled up the ladder to a perch beside him. Hagar
started to nock another arrow, but Haakon held up his
hand. He stood up on the catwalk with his shield in front
of him, hoping that if the Irish were shooting arrows, they
wouldn't hit anything vital.

"Dal Crimthann!" Haakon bellowed, making his voice
carry. It sounded only faintly over the fighting. Someone,
seeing what the jarl was doing, blew on a horn. At the
horn blast, a ripple of hesitation went through the milling
fighters. Haakon bellowed again. "Dal Crimthann! I want
no quarrel with you! Lay your swords down and talk peace
with me, and you'll go free!"

"We want no more of Olaf Haraldsson's kind in the
valley of the Bann!" A black-haired man on a gray roan
horse wheeled his mount around and shouted up at Haakon.
The sun winked off a spiraled gold brooch that pinned his
heavy cloak. Haakon saw that there was gold on his arms
and around his throat as well. His horse's bridle and
trappings were beautifully dyed with scarlet and set with
enameled plates. Like the rest of the Irish, he rode
bare-legged and wore no armor. Better the Dal Crimthann
lord should have put his wealth into a coat of mail, Haakon
thought sourly, with the insult ringing in his ears.

"You're a liar!" another man yelled at Haakon. He also
was wearing gold, as fine as the first. "All the Norse are
liars!"

"Keep a rein on your red temper, Conor MacLorne,"
Cormac shouted from below, "before you sully the cross
you carry!" His words were lost in the challenges screamed
by the Irish and the answering howls of fury from the
Norse.

Conor raised his red and white banner and set his
horse at a charge again for the Norse ranks, with Fergus
MacAiden neck and neck with him to be first.

"Odin take you, no man calls me a liar!" Haakon slithered down the ladder again in a fury.

"*Odiiin!*" The name rose from the ranks of the Norse. Haakon heard Donal shouting as loudly as any. The Norse surged forward. Haakon grabbed Thorfinn Solvisson and Knut One-Eye by the arms.

"Go and get the women and the thralls in a defensible chamber and put a guard on them. This has gone on long enough."

Thorfinn looked startled. "What are you going to do?"

"I'm going to let them in," Haakon said grimly.

Haakon could tell by looking at the Irish charge that their discipline was ragged compared with the orderly formation of the Norse. The red-haired man and the black one seemed both to be commanding, and each had followers reluctant to take orders from the other. So much to the good. When he thought that Knut and Thorfinn had had enough time to carry out his orders, Haakon pulled his men back from the gate, keeping them always between the Irish and the hall. The Irish howled after them.

Herd animals stampeded wild-eyed between the outbuildings. Fleeing Norse footmen and Irish riders careened among them. A flock of chickens ran frantically this way and that and finally flew squawking onto the turf roof in a flurry of blood and feathers.

"Now!" Haakon snapped. He signaled to Kalki Estridsson and Donal, and the twenty Norsemen Haakon had kept in reserve out of sight in the hall swarmed in on the Irishmen's backs, while the fleeing Norse halted, spun around, and locked shields with a clicking sound that was as deadly as the whistle of an arrow.

Fergus, seeing his Irish in a box, began to curse Conor. He had *tried* to keep the fool from going through the gate—Norse very rarely broke and ran. But Conor would take no orders from Fergus, ordering Fergus instead to hold the perimeter. Fergus, in a fury and taking no orders from Conor, had followed him through the gate lest Conor should steal the glory for himself. Surely that was Conor's fault!

Fergus's horse reared, and he fought the beast under control. Now they were surrounded, and the Norse fought

as one man, while the Irish were unmanageable at best.
The Irish drew in a little on their center, gathered their
reins, and prepared to kill all the Norse they could. They
could still give the Norse interloper such losses that he
would think twice about staying in Haraldsson's Hold with
the rest of the Dal Crimthann no doubt on his heels by
morning.

Haakon found Abbot Cormac conveniently beside
him. He wasn't overly surprised. "Now," Haakon grunted,
"*you* talk to them. If you don't, I'll kill every one of them."

"If I don't, you'll have to," Cormac said. Conor and
Fergus were not men who surrendered easily. The abbot
stepped forward before the Norse or Irish could charge,
trusting the jarl to keep the Norse in check. He hefted his
mace, and his eyes dared Fergus MacAidan to ride him
down.

Fergus checked his horse. "You keep ill company,
Abbot."

"I keep the word of God," Cormac said, "which bids
you live in peace." He tapped the ridged iron head of the
mace into the palm of his hand. "This was an unasked-for
quarrel, Fergus."

"When have the Norse done aught with the Irish but
quarrel and steal our land?" Conor snapped.

Cormac snorted. "When have the Irish done aught
but quarrel with each other? The two of you cannot even
agree who shall rule the Dal Crimthann. Why come here?
If you need a fight, go home and fight each other. You will
imperil your souls just as surely, but at least you will spill
no *innocent* blood."

"The Norse are as innocent as wolves." Conor gave a
long, hating look at the Norsemen: fighting-bred men,
harsh-eyed under their helmets.

"Fine talk for the Dal Crimthann!" Cormac said.
Crimthann was the name of the *tuath*'s first king. It meant
wolf.

Fergus laughed. "Are you expecting peace when wolf
meets wolf?"

"You bear Christ's cross on your banner," Cormac said
flatly. "You damn yourself when you make a needless war
in His name."

"Needless?" Conor snapped. "Needless, with a nest of thieves in our back garden? What are you doing among Norse thieves, Abbot?" The white horse danced sideways under him.

"The jarl permits my people to build our church here," Cormac said blandly "Lay down your sword, Conor, or you will be fighting Holy Church."

Haakon stepped up beside Cormac. He had been taking stock of his losses, and they were not so great: three dead and Kalki Estridsson wounded slightly. The Irish had lost more. He could afford mercy. He glared from Conor to Cormac. "That is enough! There has been a certain disagreement between this priest and myself already as to who is the thief," he said. "And I have not come here to waste my time fighting young lordlings who want to make a name for themselves. This is my land. It was my father's before Olaf Haraldsson stole it from him. Now Olaf Haraldsson is dead—by *my* hand, for which you should be grateful—and I will take back the land." He stared first at Conor and then at Fergus. "Also, I am very likely kin to some of you."

Conor's green eyes glared back at him, but Fergus's hands relaxed very slightly on the reins, and he looked at the Norseman with a growing interest. Truly the jarl looked different from most of his kind—broad of shoulder but shorter than most and dark of hair and beard. "How would that be?" Fergus said. He made some imperceptible signal, and the men behind him lowered their swords. Conor's men, Haakon noted, didn't twitch.

"My mother's birth name was Deirdre, and she came of the Dal Crimthann," Haakon said. "She married my father, Ole Ketilsson, when he held this land. She still lives, if that matters to you."

"She is here?"

"No. She is Norse now. She married again in Norway after she was widowed. I have been told I look like her."

Abbot Cormac looked from Haakon to Fergus and burst out laughing, while the two men stared at each other with a growing and unpleasant recognition. If truth were told, the Norse jarl and Fergus MacAidan had a family resemblance.

"*My* mother was Dechtire, who was youngest sister to Deirdre," Fergus said thoughtfully. "I am not sure I have a mind to be cousins with a Norseman."

"And I've no mind to be cousins with a fool who fights first and asks questions later," Haakon said sourly, "and who calls me a liar in the bargain. I killed Olaf Haraldsson for you. You should send me a chest of silver for the service. Now go home and leave me alone."

"There is treachery in here somewhere," Conor growled. "We make no truce with Norse."

Fergus turned his head lazily, resting blue eyes on Conor, enjoying his discomfiture. Fergus was beginning to have a mind to make peace with the Norseman. He had a fair opinion of Abbot Cormac's judgment, and it might be useful to have this jarl for a buffer between the Dal Crimthann and the other Norse in Antrim. Also it would make the O'Neill at Aileach nervous.

Fergus watched Conor glaring like an owl at the Norseman. "I do not see that we have a great choice," Fergus said.

"We can fight like men!" Conor said. "Like Dal Crimthann and not tame puppies. They will slaughter us before we are out the gate if we lay down swords! When have the Norse been aught but butchers?"

"When have the Irish known truth when they were told it?" Haakon said. "Lay down your swords, or I'll send you back to your kin in four different sacks."

Fergus slid off the gray roan's back and stuck his sword in its sheath. "I lay down swords for no man." He gave Haakon a wry grin. "*Especially* for kinsmen. But I will give my word—on your cross, Cormac, if you like—to ride out in peace."

"And that one?" Haakon nodded at Conor MacLorne.

Fergus rubbed his chin thoughtfully. "No, I can't guarantee Conor. But if he fights you, I won't help him. Will that content you?"

Haakon thought that very likely that would more than content Fergus. Cormac had said that the red-haired man and this one were fighting over a kingship. Ireland seemed to have more kings than Norway had carls. He nodded.

"Done. But unless the rest make peace also, you don't ride out together."

Conor gritted his teeth. He would look a fool, bending now to follow Fergus MacAidan's lead. But without Fergus's men, he hadn't the strength to argue or even to go under and take some Norse with him. "For a man of God, you choose sides oddly, Cormac, bedding down with pagan folk," he spat at Cormac.

"The jarl's wife is a Christian," Cormac said mildly. "The jarl allows us to build a church here. We are all in God's hand, pagan or no."

Furious, Conor jammed his sword into its sheath and kicked his horse. Haakon snapped an order, and the Norse pulled back and let him ride through them, with his men behind him. Fergus swung himself into the saddle more leisurely.

"I'll be taking up my dead first, jarl. Then we will go." He reined his horse around. "But if it's a bad bargain we are making today, you'll find yourself looking down a spearhead. I shouldn't like it to come to that."

Haakon shook his head. "It will come to no more than the Dal Crimthann choose to make of it."

Fergus nodded, saw that his men had put seven bodies across their horses, and kicked his own mount through the gate. It occurred to him that by *tuath* law this Norseman, as Deirdre's son, had right to a voice in *tuath* councils, even a fair claim on the kingship. The Norseman wouldn't know that. Fergus chuckled. He would put that point to Conor one day if it seemed useful.

"The jarl has given no permission to build so much as a chicken coop on this land!" Haakon advanced on Cormac as the last of Fergus's riders cleared the gate.

"Perhaps you should, you know," Cormac said, "since I have told that to Fergus MacAidan and you were not denying it just now."

Haakon took stock of the abbot again. "You've a fair hand with that mace," he admitted with grudging respect.

"God has need of soldiers as well as saints," Cormac said. "We all serve Him in our way."

"I'm not interested in your god," Haakon said. He hefted the golden ax thoughtfully, to see if his own god had an opinion in the matter, but it seemed that Thor Odinsson would leave it to him. "But my wife goes to pray in your church, and I am reasonably interested in keeping my wife happy. Also I want peace with my mother's kin."

"That would be wise," Cormac said, "especially if you intend leaving the lady here while you are gone."

"I also intend leaving half my men for assurance," Haakon said. "Still, I have been thinking, and what I have thought is that I will give you your church, Abbot. But I will give you something else with it, and you must take both or neither."

Cormac's eyes narrowed suspiciously. If it was a pagan temple on the same land, he couldn't permit it, and then surely they would come to blows. Cormac hadn't tried to convert the jarl; there was something in the oddly dark Norseman that told the abbot it wasn't possible. And one must occasionally deal gently with one unremitting heathen in order to bring others to God. But a Norse temple was blasphemy on holy ground and beyond even considering. He couldn't offer the jarl's faith the same tolerance that the jarl was offering his. Cormac sighed. He had come so close. "What is this second thing, jarl?"

"Twenty Norse children," Haakon said.

Cormac blinked. "Twenty?—"

"They aren't mine," Haakon said hastily. Many of his own men were still there, and Abbot Cormac's folks had begun to edge nervously out of the hall with Rosamund. He beckoned Cormac toward the hall, and the abbot came with him thoughtfully. Haakon put a hand on Rosamund's arm. "My dear, I think I have found the answer for Rogaland."

Rosamund's eyes widened. "Of course!" But then her face turned dubious. "They won't like it," she said, nodding at the knot of men bending over the dead, who had been carried into the courtyard. They were stripping the coats of mail off the two who had owned them. Mail was too valuable to go into a funeral fire.

"Then let them think of something else," Haakon grunted. He pulled Cormac into the hall.

When the abbot had heard the story of Rogaland, he was of the opinion that his own folk wouldn't like it, either.

He struck a bargain with the jarl anyway. The fact that the children had suffered at the hands of Olaf Haraldsson's son, Harud, gave them a common ground of sorts with the Irish. And children were children. They all belonged to God.

When he parted with the jarl, he gathered his flock about him in the half-built chapel and left Haakon to instill agreement in his own men in whatever way the jarl saw fit.

"*Norse* children?" Brother Kevin looked outraged, and the tautness of fear stretched the skin on his small, freckled face. He was young, not much more than a child himself. Norse had killed his mother after they had raped her.

"*Any* of the lost and abandoned, Kevin," Cormac said gently, "that God sees fit to send us, we will take."

"You put too much faith in this jarl, Cormac," another man said.

"He has given us our church," Cormac said. He tilted his head back to look at the sky through the unfinished roof. "God has promised us this church to His glory, and if He sees fit to use a Norse jarl to bring it about, we are not to question Him. These are babies, no more than that, and we will take them as our Lord took the little ones to Him."

"The Norse are the enemies of our blood," Brother Gilbert said. "Not even prayer can change Norse."

Abbot Cormac studied him. Brother Gilbert was of the Ui Neill and somewhat too lordly in his ways yet for a man of God, but Cormac thought that Gilbert's calling was a true one. "As to that, Gilbert, if we take these heathen children now and raise them to honor God as Christians, then they will not grow up hungry in Norway and come raiding in Ireland when they have grown. There is a middle way to fight that falls somewhere between prayer and sword. If you are to follow me, you will have to understand that."

Brother Gilbert bit his lip, but a genuine awe of Cormac, more than he would admit, bade him to silence.

Haakon's fighting men were louder in their protests but somewhat easier to quell. The jarl merely hefted his ax, glared at them, and asked if anyone else had another idea. When no one did, except those that involved a perpetual outlay of the jarl's silver—already stated as unacceptable—the furor gradually subsided to grumbling. But they disliked it all the same.

"They will make them into Christians," Hjalmar said, fingering the little silver Thor's hammer that hung around his neck. More and more the Christian faith encroached on the Norse world, and Hjalmar feared it with more than the usual suspicion he accorded any new and unknown thing. The gods of the Aesir held out the promise of Valhalla if a man died a good death: an eternity of ale and meat that never ran out, the company of good comrades, and a place on the side of the gods when the day of Ragnarok came. Beside it the Christian heaven was thin and insubstantial. More than wounds or death, Hjalmar feared losing Valhalla.

"Better Christians than starving in Rogaland as Norse," Haakon said. He thought about what Thor had told him, that a new age with new ways was coming. Maybe the White Christ was part of it. Maybe for these children, that was the pattern. Only the Norns knew that. But Haakon couldn't let the children go hungry in Rogaland only to save them from the Christians.

The Norse were still grumbling when Haakon left to find a trader in the Norse city of Larne who could fetch the children, but he knew there would be no more open protest unless someone could think of a better answer. Since there wasn't one, the matter seemed to be settled.

It was mountainous country between Larne and Haraldsson's Hold—which Haakon firmly said was now Ole's Hold again, and Norse and Irish both had best be remembering it—so Haakon took the water route with *Raven* and a small crew, downriver and along the coast to Larne to talk to his trader. When he had gone, Rosamund set about helping Abbot Cormac make ready to receive twenty extra folk, many of whom would be unable to work for their keep. Although one wouldn't know it from the rough cloth of their robes and the dreary sameness of the meals they ate, she discovered that there was a great deal of gold and silver in the community. Cormac was a lord's son and so were many of his followers, but the silver was kept for God. Certainly that would make things easier, although she made no mention of it among her husband's people. That might be setting *too* much temptation in their path, she thought wryly, when many of them were still surly over the presence of the Irish on the land at all.

In truth it was Rosamund who gave stability to the oddly assorted community of Ole's Hold. Her husband's men had a great respect for the jarl's Englishwoman, both for her courage and for her kind heart. There were few who hadn't in some way benefited from that, from being nursed through a fever to the quiet gift of a gold piece when it was sorely needed. They no longer took much note of the silver cross around her throat, and by now they would cheerfully have died for her.

The monks saw the lady Rosamund's Christianity as a bulwark against whatever evil her pagan husband might suddenly decide to do them. After a day or so, even Brother Kevin said worshipfully that if Lady Rosamund had consented to wed the jarl, then perhaps he was indeed unlike the rest of his kind. He was, after all, half-Irish. Abbot Cormac, chuckling to himself, thought that the lady was a born peacemaker. If they had sent *her* to talk to Fergus MacAidan, no doubt they would not have had to break so many heads.

V

Earl Edmund

Edmund of the Ram's Head stalked into the hall and scraped the horse dung off his feet on the stone hearth. The fire was smoking. Edmund swore and shouted for a thrall to see to it. He held out his hand, and another thrall put an ale pot in it. Edmund grunted. He sank into the chair that was drawn up to the hearth for him. They had missed the stag they had hunted all day, and now his knee pained him—it was aching worse of late, especially if there was rain. Earl Edmund was growing old, and the knowledge did not sit well with him.

Edmund of the Ram's Head had outlived his wife and his youngest son, and very likely his only daughter as well, for all that Edmund knew. *She* had been taken by Norse, although some of Edmund's thanes had said that the whore had gone willingly enough. Earl Edmund kicked irritably with one booted foot at the ragtag pack of dogs that lay in the straw and rubbish on the floor. Now there was no one to keep his house for him. He kicked again, this time aiming at the thrall who was crouched on the hearth trying to mend the fire. It had been ill-made to start with. Edmund cared very little whether the hall was clean or not, but it irked him to be unable to command a fire that did not smoke or a meal that was not either underdone and cold at the center or burned to a crisp by the thieving thralls in his kitchen.

The earl tipped the dregs of the ale down his throat and wiped his graying blond beard with the back of one hand. That was almost the last of the ale in the keep, and no doubt his sons were drinking what was left. Money would have to be found for more. There was never enough money; most of what came in went out as fast again in arms and pay for the men he owed to King Alfred's service.

"That will do! Get out!" The earl gave the thrall another kick and stared balefully at the empty ale pot. He should have had forty armed men and an alliance with a Norse jarl in Ireland in exchange for his daughter. Instead he had three chests of treasure missing along with the girl, and thanes who laughed behind his back because she'd given herself to the first man she could get into her bed, just to get away from the match he'd made for her. Earl Edmund had thought about going to fetch her back, but that cost money too, and his youngest son, Mark, had already been killed in Norway trying it. Very likely no man would have the girl now anyway.

Angry voices erupted suddenly in the courtyard. Earl Edmund snapped his head around. He recognized the source of the row—his sons, Oswain and Wilfrid, both full of ale and quarrelsome from a long day in the saddle and no quarry to show for it. They would be fighting over whose fault that had been, no doubt. Earl Edmund heaved himself out of his chair and stalked grimly for the door. The dogs looked up, raised an ear or two, and put their noses back in the warm straw by the fire. They didn't care greatly whether the earl's sons did each other an injury or not.

Oswain and Wilfrid were rolling in the mud of the courtyard that lay within the keep's inner wall and apparently trying to strangle each other. The earl's men-at-arms stood looking on, reluctant to lay hands on the master's sons—or hoping they *would* kill each other, Edmund thought sourly.

"What do I keep a steward for?" he shouted wrathfully at Theofric. The running of Ram's Head Keep was Theofric's charge.

A burly thane with graying black hair looked stolidly back at the earl. "Not to stick my hand in an adder's nest," Theofric said bluntly.

Earl Edmund glared at him. He reached down and pulled his sons off each other by the hair. He flung them apart so that they sat, legs sprawled in front of them, in the mud.

"Puppies!" Edmund bellowed at them. Then he swung his head around and fixed his furious blue-violet eyes, incongruous in his florid face, on the grinning men-at-arms. "Are you watching a May dance? Get out! Get to work!"

Wilfrid looked at Oswain and started to rise. Edmund pushed him down again with his boot. "What was it this time? Some wench at the farm? Or were you just feeling idle? God's body, I'll put you to work haying with the thralls if you are!"

Wilfrid compressed his mouth into a tight line, and Oswain looked surly. Neither of them had quite the nerve to flout their father when he was in this mood. They rose carefully, watching his eyes and keeping well away from each other. Their clothes and hair were mired with mud and dung and bits of straw. Under it they were much like the earl to look at—tall, blond, and swaggering, better looking now than they would be when they had grown to their father's age. Earl Edmund had been handsome in much the same fashion before he had begun to lose his hair and get a stomach. Unlike the earl's, their eyes were of the pale, clear blue more common among the English. Only the daughter, Rosamund, had inherited that peculiar shade of violet blue.

Earl Edmund regarded them stonily and seemed to find very little worth looking at.

Oswain opened his mouth. "Wilfrid—"

"Damn Wilfrid! And damn you! Go and get clean, or you can dine with the pigs. I don't want to hear it!"

They stared at him sullenly, faces flushed, but they held their tongues. The last time Theofric had found them fighting, the earl had taken a hound's leash to them. He could still do it.

Earl Edmund gave them a final baleful glare and then stumped up the steps to the hall again, shouting for his dinner.

His sons made a late entrance, with the dung combed out of their hair but otherwise unchanged. They took their places at the table while the earl gnawed at an underdone rib bone and regarded them moodily. They were only four at table: the earl, Oswain, Wilfrid, and Theofric. The men-at-arms ate at their own table in the lower end of the hall. Besides the servants, there were no women in the keep. For the past year there had been no chaplain either, although no one seemed to feel the lack. The last one had gathered his skirts about him, mounted his mule, and ridden off in indignation after the earl had brought his dogs to mass with him. Without a woman in the keep to natter at him over it, Earl Edmund had seen very little need to replace the man.

The earl watched Wilfrid wolfing down rabbit pie from the best dish on the table and considered the uselessness of the departed chaplain, who had failed to interest Wilfrid in the Church as he had been told to do. When the earl had taxed him with that, the chaplain had said vitriolically, jamming his flat straw hat on his head, that not even St. Cuthbert could have brought the devil's kin into holy orders.

Neither the Church nor service in King Alfred's retinue, the two traditional paths open to younger sons, had proved enticement enough to shift Wilfrid from the Ram's Head. He was content where he was, hunting, hawking, prowling among the farmers' maids, and picking quarrels with his brother. Oswain was somewhat easier to control than Wilfrid, although he was as quarrelsome by nature. But Oswain as the eldest would inherit the Ram's Head when his father died, and that in itself kept Oswain from pushing the earl too far. Wilfrid would have only a younger son's portion, and, that being nothing to light a candle for, Earl Edmund knew that Wilfrid would fight Oswain for the Ram's Head. And he might win.

Very few things mattered to Earl Edmund. He had cared greatly for neither wife nor daughter, nor if truth were told, for his sons. He paid service to God at mass when he remembered it and would repent of his sins with his dying breath, but the Church held no sway for him in this world. Ram's Head Keep and the power that went with it, the continuance of his line—those mattered. Oswain and Wilfrid would never share it peaceably and thus could not be allowed to share it. Earl Edmund by right could *order* Wilfrid into the Church if he chose, but Wilfrid would be disinclined to go. More likely he would raise an army somewhere and come back and start a war. More foolish still would be forcing him into the king's service, where an army would be easier to come by. If Wilfrid won, King Alfred wouldn't waste his time on the matter. Alfred had the Danelaw breathing down his back. He expected his earls to take care of their own.

Oswain threw a bone over his shoulder to the dog pack, belched, and wiped his hands on his hose. He looked at Wilfrid. "The bay's gone lame," he said. "I told you not to jump that ditch on him."

Wilfrid shrugged. "You rode him yesterday, and the trouble started then. You put too much weight on him. You're getting fat, Brother. You'll have a paunch like an ale barrel in a year or so."

"You whey-faced pup," Oswain said. "That's not the

first horse you've ridden lame. Keep off my beasts from now on!"

"Be careful, Oswain," Wilfrid said. "You might have a nasty spill next time you ride."

"When you're through fighting like a pair of sulky maids," Theofric said, "I picked up a bit of news today. If it doesn't interest you, it'll interest your father."

"If the king's coming, Theofric," Wilfrid said, "you'll have to take the men and find someplace to raid. His retinue will graze Ram's Head down to the ground like sheep, and the larder's nearly bare as it is." The first planting wouldn't be in harvest for a month. They were still living on the tag end of the winter stores.

Theofric grinned. "*You* do it, young master. Earn your board. No, there's been a death in the family, so to speak."

Earl Edmund raised his head from his rib bone, interested.

"Harud Olafsson. Your sister's intended. He died in Sweden last year. The only wonder is that someone didn't kill him sooner. But it leaves his hold in Ireland bare. With him and the old jarl both under sod, their men have all gone away to other masters. Naught but a few village folk on the land now."

"Where did you have this, Theofric?" Edmund said.

"My sister's son's a monk at Armagh," Theofric said. "He came over with his bishop for some high conference here and came to see me."

"Do you trust him?"

"No," Theofric said, "but I sent two men to Ireland to see for themselves. They came back today. There's good land lying fallow, with nothing but a few churchly hermits on it."

Oswain put down the dagger with which he had been sawing at a tough joint of meat. "We've as good title to that land as any."

"Better," Earl Edmund said. "Your whore of a sister was betrothed to Harud Olafsson. That's as good as a marriage."

"Our sister went with a Norseman before Harud died," Wilfrid said, amused. "You can hardly claim a widow's right."

"I made the betrothal," Edmund snapped. "If Norse took her, I can't be blamed for that."

"Are you trying to talk yourself out of a hold of your own, Wilfrid?" Theofric said.

"If anyone has a claim—" Oswain began.

"You will have Ram's Head," Wilfrid said, "as you are so fond of pointing out. Aye, I'll fight for that Irish land, Theofric, *if* it comes to me. To add to Oswain's estate, I'd sooner set fire to it."

"*Silence!*" Earl Edmund stood up. He put both hands on the table and looked down its length at them. "We have a right to the land, so we'll have it. It goes to Wilfrid. And if you are such a fool that you can't see that you are better off with your brother in Ireland than lolling about Ram's Head thinking of ways to put poison in your soup, Oswain, I am not."

"I'll need men to hold it," Wilfrid said.

"I should point out," Theofric added, "that Norse law doesn't allow inheritance through marriage. If there are no children, the husband's land goes back to the husband's kin."

"There *are* no kin," Earl Edmund said, "unless you've a mind to look for fourth cousins in Norway. And a third of that land was the bride-gift, which should come to *us* as kin. Also there were two chests of silver promised for a morning-gift, so we'll take that in land too." In betrothals of state, the morning-gift, traditionally the present given by a Norse husband to his bride on the morning after marriage, was arranged ahead of time and might be larger than the bride-gift. What had become of the bride-gift, morning-gift, and dowry of Harud Olafsson's two previous wives, no one had inquired, but Earl Edmund was fairly certain they had not been given back. No doubt the dead brides' kin hadn't had enough men-at-arms to ask for them. That there was any silver left on the steading, he hadn't a hope, unless Olaf Haraldsson had managed to bury some of it—but the land was good.

"I'm not a fool," Earl Edmund growled at Wilfrid. "You'll have enough men to hold it. I'll leave you Ram's Head men for a year. By then the land should be bringing in enough to pay your own. The Norse in Ireland will honor our claim—they haven't raided here since we made alliance with Haraldsson." That had been the point of it. English lands were vulnerable both to raids from Norway and from the Norse settlements in Ireland. The marriage to Olaf Haraldsson's son, Harud, had been meant to eliminate the latter.

"What about the Irish?" Oswain said, looking sulky. He was disinclined to go and fight in Ireland for land that Wilfrid would rule.

Earl Edmund dismissed the Irish. "We are Christians as the Irish are. Better Christians on the land than pagans."

Theofric hid a smile under his hand and drank his ale. Earl Edmund hadn't been such a Christian that he couldn't betroth his only daughter to a pagan when the price looked good. Theofric kept the thought to himself. As steward, his charge was the orderly functioning of life within Ram's Head Keep and the orderly succession of its heir. The removal of Wilfrid would go a long way toward achieving both. Earl Edmund was as tough as a bull and, at least in theory, would make his serfs' lives a burden to them for years to come, but his temper was choleric and Theofric had seen men of that nature who had died of an apoplexy after no more than a bad mood and a rich meal. It wouldn't have surprised him if death should come for Earl Edmund in that fashion, and Theofric had no wish to fight a war with Wilfrid when it did. Better an ally in Ireland than a rebellious younger son in the Ram's Head.

Theofric glanced at his lord. Earl Edmund had put his meat down and was counting on his fingers, reckoning the number of men it would take to secure the Irish land and how many his two ships would carry.

"Half a hundred," Theofric said.

"Eh?"

"Half a hundred men, allowing room for horses. We can leave forty behind with Wilfrid."

"Generous," Wilfrid said sarcastically. "I'll need a hundred, Theofric."

"Forty's too many," Oswain said in nearly the same breath. "You could hold it with twenty if you look to your walls instead of chasing dairymaids."

Wilfrid leaned back in his chair and put his feet on

the table so that a sauce dish spilled on his brother's sleeve. It had come cold from the kitchen and was nearly congealed now. "*You* couldn't hold a piss pot with forty men, Oswain," Wilfrid informed him.

Oswain kicked his chair back and stood up, glowering. He drew his fist back.

"Get out!" Edmund snapped at Wilfrid. "Go and pick your men and bring the names to Theofric."

Wilfrid swung his feet down again lazily. "A hundred then?"

"*Half* a hundred. That is what I keep a steward for, to know more than whelps like you. And ten of those come back to Ram's Head."

Wilfrid sauntered from the dais, where the high table was laid, to the end of the hall, where the men-at-arms were throwing dice among the leavings of their meal. Theofric would allow him no more than ten of these, he thought, with the rest to come from the carls who owed Earl Edmund service at arms, but he would try for twenty anyway. They would be glad enough to go. There would be more chance to rise in the world in Ireland than under Earl Edmund. The rewards for service to be gained from Edmund and the other powerful earls of Wessex were meager—no more than necessity forced them to dole out.

At the high table, Oswain stood with his fist still clenched. Earl Edmund regarded him sourly. "If you have any quarrel with your brother's choice of men, take it to Theofric."

"My thanks, lord," Theofric murmured. The day he could find no quarrel with his brother, Oswain would be underground. The only peaceable nature in the earl's brood had belonged to Rosamund, and even she had not been biddable. She had sailed for Norway with her dog, jewelry, and dower chests while Edmund had been fighting Danes with Alfred. It made her the only person Theofric knew of who had ever successfully defied Earl Edmund.

Oswain scowled and went away to find something to object to in his brother's choice of men. Earl Edmund barked at the thrall who was clearing spilled dishes off the table. "Get me some mead. And a savory if you have left any unburnt." He turned back to Theofric. "Now, do I leave you or Oswain behind to hold Ram's Head?"

Theofric considered. "You think it's needful?" The Ram's Head was a steep-sided cape jutting out into the sea. The only landward approach was through a narrow valley with a walled farm across the narrowest part, like a stopper in a bottle. When the Norse had stolen Lady Rosamund, they had had privy information from an escaped and vengeful thrall to get them in. No one else had ever done it. Ram's Head was one of King Alfred's most valuable outposts. It could easily be held by only a few men, and there were several among the men-at-arms capable of commanding.

"I'm not sure," Earl Edmund said dubiously. "But I want you in Ireland with me."

"I'm flattered," Theofric said. He was the scarred veteran of many battles, as tough an old warrior as the earl. Theofric had served Edmund since he was sixteen. It gave him the privilege of free speech, which Edmund accorded no one else. "And you don't trust Oswain on his own." That was statement, not question, and the earl didn't bother to reply.

The thrall had returned eventually with a pot of mead and a savory of spiced quinces in a scorched crust. Earl Edmund stuck his nose in the mead pot and threw the savory across the room.

"You should wed again," Theofric said. "Better that than to die of a colic out of the kitchen."

"*You* wed," Edmund said. "It would serve the same purpose and save me the trouble."

Theofric chuckled and signed to the thrall to bring him some of the mead as well. "Nay, I've never wed yet. I doubt I could get in the habit of it at my age. Find a wife for Oswain." He felt a fleeting moment of pity for any woman who came to the Ram's Head as a bride. It had been overwork and neglect as much as a fever that had killed Earl Edmund's countess. Still, Oswain had to wed one day. There was no point in insuring his inheritance else, if it would only go to the king in the end.

"I had half a bargain once with old Ecgbert of Appleyard," Edmund said, "for that tall daughter of his, but he wanted Rosamund for his son Athelwulf as well and took an offense when I gave her to Harud Olafsson."

"Well, Ecgbert's dead now, and the offense with him maybe," Theofric said. "And his girl's still unwed. A bit long in the tooth though, isn't she?"

"A year older than Oswain," Edmund said. "And she's no beauty—I've seen comelier she-goats. But she's a good housekeeper, and none of her sisters was barren, so I expect she's a breeder."

"Well, you might put the matter to Athelwulf again," Theofric said. The thrall brought him his mead, and he drank it, noting that the silver pot was black with tarnish and filthy along the beaded rim. He wiped it on his sleeve distastefully. "A good housewife is a better bargain than a pretty wench who's too fine to put her foot in the kitchens." She might also be more grateful to be wed, and gratitude would go a long way to resigning a girl to living out her life on the Ram's Head.

Edmund pushed his chair back. "It might serve at that. It's young Athelwulf I'm thinking of when I don't like to leave Ram's Head without a good captain. He's an itch in his hand for more land than his father left him, and he knows the way here well enough. If I make an offer for his sister, Athelwulf won't cut his own nose off by raiding here while we're gone." Neither of them considered asking Oswain what *he* thought of the idea.

Theofric chuckled and swallowed his mead. It was very good, pure honey mead, well spiced and strong enough for a pot or two to make a man forget his age. He scratched indulgently at an itch under his woolen shirt. The floor straw, bed hangings, and clothes were all inhabited. A man got used to it, up to a point. The rosemary and pennyroyal among the straw had long ago lost their sweet scent, and the odor that emanated from them now was unwholesome. Theofric stretched his legs out and put them on a sleeping dog. "I doubt the floor strewings have been changed in a six-month. One of us has need to wed, Earl. Best it be Oswain."

In the morning, Earl Edmund swung his bulk up onto his war-horse, took a troop of men, and rode to

Appleyard Keep to put the matter to young Athelwulf. It
was a pity that out of old Ecgbert's numerous brood, all
the beauty should have gone to Athelwulf, Edmund thought.
The girl, when Athelwulf shouted to her to come down
from the bower for the earl's inspection, was still as goat
faced as he remembered her, but her eyes were clear and
she looked strong. Oswain could close his eyes at night if
he didn't like it. Her name was Eadgytha, Athelwulf
informed him, assuming correctly that the earl wouldn't
remember it.

Her brother dismissed her again without telling her
why she had been wanted, but Eadgytha knew anyway.
The only doubt in her mind was for whom she had been
proposed as a wife: the earl or one of his sons. Earl
Edmund's countess had still been alive the last time a
match had been mentioned. It might be that now he had
decided to marry again himself. Eadgytha sighed. They all
looked equally undesirable, but she had begun to be afraid
that she might not marry at all, and on the whole she
thought she would prefer Earl Edmund. He wouldn't live
so long, and then she could be a widow.

In the chamber below, Athelwulf listened receptively
to Earl Edmund. An alliance with Ram's Head would be
useful, and the slight arising from the earl's rejection of
Athelwulf's suit for Rosamund, Edmund's daughter, was
not mentioned. There was very little point since the
daughter was no longer in the earl's possession. Athelwulf
was young, ambitious, fair of face, and wishful for an
avenue to let these attributes take him as far as they
would. He had green eyes, light brown hair streaked with
gold by the sun, and a beautiful, finely carved face that
belied a nature that was nearly as ruthless as the earl's.

From Athelwulf's point of view the only fly in the
wine cup was Wilfrid. There was no point in making his
sister a prospective countess if Wilfrid was likely to murder her husband as soon as she had achieved that rank.
When the earl had explained the matter of the Irish land,
Athelwulf struck a bargain. He knew that part of the earl's
offer was to keep Athelwulf from eyeing Ram's Head in his
absence, but Athelwulf considered it easier to marry his
sister to it than to take it by storm. And Edmund was

offering a good price. Athelwulf decided that Lady Rosamund had indirectly brought him fortune after all, and a man who was ambitious needed to know how to change his plans to suit events. To stick stubbornly to a demand that was no longer in the earl's giving would take him no farther down the road. Earl Edmund left Appleyard with an agreement, and the next day he began to load his ships.

While Earl Edmund was preparing to enforce his dubious claim on the Irish land, the rightful owner put his arms around the earl's daughter and gave her a long kiss. *Raven* was loaded and ready, and Rosamund could feel the itch in Haakon's foot even through his passion. She wondered wistfully if he would ever be content to rest more than a season or two in the same place, and decided that he probably wouldn't. So she blinked back her tears and lifted Asa up to say good-bye to her father. Rosamund had never been under the delusion that Haakon was a man who could be changed to suit his wife's requirements, nor had Haakon ever promised her that he was. Haakon only made promises that he knew he wouldn't break. Rosamund set Asa down and leaned against his chest for a moment. This farewell might have to last her longer than she cared to think about—not even Haakon knew where he was going, and Rosamund put smaller faith in whatever it was that inhabited the golden ax than Haakon did.

A furious howling reminiscent of a dragon underground gradually intruded on her notice.

"Is that Wulf?"

Haakon nodded. "This time he stays with you. I've locked him in the dairy."

It was a good thing there were no cows in the dairy as yet, Rosamund thought, or they would undoubtedly be dry for weeks. When Haakon sailed, Wulf always went with him unless locked up, and he registered his displeasure loudly. Still, she would be glad of the big dog's company. Wulf had been hers before she had ever known Haakon.

"I've been wanting some pups from a better-looking bitch than Gerd," Haakon said cheerfully, "and Ireland is full of wolfhounds. You can find some mates for him here."

"Certainly," Rosamund said, trying not to snap at him and succeeding ill. "I will have nothing better to do in this palace"—she cast a scornful glance about the half-repaired steading—"than to find lovers for a dog while you are gone."

"I knew you would think so," Haakon said, ignoring her temper. "Cormac will know who has a likely female."

Rosamund glared at him, gave up, and burst out laughing. How like Haakon to be thinking of breeding a dog, on the eve of sailing for God knew where. And she didn't want to quarrel with him as he left. She hugged him again and watched wistfully as he strode down the track to the river. There was a spring in his step. *He won't be happy until he has found it*, she thought. She turned back to the hall with her throat tight, suddenly unable to watch him sail away. Idleness bred misery, but certainly there was enough to do to keep her mind from that. Putting the steading itself into proper order would take the rest of the summer, even with the labors of the forty men whom Haakon had left behind. The first thing was to get the gates rebuilt. There had been no further quarrels with Haakon's Irish kin, but a hold with no gates was a foolhardy invitation.

VI

The *Kraken*

Raven first turned her prow not west but north with the prevailing wind and current to the Faeroe Islands, and thence, with the guidance of the Faeroe men, to Iceland. Iceland was the farthest that any known man had gone into the Western Ocean, and if any man knew what lay beyond, it would be an Icelander. Haakon was not such a fool that he wished to sail blinder than need be, even with a god for navigator. The gods had a way of considering things funny that did not amuse men at all.

Two days out from the Faeroes, *Raven* slid beneath the shadows of the towering black basalt cliffs that had been their guide to landfall on the southern coast of Iceland. As the crew beached her beyond the cliffs and waded through the sun-tinged foam to shore, Haakon was not overly surprised to find a delegation of Icelanders awaiting them, mail clad and armed to the teeth. Viking folk were not above preying on their own kind, and Iceland had been settled largely by Norse who did not care for Harald Fairhair's method of ruling Norway. It inclined them to suspicion.

Haakon's men kept their weapons to show that they were no easy prey but left them sheathed to show that they also meant no harm, a universal gesture like the peace shield that hung atop *Raven*'s mast. Political differences had never stopped the constant trade that flowed between Iceland and the rest of the Norse world, and it took only a few sentences for Haakon and the burly graybeard who was the Icelanders' spokesman to strike a bargain. Haakon wanted fresh water, a day or so to talk with any man who had gone a-voyaging in the Western Ocean beyond Iceland, and a healer for Kalki Estridsson, whose wound taken in the battle with the Irish had begun to fester. He should have left Kalki in Ireland, Haakon thought as Hagar the Simple lifted the sick man over *Raven*'s side, but Kalki had seemed well enough a week ago. Now his face was flushed and burning hot to the touch. The wound in his thigh was an angry red and hotter than his face. The graybeard, whose name was Mord Frey-Priest and who was also a healer, tut-tutted professionally and had them bear Kalki inland to his farm.

"That does not look so good," he said in a low voice to Haakon as they marched along.

"He is a good man," Haakon said shortly. "Also a good helmsman, and I need him. I will be grateful if you can heal him." It would be a bad omen for Kalki to die at the start of the voyage.

Mord gave a noncommittal grunt, and Haakon said nothing further. It had been his experience that healers always predicted the worst at the outset so that if the patient lived, you were grateful, and if he did not, you were not surprised. At least Kalki had taken that wound in honest battle, so surely Father Odin would take him to Valhalla for it if he died. For some reason there was smaller comfort in that than there might have been.

Haakon concentrated on taking in the sights of the Iceland coast as they marched. It was fair country, and he could see why a man with no mind to acknowledge Harald Fairhair as an overlord might come here to live. The green hills were flecked white with sheep, and the climate bred good wool, thick and oily, which wove into a heavy cloth that was almost waterproof. Iceland was volcano born and there was no timber on it, so all the houses were built of massive turf walls on a stone foundation, with pitched turf roofs.

Mord's farmhouse lay in the center of a little valley, a self-contained village, surrounded by byre and smithy, nondescript huts for the lesser folk, and flocks of sheep, shaggy horses, and cattle dotting the valley around it. Inside, the turf walls of the main hall had been paneled with smooth wood, set a little away from the walls to protect them from the damp, a mark of their owner's wealth. That wood would have had to be shipped from Ireland or Norway.

Mord's wife, a brisk, round woman with red cheeks and a merry smile, welcomed with ale and a hot stew whomever her husband had seen fit to bring home with him. She made a motherly noise when she saw Kalki and bade Haakon's men take him into the back chamber, where she had him put in her own bed. Mord, whose bed it was also, appeared to find that unnecessarily hospitable, but his wife gave him such a look that he made no protest.

Mord collected an array of pots and bottles from a chest at the end of the hall and followed Kalki, while the rest sat gratefully around the fire. Haakon had left half his men on the shore for a shipguard, and the men in Mord's hall congratulated themselves heartily on not being among them, as Mord's wife went around with another pitcher of ale. Haakon drank his moodily, and when Mord reappeared, Haakon was at his elbow.

"I will tell you, Jarl Haakon," Mord said solemnly,

and Haakon did not think that the old man was only playing it safe, "it does not look good to me. He has the wound fever, but I think he is sick with more than that. Sometimes it happens that when a man has one illness, it weakens him so that another comes in also. And the two of them, neither one of which might harm him separately, together may kill him."

Haakon looked through the open doorway.

"Go to him later," Mord said. "He is sleeping now. Sleep will do him more good than salves just now."

Haakon grimaced. Not being taken on a week's voyage from Ireland would no doubt have done him more good than either. Hindsight serving no more purpose now than ever, Haakon went back to the fire and prodded Donal out of his ale pot until Donal took out his harp.

Once assured of *Raven*'s intentions, the Icelanders proved a friendly lot. Mord's hall filled up with men from the outlying farms as they came in from their work and heard the news of a strange new kind of ship and a crew that claimed they were going viking beyond the Western Ocean. By nightfall there must have been thirty men in the hall besides Haakon's own, drinking Mord's ale and arguing about what, if anything, the *Raven*'s crew would meet with in the west.

"Aye, there be land out there," a red-faced man with his hair in two braids said loudly. "Didn't Flosi Ormsson come back to say he'd seen ravens blown out by a storm, and the raven be a land bird! But there's other worse things west-over-seas, mind you—giants and the like."

"I know a man who saw a serpent big enough to swallow his ship," another said.

Hagar the Simple thought that one over. "Why didn't it then?"

"He killed it with two strokes of his ax," the man assured him. "And all the skalds made verses on it."

"Reckon it must have been a big ax," Hagar grunted.

Donal chuckled and picked up his harp again. To his mind none of them had seen any of these beasts in anything but an ale horn. That wouldn't mean they weren't out there, though.

"I myself have seen a *kraken* in these very waters," a

third man said. His name was Eilaf Eiriksson. He had a red face and pale hair going bald in the front, although he didn't look to be over eight-and-twenty. He glared huffily at Donal as the harper drew a finger along the strings in a little amused tune. "It was like a tree stump uprooted—a fat body with a hundred legs on the end."

"And likely the skin of the thing is hanging on your wall at home," Donal said with a raised eyebrow.

"It would have been," Eilaf said, "but that the beast was cowardly, and swam from us when we pursued it."

Donal thought that of Eilaf and the *kraken*, he knew which one had run from the other, but Haakon was glaring at him to mind his manners, so he kept the thought to himself.

The conversation turned from monsters to land again. One man who had hitherto kept his silence said briefly, "There is land there, jarl, of a certainty, but you won't like what lives on it."

"Don't be minding him, jarl," Mord's wife said. "That one always sees the worst. Storm-driven west, he was, and came back all grim faced and closemouthed about it, and only making black warnings when another man has a mind to go voyaging, the use of which I *don't* see"—she glared at the man who had spoken—"if you can't be speaking plain." At the end of this somewhat convoluted speech she bustled off, and Mord Frey-Priest laid his hand on Haakon's arm.

"I'm afraid he is worse, jarl. Best you should come."

Haakon followed him into the back chamber and sat down on a rug by Kalki's bed. Kalki's face was white now with just the burning fever spots in his cheeks. His eyes were open, but they had a hectic glitter and seemed not to see Haakon. A harsh rattle in his lungs spoke, as Mord had said, of more illness than the wound fever. Kalki's hands roved restlessly over the coverlet, plucking at it. Haakon put his own hands over them, but Kalki was too far gone in his fever dream to feel it.

"At least he can be howe-laid on dry land and not in Ran's lair," Mord said. Ran was the sea goddess, who dwelled beneath the water.

If the words were meant to comfort, they succeeded ill. "He is not dead yet!" Haakon snapped.

Mord shook his head sorrowfully. He would be, what-

ever this dark jarl thought. And it was no pleasure to
Mord to lose one in his care.

Haakon relented. Like all seafaring folk, the viking
kind most courted and most feared a death by drowning.
The old man had meant well. "I am sorry, old father,"
Haakon said gruffly.

Mord pulled the door shut behind him and left Haakon
to sit by the bed through the long, light summer night.
Haakon went to sleep at last with his face against the down
mattress and woke to find Kalki still and cold beside him.

Mord sent a shipguard of his own men to *Raven* so
that the rest of Haakon's crew could come inland for the
howe-laying. They gathered sorrowfully on a hill above
Mord's farm, where other Norse dead already lay. Haakon,
Thorfinn Solvisson, and Knut One-Eye set the stones that
outlined the bow and stern of a dry-land ship, and they
laid Kalki's body between them and covered the grave-
ship over with green turf. Haakon paid Mord for a horse
and two yearling bulls to go with Kalki for a grave offering.
Yazid stood a little ways away, wishing to give no offense
but unable to join in heathen prayers. Donal MacRae
knew that likely he should not be here either, but he had
liked Kalki, and, he thought stubbornly, God would have
to understand.

Thorfinn and Knut One-Eye stood side-by-side, mourning Kalki and thinking of practical matters. "This leaves us
one helmsman short," Thorfinn said quietly after Haakon
had killed the animals beside Kalki's howe and the men
had begun to stream back down the hillside to Mord's
farmstead. For ordinary voyages, only one helmsman was
needed besides the captain of a longship, for the ships
were run ashore at night. But *Raven* might be out of sight
of land for days at a time, so she needed enough men to
stand day and night watches.

"There are others of us who have taken a helm before,"
Knut said. "Not on *Raven*, though," he added thoughtfully.

"And not that the jarl would trust," Thorfinn said.
"You can tell by looking at him. Haakon doesn't like it
either, but it isn't a seemly matter to talk of at Kalki's
howe-laying."

"There's Yazid," Knut said. "He built her."

"Oh, no," Thorfinn said flatly. "Yazid is in command of those troll-taken *things* he's planted all over the ship. No other man will lay a hand on them."

"Ah, well, I daresay the jarl will think of something," Knut said. He gave a thoughtful glance at Haakon, walking beside Eilaf Eiriksson, the man who had seen the *kraken*. "There will be men in Iceland who haven't done with viking, and maybe a helmsman among them."

"You have run mad," Donal MacRae said. He looked at Haakon as if to see if it showed in his face. "That braggart is no more a helmsman than I am the king of Scotland!"

"Neither are you," Haakon said. He stuck his head in the rain barrel and lifted it up again, dripping. It didn't seem to help his headache. "He claims he is, and we are short one man, so he will have his chance." Eilaf Eiriksson had put the matter to him at Kalki Estridsson's funeral feast, and now Haakon found himself reluctant to admit that his good sense might have gotten lost in his ale horn. The sun on the meadow was blinding. He closed his eyes. When he opened them again, Yazid had appeared beside Donal, twin voices of doom.

"Donal is right," Yazid said quietly. "This Eilaf makes too much large talk for a man who has actually done all the deeds he lays claim to."

Yazid's dark eyes were clear under the red and white cloth of his headscarf, and he appeared to be the only one of *Raven*'s crew without a bad head this morning. Haakon thought that perhaps Allah was right in prohibiting his followers strong drink, but Haakon would be dragged into the hills by trolls before he would admit it. He knew why he had drunk too much—in some way he felt that Kalki's death had been his fault and it was no pleasant thing to wake up with a corpse in the morning. Dimly through the ale and the hot, thick smell of roasting horseflesh, which was the Icelander ritual funeral meal, he had heard Eilaf Eiriksson telling him of the voyages he had made and the monsters he had met and vanquished. He thought that Eilaf had told him several times about the *kraken*, and that it had gotten somewhat larger with each telling. Somehow by the time that Eilaf had asked him for a place in *Raven* as third helmsman, Haakon had thought it a very fine idea indeed.

"I have given him a place," he said gruffly. "He stays."

Yazid shrugged. "It is yours to command, jarl." The Arabs, Haakon had discovered with pleased surprise, were not given to arguing with their lords in the fashion that the Norse considered their right.

No such reticence afflicted Donal, however. "You'll be sorry. That man is walking trouble, Haakon. He has—what is it the Norse call it? Thief's eyes. He has thief's eyes, and you had best keep your own on him."

"*Enough!*" Haakon gave Donal the look of a man much tried and put a hand to his head as the sound of his own voice made it ring. "He stays. He sails with us. Keep *quiet!*" Donal spun around on his heel, prophesying doom, and Haakon stuck his head in the rain barrel again.

The Icelanders gave Haakon all the information they could on wind and current west of their land, and *Raven* turned her face into the unknown. Haakon stood on deck with the golden ax over his shoulder, and he could almost hear it singing in his ear, *West, West*. The black raven spread her wings on the sail, and the proud, carved bird at the prow rose like a live thing from the foam. "I keep my promise, Lord," Haakon said under his breath, and the ax whispered back to him, *West*.

Haakon wondered if Kalki in Valhalla could look down on them and be pleased, and then he put that thought away from him because it made him think of Kalki's replacement, and that, he had known one day out of Iceland, had been a mistake. Haakon was too prideful to admit it and put about for Iceland again, so he clung to the fact that Eilaf was indeed a fair helmsman. It was no doubt the only thing he hadn't lied about, Haakon thought sourly. Eilaf Eiriksson was a loud braggart and had no doubt left the other ships he had served on because their captains had grown tired of his troublemaking. Mord Frey-Priest had even said something to him the night of Kalki's funeral, Haakon dimly remembered now, but Haakon hadn't been listening to anything but the ale and his own guilty grief. He wondered vaguely if Thor Odinsson might have sent him Eilaf to keep him from being too pleased with himself. Certainly it was not a thing that was beyond the gods, and Thor had found Haakon's pride overgreat before now. Eilaf Eiriksson might have struck him as a fitting warning. Haakon looked at the ax, but it had no word to say.

In these latitudes in summer the darkness was only a hand briefly brushed across the sun. Raven's crew left their tents pitched on the middeck, moored to pegs set in the planking, and slept in turn whenever they came off the oars. They had picked up a fair westerly wind, but Haakon kept them to the oars anyway, both for better speed and to stay boredom. With no enemy to fight and confined in the close quarters of the ship, they would fight each other if they had naught else to do. There were animals in the hold to be tended, but that used up only a small part of an endless day. For the rest there was nothing to do but watch the boundless gray water and dodge the drifting ice floes.

The only living thing they saw besides each other was a walrus, perched on his floe like a toothy jarl in a fur cloak. Once they passed a pod of spouting whales, but Haakon refused to give chase. Whale meat would have enlivened their diet, but if Raven were damaged, there would be no known place to put in for repairs. Distance from Iceland had quickly made him cautious. Too cautious, Eilaf Eiriksson seemed to think—he told in a loud voice how in a single ship's boat he alone had taken three whales not a season past. Donal suggested rudely that he take Raven's boat and try it now, and Haakon pulled them away from each other. Privately he thought that was not such an ill idea, but he had no wish to lose the boat. The brief darkness was just beginning to fall when he climbed into the leather double sleeping bag he shared with Donal and left the helm to Eilaf.

Eilaf took the tiller moodily and stared into the gloom. This jarl was too cautious. He hovered over his strangely fitted ship like a nursemaid. Eilaf enviously regarded the catapult bolted to the foredeck. No one was allowed to touch it but the jarl and the Arab who kept his hair under a headrail like a woman. The other crewmen seemed more pleased than not to let matters rest that way, but the thing did not look so greatly complicated, Eilaf thought, deciding that the jarl was prideful and wished to keep the catapult a mystery. Haakon Olesson no doubt kept his crew's loyalty through the Arab's strange devices and the golden ax that was said to be magic. Certainly he appeared to be an ordinary man in other ways, and not even so tall as most. Haakon Olesson was no more deserving of his riches and his fine red and black ship than any other man—Eilaf Eiriksson, for instance, Eilaf thought, aggrieved.

Eilaf Eiriksson was a man who felt that somehow life had shorted him of that which he deserved. Other men, not so brave or clever, gained fortune, but always, Eilaf thought, luck ran against him, or some enemy stepped in his path from spitefulness, and it all came to nothing. He leaned on the tiller and cast a professional eye at the gathering stars. It was easy to keep a course with the wind obligingly steady. It had even picked up some in the last minutes. In fact, it was *too* fair, Eilaf thought. These fools would follow the jarl like sheep for as long as the jarl's luck held. Eilaf grimaced. He should have been master of his own ship by now, not third helmsman in Haakon Olesson's. A small island had been rising to the northwest, and Eilaf shouted an order to trim the sail to give it a wide berth. He could see through the gloom that the water around it was littered with jagged reefs. Then his eye caught a movement through the spray, and he changed his mind with the next breath. A formless shape with writhing limbs clung to the reef. A *kraken*!

Whatever the jarl's harper might think, Eilaf Eiriksson had seen a *kraken* before, although it was true that he had had no mind to fight it with a whaling spear. But the catapult on *Raven*'s foredeck could smash the beast against the reef at a safe distance and give credence to all of Eilaf's tales. *Then* they would see if he or Haakon Olesson was best fit to lead them!

Eilaf shouted at the nearest man to take the helm and another to retrim the sail. *"Out oars!"* The men drowsing on the oar decks brushed the sleep from their eyes, and the scarlet oars ran out through the oar ports in unison. No one questioned Eilaf's orders. The man at the helm was the man in command. Eilaf dodged through the tents

of the sleepers to the catapult on the foredeck. As he had
thought, it did not look so mysterious. Eilaf loaded the
sling with a stone from the basket tied to the deck beside
it and wound the levers back until the skeins hummed
tautly. He gave no thought to the rising sea and the darker
clouds that had gathered swiftly across the stars. The
kraken reared up on the reef, tentacles writhing, as it
sensed *Raven's* bulk bearing toward it.

Hjalmar, leaning on the tiller, yelped and tried to
turn it back again. He had followed Eilaf's orders as he
was meant to, but he hadn't seen the reefs until now.
Blind obedience did not include running the jarl's ship
onto the rocks and into a sea monster's mouth.

"Hold her steady!" Eilaf shouted furiously. There was
plenty of time to bring her around. "Do as I say, curse
you!" He looked around for a mallet that was meant to
knock the catapult's firing pin free and couldn't find it, so
he slammed it with his fist instead.

Haakon had reached the first stage of deep sleep,
from which it is hardest to awaken. When the shouting
began he pulled himself from it laboriously, trying to push
the fog from his brain. Suddenly a piercing shriek cut
through the other noise, and he sat up, awake and cursing.
As he staggered out from under the tent, a bolt of lightning from the storm that had gathered above them illuminated *Raven's* deck and the sea beyond. They were close
to rocks, where no rock had been when he had gone to
sleep, and some huge and hideous thing was visible
through the spray that battered at the reef. On the foredeck, Eilaf, who should have been at the helm, clutched a
bleeding hand and screamed that the catapult was an
ill-luck thing possessed of Arab demons. Some piece of its
works had flown back and torn the sail, and half the crew
were struggling to bring it under control.

"Knut, take the helm!" Haakon shouted. He could
see Thorfinn among the men wrestling with the sail.
Several lines of the rigging had parted, and the half-
lowered yard tilted dangerously. Even in full night at this
latitude it was never quite pitch dark, but the storm
clouds and now a driving rain greatly increased the darkness. Haakon didn't see the *kraken* slide from its rock into

the boiling sea, but he was eye-to-eye with it when it erupted on *Raven*'s starboard bow. *Raven* rocked violently as three arms wrapped themselves around the prow, and Haakon saw two eyes the size of dinner plates venomously regarding the small thing that had had the temerity to shoot rocks at it. The lightning flashed again, and as *Raven* dipped under the *kraken*'s weight a huge wave came sheeting over the bow. Haakon slid backward under the weight of the water, struggling frantically to get the golden ax unslung from its sheath on his back. He righted himself, staggering, as something more powerful than an iron band, and smelling foully of ancient evil and decay, wrapped itself around his ribs. Above him the *kraken*'s eyes glowed with a ghastly phosphorescence, and a beak-shaped maw opened and closed again.

Haakon swung the ax and felt it bite through the *kraken*'s flesh, but two more arms were entangling him now, and something burned like red-hot irons across his back. *Thor aid me*, he thought. He wasn't going to be this thing's meal, but he would gladly give it Eilaf. He swung the ax again, and another arm, half-severed, recoiled and slid over the bow into the sea. Haakon, tangled in the third arm, felt himself dragged against the oar ports and lifted half over their edge. He cut the last arm away frantically and then raised the ax to smash it down between the *kraken*'s eyes. The horrible beak opened and closed, and the *kraken*'s arms flailed wildly as the creature slid down beneath the sea again. Haakon dived out of the way of those writhing arms. If one caught him in its death throes, it could yet pull him into the sea.

The last tentacle curled over the side, and Haakon stood leaning on the bow, gasping. His shirt was in ribbons on his back, which felt like fire where the suckers on the *kraken*'s arms had drawn blood. Something soft twitched at his feet, and Haakon stumbled back in horror, then saw that it was a severed arm of the *kraken*, curling and uncurling with some last muscular contractions of its own. All along the underside were saw-toothed rings to match the wounds on Haakon's back. He thought for a moment of keeping it, to flay and take home to Norway. But there might be more of the *kraken*'s kind in these waters. If so,

Haakon had no wish to attract them, he thought wearily. He lifted the arm with the blade of the golden ax and flipped the limb overboard into the storm. The sea pounded at *Raven* like a fist, and a jagged bolt of lightning showed Haakon the danger he had forgotten while he battled with the *kraken*—the jagged reefs were perilously close, as openmouthed and fearsome as the *kraken*, and *Raven* was nearly on them!

Rosamund quickly sat upright in bed, her heart pounding, and reached automatically for Haakon. She did that every morning when he was gone and couldn't seem to break herself of it, but this morning some dimly remembered horror had crept into her dreams and made her reach more urgently for him. Rosamund rubbed the sleep from her eyes, indignant with herself, and burrowed down under the coverlet again. The air was damp, and she could hear the sullen sound of rain sheeting down outside. The bulge that her body made under the coverlet suddenly looked very small to her in an ocean of bed. All the beds she shared with Haakon were as large as they could be made. He twitched and writhed like a nervous horse all night, and it was either share a large bed with him or share no bed at all, she had discovered. But a big bed was a lonely place to sleep by oneself.

A patter of feet outside the door proclaimed that the thralls were up, and a provident mistress should be up with them. Rosamund sighed and pulled her fur wrapper around her, trying to wriggle out of her night shift and into her day one within its folds. It was not unseasonably cold, but the rain made the air clammy. The men would be getting dressed by the fire in the great hall, but they had less modesty and mostly slept in their clothes anyway.

"My lady! I was just coming!" Tordis, her maid, bustled in, took the undershift indignantly, and trotted out again with it. In a moment she was back, and the fine white wool folds were warm from the hall fire.

"Thank you, Tordis. You spoil me." Rosamund slipped it on gratefully and stood while Tordis dropped a heavy red woolen gown over it. Next was the apron, really only two oblong lengths of cloth, front and back, held over the shoulders by thin straps and two elaborate filigreed gold brooches at the front. "Not that one," Rosamund said as Tordis held out her best apron, richly woven with red and gold thread a foot wide on the hem. "I have work to do today."

"You have company," Tordis said firmly. She dropped the apron over Rosamund's head, pinned it, and hung a necklace of gold and glass beads between the brooches.

"Company?" Rosamund looked blank.

"One of these Irish that the jarl says are blood kin to him," Tordis said disapprovingly.

"Only one?" Visions of a horde of armed men at the gates passed through Rosamund's mind, but if there were, Tordis wouldn't be worried about which gown she should wear.

"One of those Christians' priests," Tordis said with loathing. Then she remembered the silver cross that Lady Rosamund wore under her shift, gulped, and blushed.

"It's all right, my dear," Rosamund said. "Maybe he has only come to see Abbot Cormac," she added hopefully.

"Oh, no, my lady. He asked for you." Tordis shook the braids out of Rosamund's long hair and began to comb it with a wide-toothed ivory comb. "He's in the hall now, standing by the fire and looking as friendly as a troll."

"Oh, dear. Have the men had their breakfast?"

"*If* it hasn't curdled in their bellies from having the man watch them eat it," Tordis said. "I'm not meaning to offend, my lady, but the looks he gave us all . . . he wouldn't stop to spit if we were all ablaze."

"Well, send them about their work as soon as they've eaten," Rosamund said, "before one of them takes offense." She racked her brains, trying to think what the man could want with her. She had been good, she thought rebelliously. She did not deserve that God should send her a truculent priest to be her cross. Tordis piled her mistress's waist-length hair on her head, secured it with a handful of ivory pins, and tied a clean white kerchief over it. "Bring him something to eat, Tordis," Rosamund said. "It may sweeten him. And tell him I will be with him as soon as may be."

"Yes, my lady."

Tordis bustled out, and Rosamund felt on the thick rug for her fur slippers. What next?

She knew who the man was as soon as she saw him. The priest was of medium height, slender, straight backed, dark of hair and eyes. His hair had the same streak of gray across the temples, where his tonsure ended, that Sigrid's had, and his face might have been Sigrid's cast into a masculine mold.

"Bid you welcome, Father," Rosamund said gently in her halting Gaelic. "I am thinking that your name must be Kilian, for you have such a look of my husband's mother, Sigrid, about you."

"Her name was Deirdre," Kilian said, "and she is dead to us."

Rosamund blinked. Sigrid had said that her brother was bitter but not that he carried the sort of gall that ate away the heart. "The man that she grieved you by marrying is long dead and buried," Rosamund said. "And before we sailed she asked that we learn if it was well with you."

Kilian made no answer. He was dressed all in black, and his face was white and intense against the black robes.

"I told my maid to offer you food and drink," Rosamund said, wondering what on earth to do with him. "You must be wet to the skin and have been up with the sun. Have you eaten?"

"I cannot eat in a house of the heathen!" Kilian said. His eyes glittered.

For Sigrid's sake, Rosamund checked her temper as she would check a bolting horse. "I assure you that Abbot Cormac has done so," she said. "I am a Christian, and so is one of my women."

Kilian strode toward her suddenly. "You imperil your soul!" he hissed. "It is for that I have come, when I heard that there was a Christian woman living in this unholy place! If you fear hellfire, lady, you must leave here!"

Rosamund sat down on one of the benches that was still pulled up to the long trestle table, thankful that the men had gone and there were only two thralls clearing the mess away. "You don't know what—"

Kilian pursued her to the bench. The intensity in his voice was unnerving. "You abandon yourself to the fires of hell, and you commit a mortal sin so long as you fornicate with a pagan!"

"*Fornicate?*" Rosamund sat bolt upright on the bench. Asa toddled up to her, apparently escaped from her nurse again, and Rosamund scooped the child up and set her on her knee. She would be less likely to throw the soup pot at Father Kilian with Asa watching. "The jarl is my *husband*," she said icily, "and *your* nephew, for whom I would have thought you would have a greater care." She felt that her Gaelic had got tangled somewhere in the last sentence, but she thought that Father Kilian had got the gist of it.

"Deirdre is dead," Kilian said. "A child of the woman who calls herself Sigrid has no place in my family."

Rosamund took a deep breath, grateful that Sigrid hadn't come to Ireland with them after all. "I am told that Fergus MacAidan recognizes kinship," she said, "and he is cousin to my husband."

Kilian stiffened. "Fergus MacAidan is as great a fool as you, lady, if you continue in this place." He looked at Asa, who was watching him curiously. "Take the babe and leave this place, for your soul's sake. You may come to us if you wish," he added stiffly.

Rosamund thought that she would rather be found dead in a ditch. "My soul must be in my own keeping, Father Kilian," she said firmly, "and I cannot agree with you as to its peril. But I thank you for your care."

Kilian's face darkened, and Rosamund said hastily, still trying to smooth matters over, "But there is a holy office that I should be grateful if you would perform for me. Asa has not been baptized, and it frets me that that should be so." That much was true, although she had never spoken of it to Haakon. When Asa was grown, she would have to choose what path to follow, as both Sigrid and Rosamund had done in their different ways, but in the meantime Rosamund knew that she would be more comfortable if the child's soul had been spoken for to God.

"No," Kilian said flatly, his eyes dark with righteous anger. "I will not make a mockery of the Holy Church as you have done and read the baptism over a pagan Norseman's child!"

Rosamund sat looking at him with her mouth open for no more than a moment. Then she rose, Asa under one arm and fire in her eye. "You would damn a *child*, for spite against its parents? Get out of my hall, Father Kilian, and take your pious words with you! It takes more than a tonsure and a monk's robe to make a Christian!" She turned and shouted "Leif!" at the top of her voice, and the hold's steward came running.

"Escort this man to the gates, and see that he is not harmed," she said in Norse. "See also that he does not come back. *Ever.*"

Leif and Father Kilian departed, each eyeing the other as he would a snake, if there had been snakes in Ireland. The holy Patrick was said to have driven them all into the sea, Rosamund thought furiously, and it was an embarrassment to God that he had not taken Kilian with them. She was still holding Asa to her breast and steaming like a kettle just on the boil when Cormac shouldered his way through the door at the end of the hall. He had been gardening apparently—even in the rain. He had a bunch of herbs in one hand. He set it on the table and listened while Rosamund sputtered at him.

"He told me I should leave Haakon! That I—I am *fornicating*! And then when I asked him to baptize Asa, he *refused*!"

Cormac sighed. "I imagined as much, when I heard he had come. Kilian is an uncharitable man, child, and always has been. But you mustn't blame Holy Church for it. The world is full of men like Kilian. A priest is only a man; a calling to God does not always make us holy. We have still our pride and our faults to conquer. Pride is Kilian's cross, I fear."

Rosamund ground her teeth, and Cormac scooped Asa out of her arms. "Come with me, child." He pushed the door open and set out across the yard for the well, with Rosamund trotting after him through the rain. Asa watched with interest while Cormac raised the bucket with his free hand. He also had found it troublesome that the little one was unchristened. He wasn't going to whistle the chance away when it was handed to him. His outstretched hand formed a cross above the bucket. "What is her full name?"

Rosamund hesitated. "Just Asa Haakonsdottír. The Norse don't give but one name."

"*Asa, credis in Deum, Patrem omnipotentum, Creatorem caeli et terrae?*" Do you believe in God, Father almighty, Creator of heaven and earth? Cormac smiled at Rosamund. "You may answer for her."

"*Credo,*" Rosamund said firmly. I believe. She wondered if Haakon was going to like this.

"*Credis in Jesum Christum Filium ejus unicum, Dominum nostrum?*" Asa had begun to wriggle, trying to put her hands in the bucket, and Cormac hastened the ritual. "*Credis in Spiritum Sanctum et sanctam Ecclesiam?*" He dipped his hand in the bucket. "Asa Haakonsdottír, will you be baptized?"

"*Volo.*" I will.

"*In nomine Patris, et Filii, et Spiritus Sancti.*" Cormac splashed the water three times on her brow in the sign of the cross while Asa screwed up her face in surprise. She had the jarl's dark hair and her mother's purple-blue eyes, he noted. An interesting combination. "*Asa, vade in pace, et Dominus sit tecum.*" Cormac wiped his hand on his robe and gave the dripping child a kiss. "There then, little one, that was not so dreadful, and now you are part of Holy Church, and holier no doubt than Father Kilian." He handed Asa back to Rosamund with a smile, and patted Rosamund's shoulder. "Take her back in out of the wet. You needn't tell the jarl, you know, until you think the time is right. There is no sin in silence." He looked thoughtfully at the bucket of water, now sanctified, then with a faint smile poured it back in the well. It would do the Norse no harm to drink of it.

Rosamund ran a hand through Asa's hair, comforted, Abbot Cormac's friendly presence beginning to dim her fury at Kilian. She kissed Asa, glad of the surety of a place with God that baptism had given her. There would be time enough to decide how to explain that to Haakon when he came home. Rosamund crossed herself, the dimly remembered terror of her dream blotting out the last of her anger. *Holy Mother, send him home safe*, she thought. And then, guiltily, hoping Cormac couldn't read her thoughts, *Thor Odinsson guard him.* Haakon believed in Thor's power, and Haakon was not an evil man. Rosamund had reconciled that with her own beliefs long ago. Now she would cheerfully pray to *anything* who could send him back to her.

The storm that merely dumped rain by the bucketful on the north of Ireland had grown to a living fury over the waters west of Iceland. Haakon took Eilaf Eiriksson by the throat and kicked him into the open hold with the cattle. "I ought to put you over the side for that thing to eat!" he bellowed over the crack of the lightning.

Eilaf yelped as he landed, but Haakon was already at the helm, pushing the struggling Knut out of the way. "Go and help bail," he gasped, "or we'll go under before the rocks get us!" Bailing was a constant task and critical when a ship was taking on water at the rate that *Raven* was. "Thor Odinsson, call off your storm!" Haakon shouted into the teeth of the wind, fighting the tiller. He was heavier than Knut, and in this raging sea, that made a difference. The crew had gotten the sail reefed and were struggling at the oars. The rock-fanged reefs that guarded the island snapped at them as *Raven* plunged by. There was no turning in this storm. They would have to go in and beach on the island. Haakon hoped there would be a place to do it. It might be rock all the way in, enough to tear out *Raven's* hull. Another rocky outcrop slid by, menacing behind its veil of spray. But the air was growing lighter, and Haakon thought that the wind had dropped just a little. If Thor Odinsson wanted his land in the west found, Haakon thought grimly, he had best heed Haakon's prayers now. Suddenly a clear space opened, and *Raven* shot through it with a jarring thud onto the beach. "That was somewhat late in coming, lord," Haakon said gruffly, "but my thanks for it." He thought he could hear just the faintest trace of laughter above the dying storm.

It was full daylight again. They pushed *Raven* as high onto the beach as she would go, lest the tide come and take her back again, and then dropped down to sleep where they stood.

In the morning the only damage they found was a broken water cask and a small hole in the hull that Snorri Longfoot and Yazid said was no great matter. Yazid got his prayer rug out of a sea chest, pointed it eastward, and touched his forehead to it in fervent gratitude. Haakon, like-minded, went to pick one of the frightened, lowing animals from the hold to give as thanks to Thor Odinsson. The god had helped when Haakon had asked for it, and a wise man didn't quarrel over a small tardiness. Donal MacRae, with a bleeding gash over his forehead from the night's work, suggested Eilaf Eiriksson as a fitting gift, and Haakon thought that he was only half joking. Eilaf prudently kept out of the jarl's path.

The island appeared to be small, but Haakon thought that there would be a fair chance to find water. It was green and tree dotted, and Haakon thought that he could see wild sheep on the hillside. He turned back to the ship. "Thorfinn! Take some men with that mended cask and have a look!"

Thorfinn didn't answer, just stood staring over Haakon's shoulder. Haakon spun around. A dozen women now stood in front of him, dressed in skins and rough cloth. They must have sprung up out of the ground. He goggled at them, and the eldest of them, a woman well into her forties but fair still, held out a bowl of apples.

"Bid thee welcome, sea man," she said in a tongue that took Haakon a moment to recognize as Gaelic.

VII

The Island

"We come here in peace," Haakon said hastily, giving his crew a firm eye to see that they remembered it. "Where are your men?" He wondered if this was a trap. The square sail and unmistakable prow of a viking ship did not generally bring out women with baskets of apples to greet it.

"Men be away sealing," the woman said. Haakon saw that most of their clothes were sealskin. "There be nothing to fear here, sea man." More folk had begun to gather behind her, coming over the green crest of the sea-grass dunes that bordered the shore. There were a few children among them, girls close to their teens, but no younger babes. One old man walked behind the children, his long hair and beard ruffled by the salt spray that blew in from the reefs. Other than he, there was no human male to be seen.

"We need fresh water," Haakon said. "We broke a cask in the storm." His crew had begun to gather interestedly at his shoulder, eyeing the women.

"Of course," the woman with the apples said. "What we have be yours. Old One has said thee would come."

"Old One?" Haakon looked questioningly at the old man.

The woman shook her head and laughed gently, a musical sound like small silver bells against the roar of the surf. She took Haakon by the hand and tugged him forward a step.

The other women flittered forward, surrounding Haakon's crew, chattering at them in gentle, silvery voices. "Do you come with us, men out of the sea."

A faint note of warning echoed through Haakon's mind and was gone. A fine fool he would look if he seemed to fear a gaggle of women. He let the woman lead him up through the dunes. On the far side, past the sour salt-marsh grass, was a village set at the foot of the spur of hills Haakon had seen from the shore. The forest grew right up to the edge of the houses, but beyond in the low-lying valley were neat fields and orchards. Fowl scratched in the narrow street, and as Haakon watched, a small girl came out of the forest driving a herd of swine before her. The sheep he had seen on the hills would not be wild ones after all.

"Who rules here?" he asked the woman leading them.

She smiled and said in her odd-sounding Gaelic, "There be no king on Bee Isle."

"Bee Isle?"

She pointed to a row of wattle-and-daub bee skeps on the wood's edge. "We do make fine mead, sea man, finer than thee has tasted yet. The kind to send good dreams at night." Her face clouded for an instant. "That be necessary sometimes, when there be little enough to make merry for in the day." Then she brightened and pulled at Haakon's hand, beginning to run. "That be gone now, though. Old One *said* the sea would send what was needed!"

Haakon followed her, with his crew and the rest of the women behind them, and they entered the village in what he felt was very like a triumphal procession. The huts were made of the same wattle and daub as the bee skeps, small and dome roofed. Some were very ancient, he thought, with signs of newer repairs. The woman pulled him under the leather flap that hung across the door of the largest one. Haakon stood blinking, trying to adjust his eyes to the gloom. The air was thick and sweetish with smoke, and the fire that burned in the central hearth gave the hut its only light. A woman of an age past guessing at sat beside it, her white hair falling around her face in a cloud like the fire's smoke.

The younger woman brought her hand to her forehead in some intricate and curious gesture. "He be come as thee said, Old One."

The old woman shifted on her sealskin cushions and fixed Haakon with a pale eye from which, he thought uncomfortably, all sanity might have fled aeons ago. "Be many men with thee?" she demanded.

"Half a hundred," Haakon said. If this was a trap, she should know that they would be no easy victims. Before either woman could protest, he jerked the door flap open and shouted for Donal. Donal appeared with a girl of about sixteen on his arm.

"Maeve," his companion said excitedly to the woman who had brought Haakon, "Look you, Maeve, a harper!"

Maeve laughed and gently pushed her out again. "Time to make friends at evening. There be no room for all in here."

"Tell them to keep watchful," Haakon said to Donal in Norse. "I can't see any harm here, but until we know what their men will do, we won't take chances. And none of the women are to be forced, mind—tell them that and tell them it came from me."

Donal chuckled. "You needn't be worrying about that, I'm thinking. Their men must be sad creatures in a bed indeed, for the welcome their women are giving us."

"Or only gone too long," Haakon grunted. "They won't be best pleased if they come home to find you've cuckolded half the village, so watch your step."

Suddenly the old woman shot a hand out at them across the fire. She wore one bracelet of shells and ivory around her wrist, and another of carved bone. Her arm was thin as birds' bones. "Men of the sea, know you that you be sent by Aengus Og and by She Who Is the Three Morrigans, and it be meant, as it be promised us. Go you and rest now. Be time to give the Three their due for the gift."

Haakon found that largely incomprehensible, and he saw Donal's expression change to puzzled curiosity as Maeve took them each by an arm and led them out of the hut again. Most of Haakon's men were waiting for them, but a few had scattered away with the women already. Maeve pointed at four beehive-shaped huts ringed around a small yard. "Those be ready for thee."

Haakon peered inside one cautiously. It was empty, the dirt floor swept smooth, and a new fire laid, but there was no sign of human habitation. "Does no one live here?"

Maeve sighed. "There be too many empty huts on Bee Isle. But that changes now." She gave him a little push. "Do thee go and rest, sea man. There be time to find thy water later, when thee hast eaten."

She turned away back to the old woman's hut, and Haakon looked after her in exasperation. It was as hard to get a straight answer from the woman as to uncurl a snake.

"Look, jarl!" Thorfinn Solvisson emerged from another hut, brandishing a handful of cooked meat and an ale horn. "There's enough to feed us twice over in there, and good food too. Taste." He pushed the ale horn under Haakon's nose, and Haakon sipped from it gingerly. It was mead, rich and very strong, with an odd flavor that might come from whatever wild plants the bees fed on here. It was the best he could remember drinking. He took another gulp and handed the horn back to Thorfinn regretfully. That was too potent a brew to drink carelessly so long as he still had his doubts about this place.

No one else save Donal MacRae seemed to share the jarl's doubts. Those who had not already gone off with some woman spilled happily into the hut, crowding each other for the mead and roast meat and sweet apples.

Donal watched them thoughtfully, wondering if the meal was magicked, like Circe's banquet that the ancient Greeks had written about, which had turned all its diners to swine. They didn't look any more like swine than usual, he decided, watching Hagar the Simple wolfing down his meal, but there was something about this place that made the hair prickle on the back of his neck. He touched Haakon on the shoulder and drew him a little way out into the street. All the women seemed to have disappeared for the moment. Haakon raised an eyebrow questioningly.

"There's something I want to look at. I saw it from up there." Donal gestured back at the low sand hills that divided the valley from the beach. He drew Haakon into the wood with him in what he thought was the right direction. The wood grew very close to the houses here. There must be no wolves on the island, Donal thought, or they would have kept it properly cleared.

"There," Donal said.

Haakon saw that they were in an old clearing, now grown wild. From the hills above the beach, it had showed as a lighter patch in the darkness of the wood. Young trees had sprung up around the leveled stumps of the old ones and were already thick with creepers in their upper branches. In the dimness at the center of the clearing, half hidden in a tangle of new growth, was a small stone building with an arched wooden door, now nearly rotted away. Something about the shape of it nudged Haakon's memory.

Donal nodded. "That is a monastery church such as the Irish build. You saw its twin in Abbot Cormac's meadow."

"Are they Christians here?" Haakon had seen no sign of it.

"No," Donal said shortly. "I don't know what they are, but it is not Christians."

"Could you understand what that old woman was saying?" Haakon asked.

"Mostly," Donal said. "Their language sounds—old, somehow. They may be very isolated here. This place was settled from Ireland, though, I'm sure of that."

Haakon shrugged. That was not so unusual. The Irish had their explorers too, monks mostly, looking for some lonely place to serve their god. There had been a few in Iceland when the Norse came. "Who are the gods the old woman spoke of then?" They were no deities of whom Haakon had ever heard. He wondered if they might be spirits peculiar to the island.

"Old gods of the Irish," Donal said slowly. "Names out of—out of legend, Haakon, from pagan times. Very old and, for a Christian, very evil."

"You've never quarreled with another man's gods before, Donal," Haakon said. Donal was endlessly curious about everything under the sun, and Haakon had found that his Christianity sat but lightly on him.

"This is different," Donal said. "Ireland has been Christian for centuries, since before my own folk left Ireland for Scotland. Even the old Druidical families have sent their scholars into the Church. The people who came here couldn't have known any more about the old gods than their names from fairy tales. Why should they worship them? I tell you, Haakon, I don't like it."

Haakon didn't care if these people gave their worship to the Christian god or to the Whale King, as some villagers of the far north were said to do. What he did not like was that the old woman had seemed to feel that her gods had brought him there personally at her request. Haakon Olesson was at no god's beck and call save Thor Odinsson's, much less that of a mad old woman in a sealskin dress. The other troubling question was what these folk wanted with them. They couldn't be planning to make thralls out of fifty armed men.

"Sea man!" The gentle voice at his elbow nearly made Haakon jump higher than the ruined church roof. Maeve had a softer footfall than a cat. "We did wonder where thee had gone. Be nothing here for thee." She took his hand and tried to tug him away from the clearing. Her white hands were work worn, and she was some ten years older than he, but there was great beauty in her face. She smiled at Haakon and then at Donal. "Morna be waiting for thee, harper."

The girl whom Haakon had seen earlier came running lightly through the trees and beckoned Donal to follow. The harper was gone before Haakon could open his mouth to protest, and Haakon burst out laughing in spite of himself. Whatever misgivings Donal might have about these people's gods wouldn't keep him out of any bed one of the village maids might see fit to invite him into. Nothing ever did.

"What be so funny, sea man?"

"My harper and your little maid Morna," Haakon said. He frowned. "Has she got a husband?" That might make trouble.

"It be meant," Maeve said. "Thee mustn't worry." Again Haakon had the feeling that his question had not been so much answered as turned aside. Maeve slipped an arm through his and drew him away from the clearing with her, but before they reached the edge of the trees, she stopped in the deep shadow and laid her head against his breast. "It be all meant, sea man. Thee must not go against it."

She smelled faintly of the sweet smoke in the old woman's hut, and either that or the mead he had drunk was dizzying. He could feel the shape of her body clearly through the woolen gown and soft sealskin tunic she wore over it. Her eyes were warm and blue like a still sea, and her pale hair, only faintly touched with gray, rippled down her back like the breeze on a summer wheat field.

Haakon tried to push her away, but she clung to him, half-avid and, he thought, half-fearful. "I be too old," she sighed gently, "not like Morna. There be no blood from me with the new moon anymore. But must anyway. Old One has said it." She pressed herself against him and gave a little murmur of satisfaction as she felt him stiffen. Her hands sought him eagerly.

Haakon swayed drunkenly on his feet. Men, ships, and wife faded from his mind with the intoxicating closeness of her. She pulled the thongs from her sealskin tunic and put his hand on her bare breast. There was the smell of honey in the air. His need for her was suddenly overpowering. Maeve's hands were pulling at his belt, and her head was tilted back so that he could see the fine blue veins in her throat. He felt drunk. He bared her other breast and bent his head to it.

"Thee must love me, sea man," Maeve whispered. "Thee must love me so we do not die."

Maybe it was the mention of death or only that his own god watched over him. A sudden unreasoning terror came into his mind, and he thought of insects mating, when the female kills her lover at the moment of copulation. He pushed the woman away from him and staggered back, fighting the dizziness. "No!"

Maeve gasped and held out her arms to him. He turned and fled, like a child fleeing a nightmare. At the edge of the wood, where the cleared land of the village began, he stopped, gasping for breath, and looked back into the trees. She had gone.

In the sunlight of the village street, he felt somewhat foolish, but the fear in the back of his mind was not entirely gone. The street seemed empty save for the old man tending the bee skeps. He turned as Haakon passed, and shot a sideways, fearful glance at the old woman's hut. "Do not thee go in the woods with Maeve, sea man, if thee's a mind to see home again," he hissed.

Haakon started toward him, but the old man turned his back quickly, his hands moving again expertly, unstung, among the bees.

Feeling more unsettled than ever, Haakon strode down the street and stuck his head in the door of the hut where the meal had been laid. There he found his men sprawled around the remains of it.

"This is a fine place, jarl," Eilaf Eiriksson said, any shame at the previous night's work seemingly fled. He raised his horn, slopping mead down his wrist. "These women give a fine welcome. We've a mind to stay here a while."

A satisfied murmur of assent rose from the others. "Drink while you can!" Haakon snapped. "When Snorri has the water cask mended, we sail!" He stalked out before they could protest, went into one of the empty

huts, and rolled himself in his cloak. Suddenly he was
bone weary.

He woke in the long midnight twilight with the
sounds of merrymaking in his ears. Six of the women and
as many of his men were dancing on the grass between the
huts to the high thin music of some unseen piper. Haakon
stepped through the doorway, skirting around the dancers,
and nearly put his foot on a man and a woman coupling in
the shadow of a hawthorn hedge not ten feet away. Had
they all run mad? he thought. There was still no sign of
the Bee Isle men, but the sealing boats could return at
any time, and the men wouldn't be best pleased to find
their women coupling in hedges with a shipload of strangers.

He stared through the fading light at the old woman's
hut. A fat plume of smoke still rose through the smoke
hole like something alive, coiling around itself in the last
gold glow of the sun.

"Old One be watching," Maeve said at his elbow. "In
the fire she be watching."

Haakon suppressed the urge to bolt and turned toward her slowly. She wore a long gown of sealskin, cut into
points at the hem and sewn with shells, so that it swayed
and whispered as she moved. Her pale hair was knotted
with some kind of wild grass that had the same heady
scent as the mead. She smiled at him but didn't touch
him, knowing that he was ready to run.

"Thee mustn't grudge them their pleasure, sea man.
Will make Bee Isle bloom. Thee will come to it, too." She
smiled at him, and he thought uneasily that there was
something a little sad in the smile.

"My god forbids it," he said gruffly, searching for
some excuse that would give no offense. Her nearness had
begun to dizzy him again, and he wanted nothing more
than to take her in the grass where they stood. He edged
away from her, fighting it.

"Still thee will come to it," Maeve said. "Old One has
said it."

"Who is this Old One," Haakon demanded, "that
everyone leaps to her bidding like hounds to a whistle?"

"She be holy," Maeve said. "She Who Is the Three
Morrigans comes into Old One when she does speak.

When Old One be gone, she will come to me. So thee must love me, sea man. It be necessary."

The thin, piping music drew closer, a wild, compelling sound, and Haakon saw that the dancers had begun to move off in couples into the deepening night. Suddenly he saw the source of the sound—three shadowy figures with thin, bone pipes. At first he thought that they were not human, but then, as the nearest one danced by him, he saw that the odd shape of her head was only a sealskin cap, with the snout and whiskers still on it. The rest of the hide hung down her back, swaying as she danced. The other two seal-women danced behind her, and the music of their pipes seemed to fill up the night.

Maeve put her hand on his arm again. Her beauty was intoxicating, ancient and fearful. Haakon felt his own arms going out to her and fought them down to his side. He backed away a little. He still wasn't sure what it was that he feared, but he knew that if he lay with her, he would never be the same again. "Find another man, Maeve," he said hoarsely.

"Cannot," Maeve said sadly in the darkness. "Cannot. Must be thee, sea man. I do be sorry for it, though," she added, sounding suddenly human again.

Haakon turned and fled. The wild music of the pipes battered at his ears long after he reached the ship. He sat down on a sea chest, Thor Odinsson's ax across his lap, to think things out. He had no mind to spend the rest of the night in one of those huts.

In the morning he went back and kicked such of his men as could be found out of their cloaks and into the sunlight, along with Snorri Longfoot's mended cask. "Go and get it filled and stowed on board," he told Thorfinn Solvisson, and sent Knut One-Eye to take three men and help Yazid patch the hull. Away from Maeve and in broad daylight the island began to look normal again. She had spoken of something that would make the land bloom, but Bee Isle appeared to be as fruitful as land that far north could be. The fields looked placid and well cultivated in the sun.

Thorfinn yawned and grinned at him. "Are we in such a hurry then?"

"A day or two of rest, jarl, that's what we're needing," Eilaf Eiriksson said. "Aren't we deserving as much, after such a storm?"

"The storm would have been no danger but for you!" Haakon snapped.

"Aye, and we'd never have come here either, would we then?" Eilaf said. "I'm thinking I deserve thanks after all." He grinned broadly at the rest of the men, and they grinned back at him.

"Hah! Look you there!" Hjalmar Sitricsson pointed to the road. Morna and two other girls came pushing a two-wheeled cart draped with green leaves. It was piled high with food. "I'm thinking King Harald Fairhair never had a finer feast at his hall in Vestfold," Hjalmar said.

"Aye, we've a mind to stay and be kings another day or two," Eilaf said. The men shouted in boisterous agreement and ran to meet the girls with the cart.

"It may be as close as we'll ever get, jarl," Hjalmar said. He put one arm around a girl and reached for the kettle of meat with the other. "What harm in that?"

"Eat, then," Haakon growled. "But no more whoring until that water's loaded and the hull is patched!"

Donal MacRae strolled over to the cart and gave Morna a cheerful smile, but he didn't seem inclined to stay with her. He took a handful of meat and oatcake and came back to Haakon. "Those women have set themselves to bed every man on the ship as many times as his cock'll stand up for," Donal said in a low voice. "You cannot wonder they've no mind to leave."

Haakon stood glaring at them as they swarmed around the cart like the old man's bees, fondling the women and stuffing themselves with food. Even Yazid seemed to have fallen under the spell. "You're no better," Haakon growled at Donal.

"Oh, no," Donal said. "*I* think we should go. But you'll have to give it a day or two or be putting them on board with a whip."

"Two days," Haakon said. "No more. I spent the night thinking about it, and what I think is, I don't like this place. I want to get out of here before I find out why."

*   *   *

In Ole's Hold, Rosamund found that if she wished to worry about Haakon, she could do it when she slept at night or not at all. There was scant time during the day for anything but the myriad small demands on her time that added up to one overwhelming responsibility. The Norse trader that Haakon had sent to Rogaland returned with the children, having raced a scant inch ahead of the recent storm all the way, or so he said. The children had all been seasick, he added grimly as he tucked into a dish of stew in the hall while Rosamund and Abbot Cormac sorted out the children, and he would sooner transport a cargo of wild pigs the next time, they being more restful. Leif, the steward of Ole's Hold, nodded sympathetically. Twenty children underfoot wasn't what he would have prayed to the gods for either, but the jarl and the lady would have it so, and Leif was a loyal soul.

Rosamund, trying to comfort twenty sick, frightened, and occasionally rebellious children, had also begun to think that she and the jarl had run mad to bring them all here, but her heart went out to them, especially the littlest, who were so scared, and the eldest, who were old enough to know how greatly their life was to be changed, and she kept her thoughts to herself.

The middle children, the five- to ten-year-olds, were the most adaptable. They explored Cormac's settlement with curiosity, ate till they were sick, and got underfoot everywhere. The eldest—especially Njal, who was sixteen and except for a slightly lame leg might have been judged old enough to stay behind in Rogaland—were the worst. Njal regarded the Christians and everything Irish with surly suspicion, and as he was fully as old as some of Abbot Cormac's monks, they gave him a wide berth. Freydis, at thirteen the eldest of the girls, was little better. But fully the most intractable was eleven-year-old Svein. Abbot Cormac had prepared for the children's arrival by building two long halls, one for the boys and one for the girls, but the only way to keep Svein in his bed in the boys' hall at night proved to be to tie him to it. He would go and sleep in the dairy or up on the roof—anywhere except where the monks had bade him sleep.

Rosamund finally told them to let Svein sleep where

he would. There was no place he could go, and she had no time for Svein until the little ones were settled. These, who had been no more than infants when Harud Olafsson had stolen them away, were troubled only by nightmares. Rosamund, blessing the short memory of the very young, knew that they would do well enough when they had had enough love and food on which to build a sense of belonging, but in the meantime they woke howling in the night with unfailing regularity. She felt as if she had suddenly littered like a hound and produced a dozen babies overnight.

To add to Rosamund's trials, she had discovered that she was indeed breeding again. Most certainly it was not the time she would have picked, but at least she would have something more than wolfhound puppies to show Haakon when he came home, she thought with a grin. In the meantime, she prayed not to be sick, an inconvenience for which she had no time, and went about her work.

Ireland was a fair country in the summer, Rosamund discovered, green and lush, with an almost heart-stopping beauty in the hills. Even Fann seemed to bloom here. Certainly the poor maid looked less frightened and shrewish than at any time since Rosamund had known her. Every day Fann would put on an old gown, pin her red hair up out of the way, and work happily beside the jarl's lady in the herb garden Rosamund had marked out behind the hall. Abbot Cormac had told Rosamund what grew here, many of the plants close kin to English herbs. Rosamund and her women went out in the early morning with baskets and trowels to dig where Cormac showed them, and brought their finds back to plant at Ole's Hold.

The storm that had driven Haakon to Bee Isle and chased the children's ship across the sea from Norway had caught Earl Edmund's ships full in the center of it. They lost a mast, all the horses had hysterics, and Edmund, cursing the weather, put about and made for the nearest coast. It was nearly a week before they could sail again.

Rosamund was happily putting sprigs of coltsfoot and calamint into the damp earth of her garden, with Asa paddling in the water crock beside her, when Rosamund's father's ships came limping up the Bann. Earl Edmund, who had been this way once before when Olaf Haraldsson held the land, beached his craft a half mile downriver to let his fighting men and horses shake the shipboard cramps out of their legs.

Theofric pulled his horse's muzzle out of the water and swung up into the saddle with a grin at the earl. "We should sleep dry tonight!" He tightened his grip on the red-cat banner that was braced against his stirrup and swung it in a wide arc. The restive men behind him surged forward, eager for something to fight besides the sea.

A shout from one of Cormac's monks in the field came faintly to Rosamund's ears, but the hubbub that followed it made her scoop up her daughter and abandon her herbs. Leif was already calling the fighting men from their work as Cormac's folk came streaming through the newly hung gates.

Not Kilian again, Rosamund prayed. She wondered if she had offended him enough to come and fight her. She pushed Asa into Bergthora's arms and shooed the Rogaland children after them. "Get the little ones into the hall and bolt the doors!"

"You too, lady!" Tordis appeared and tugged at her arm.

"Be damned to that!" Rosamund snapped. "This is *my* hold. No meddling priest is going to drive me into a hole to hide!"

"It isn't Kilian, lady!" Abbot Cormac shouted, running across the yard with his skirts flapping about his legs and his mace in his hand. "Nor Norse either, I think." The Norse were never above raiding each other.

"I should hope not," Rosamund said grimly. "We're their buffer against the Irish, and those fools in Antrim should know it. And they ought to be too afraid of Haakon." The last time a Norseman had raided Haakon's steading when Haakon wasn't home, Haakon had come back and cut his head off and kicked it after his retreating men. The skalds were still making verses about it.

Leif had scrambled up the ladder to the catwalk, and now he came sliding down again. "No more than fifty, Lady Rosamund. Mostly mounted. If that's all, we can hold them off."

"Who are they?" Rosamund demanded. Armed, mounted men didn't just drop out of the air.

Leif shrugged his shoulders. He couldn't see that it made any difference. They hadn't come for friendship's sake.

Rosamund picked up her skirts and started up the ladder before Leif could protest. Below her she heard the new gates slam shut. They were heavy timber, iron bound, and she said a brief prayer of thanks that they had had the sense to stop all other work to get them hung. The gates would hold a long time against a ram, and the archers fanning out along the catwalk on either side of her would make anyone carrying a ram speedily wish himself elsewhere. She squinted at the mounted men who came thundering up the track from the river. Fifty men were not enough to take Ole's Hold. Were there more of them, or had they expected to find it empty? Suddenly there seemed something familiar in the leading riders. Rosamund stared openmouthed as a gust of wind caught the banner and spread it out flat for a moment. The riders' faces were shadowed by their helms, but Rosamund knew the burly form that sat a roan war-horse to the right of the banner-bearer as well as she knew his crouching red cat.

Rosamund ducked down and slid to the ground again in a flurry of bare legs and rumpled gown. She shook her clothing into place and stalked to the gates, where Leif was piling anything movable against them. Wulf appeared at her heel, growling like a demon, and she wondered if he recognized the interlopers, too. Wulf had never cared for Earl Edmund.

Cormac, who seemed to have become the man in command, took her by the arm. "Stay off that catwalk, child. We don't know who's out there, and they may not care who they're shooting at."

"Oh, yes we do," Rosamund said. "That's my loving family we're getting ready to fight, Abbot."

Cormac stared.

Something thudded heavily into the gate, and a voice shouted, "Open or we'll break it in!"

The voice was English, but recognizable enough.

"Who gives free Norsemen orders, English thief?" Leif shouted back.

"Your rightful lord, Edmund of the Ram's Head, who claims this hold by marriage right!"

"Marriage right!" Rosamund shrieked. She ran for the catwalk again.

Cormac caught her arm. "*What* marriage right?"

"My father betrothed me to Harud Olafsson while Harud was still alive," Rosamund said between clenched teeth.

Cormac looked thoughtful. Daughter fighting father went against God's law, but a man who would betroth a maid to the likes of Harud Olafsson was doubtless past praying for. "Does he know you're here?"

The ram thudded against the gate again, and a flaming arrow sailed over the palisade. Someone stamped it out with his foot. Rosamund started for the catwalk. "He is going to find out," she said grimly. She was shaking with fury as she climbed. To claim Haakon's land in *her* name! And not for her, either—Rosamund knew that well enough. She snatched a shield from the nearest man and stood up behind it. "Take your thieves home!" she shouted. With satisfaction she saw her father's head snap around. He peered up at her. Now that they were closer, she saw that Wilfrid and Oswain were with him. Her eyes slid over them contemptuously and came to rest on the earl and the tall horseman beside him. "Is that you, Theofric?" she called. "You should know better than to bring such a paltry force to push a rightful lord out of his hall!"

A bowman among the earl's men nocked an arrow, but Theofric waved him down again. Theofric gave a bark of laughter, but the earl stood up in his saddle and roared, "Open the gates, you whoring jade, or we'll push them in!"

"Get out!" Rosamund screamed. "Get off my land!"

Theofric said something to the earl, who seemed to consider that perhaps his first approach had not been best thought out. He cleared his throat and said gruffly, "So you're here, are you, lass? Come and let your father in, then. It's your rights we're looking to, you know."

"You don't tempt me!" Rosamund snapped.

"Knock them down!" Earl Edmund bellowed.

The ram hit the gates again, and they creaked but didn't budge. An archer on the catwalk nocked an arrow and sent it singing into the neck of a man on the ram. He coughed and dropped where he stood, clawing at the arrow. Earl Edmund's archers sent another hail of arrows over the walls, but they couldn't see what they were shooting at. Rosamund noted that none of them aimed at her. The earl had more sense. She was more useful to him alive if he could get her.

"Know you that we have seventy men in Ole's Hold to your fifty," Rosamund said as two of the earl's men dragged their fallen comrade back from the gates. "And enough food to sit here all summer while you eat hay. I know how much your ships will carry. If you wish to try stealing from the Irish, you may. They may kill you and spare us the trouble!" She gave Earl Edmund and her brothers a last baleful glare and disappeared from the catwalk.

There was one last thud at the gates, and then the sound of the earl's men pulling back. Rosamund bit her lip and paced the inner yard behind the gates like a penned wolf while her father made his camp in the meadow and thought things over.

There they sat until nightfall. Rosamund climbed to the catwalk and peered over the palisade at her father's campfires. Earl Edmund appeared to have settled in, but how long he would be willing to wait, Rosamund wasn't sure. She was reasonably certain that fifty was all the men he had brought. Earl Edmund had been planning to rob a handful of monks of their land, not grapple with an armed hold full of Norsemen. Cormac, having settled his flock as best he could in every available outbuilding, climbed up the ladder after her and found her sitting on the catwalk with her arms around her knees, brooding.

"What are the chances of making peace?" Cormac inquired. He wasn't inclined to, but his service to God bound him to try that avenue first. Cormac sighed. He liked to fight. It was the worst of his sins, and the one that had prompted him to heed God's call. In Holy Orders, he had thought, he would find that temptation put less often in his path.

"Nothing short of a miracle," Rosamund said. She was wrapped in a fur cloak so that only her shoes and her kerchief showed. Her face brooded angrily above the fur.

"He wants the land for Wilfrid, I think, to keep him out of Ram's Head and from murdering Oswain. Also, his pride is in it now. He wants me back because I made him look such a fool."

Cormac looked amused. He had heard the story of Jarl Haakon's wooing. It would take a humbler man than Earl Edmund to forgive that. Having unexpectedly found his wayward daughter, the earl would be singularly disinclined to sail home without her.

The truth of that was borne in upon them the next morning when the earl sent Theofric to his daughter under a white flag, with the message that the earl wished a meeting.

Rosamund fixed Theofric with a stare from the blue-purple eyes that reminded him uncannily of the earl's. "Tell my father I'll see him in hell first."

Theofric chuckled. "Not even a kind word, lady?"

"I learned none from him," Rosamund said. She eyed the scarred, graying thane consideringly. "What are you doing here, Theofric, trying to wrest an honest man's land from him?"

Theofric shrugged. "I serve the earl, lady."

"Then serve him best by telling him to pack his men and his horses back to England. You'll get nothing at Ole's Hold but a grave, Theofric."

Theofric studied her and the tall, long-limbed Norsemen standing behind her. The lady Rosamund had grown up since she had run away from the Ram's Head. She made a formidable enemy. "It's a pity *you* weren't the old man's son," he said honestly. He touched his forehead to her and wheeled his horse around.

Regretfully, Rosamund watched him gallop back down the hill to the earl's camp. Theofric had never been anything but kind to her, but he was the earl's man. He would never change sides.

The earl attacked twice more that day, each time with as little success as the first. He simply hadn't enough men to take Ole's Hold, and the defenders knew it. He lost two more men to the Norse archers on the catwalk, and when he tried burning through the gate, Cormac's folk formed a bucket line from the well and wet it down. In the meantime Rosamund paraded all the men she could, including the oldest of the children and Cormac's monks, along the catwalk with bows, to give her father a proper sense of the defenders' numbers. She hadn't let Theofric get close enough to see that fully thirty of the seventy fighting men she had claimed were monks and children. In the common danger, Norse and Christians had forgot their quarrel, and Brother Gilbert proved to have an archer's eye that rivaled Hagar the Simple's. Abbot Cormac made him say ten Paternosters after supper for the glee that he had taken in his first kill.

Between attacks, Earl Edmund sent two more messages to his daughter, alternating cajolery with threats and bluster. Rosamund proved susceptible to neither. The last time, the earl came himself, with Oswain and Wilfrid to add their brotherly pleas. Rosamund took one look and refused even to come out of the gate.

"You've sullied a truce flag before," she said from a perch on the catwalk above the gate. "I wouldn't trust you if you were laid out for burial."

"A willful woman is an affront to God!" Earl Edmund shouted.

"So is a thief!" Rosamund shouted back. An angry baying echoed her from the ground. Wulf could see no reason why they would not let *him* go out the gate and bite the earl.

Earl Edmund pulled his horse's head around viciously, leaving Rosamund standing triumphant on the catwalk.

"Look, lady!" Leif shouted. "They're breaking camp!"

Rosamund slumped against the timber palisade, sick to her stomach now, and watched her father's men draw back to the river. "They'll be back," she said wearily. "They'll be back, Leif. I know him."

Earl Edmund lost no time in departing. He was an old campaigner and knew bad odds when he saw them. But he didn't put out across the sea for England again until he had sent his spies into the Norse city of Larne, and there he learned a thing or two that dampened his fury. Rosamund's jarl had gone off on some voyage; rumor was rife, but no one seemed to know where exactly. All agreed the jarl would be a long time in coming home. Long enough

for Earl Edmund to gather sufficient men to come back and
teach his daughter just how greatly she had erred.

It would cost the earl more than he had planned to
take the Irish land for Wilfrid, but he *would* have it. It was
his. And he would also have Rosamund again, who would
be useful. Earl Edmund chuckled. The wench had served
him none so poorly maybe. He had betrothed her to Harud
Olafsson, and now he would have Harud Olafsson's land for
it. And he would still have Rosamund to betroth elsewhere.
Maybe he should heed Athelwulf's claim this time. Athelwulf
was proving a more formidable force than his father had
been. True, Rosamund was no longer virgin, but she had
borne a child, the earl thought practically, and so was
proved fertile. There was no need even to go to the expense
of having the Church set her marriage aside. Marriage to a
pagan wasn't valid anyway. With Athelwulf's men, he could
break that pitiful collection of Irish hovels into kindling, and
unless he was a fool Athelwulf would overlook, for the sake
of a good alliance, the years that Rosamund had spent
among the Norse. Men like Athelwulf could see what
mattered. Men-at-arms and land mattered. A wife was a
convenience. If Athelwulf balked at his wife's lack of virginity, Earl Edmund himself would take the brat she'd already
borne. That should salve Athelwulf's pride, and Earl Edmund
could threaten to leave the babe behind if he needed a stick
with which to beat Rosamund into better manners.

Earl Edmund looked satisfied and shouted for Theofric
to come and tell him how many men young Athelwulf kept
at Appleyard.

VIII

Fergus MacAidan

Raven's crew stayed three-days on Bee Isle because
Haakon was reluctant to drive them aboard ship by force

or to call on Thor Odinsson to do it for him. He knew that if the god were willing, he could make them very afraid indeed of the golden ax, but he was loath to captain his crew with Thor's help when he couldn't do it alone. By the third day, Haakon was beginning to think that he would have done better to raise the god against them if that was what it took. With every day his crew lingered, they became yet more stubbornly determined to bask a little longer in the pleasures of Bee Isle. The women clung to them, chattering like birds, begging them to stay only one more day. The old man tended his bees and muttered, but he said no more to Haakon. Haakon was beginning to think he was afraid to.

On the morning of the third day, some curious excitement began to run through the island. The women moved unceasingly between the men and the Old One's hut. Although he didn't see her, the old woman seemed to Haakon to be a presence everywhere on the island, a force that reached out through the women and drew his men away from him. *I have made a mistake*, he thought sourly, but he didn't know how to mend it. Even such level heads as Thorfinn Solvisson and Knut One-Eye seemed content to bask in the sun on Bee Isle for as long as the women would have them. As for Haakon, he was nervous enough to order the animals driven back on board *Raven*.

Maeve seemed to dog his footsteps, and the longer he stayed on Bee Isle, the more her presence made him drunk. Some dark terror in his mind still screamed that if he lay with her, he would never leave, but the whisper of her voice and the heady scent that clung to her hair called to him almost beyond bearing. He had begun to flee from her, feeling foolish because of it.

"Leave that one alone," Donal said darkly. "Do you know what 'Maeve' means?"

"It's just a name," Haakon said.

"It's an old name. It means 'She Who Intoxicates.' The first Maeve was a goddess in Ireland, and she swallowed men. Let her alone, Haakon."

"I am wed," Haakon said shortly. "I do not need Maeve."

"No, but you want her," Donal said. "Don't do it."

Only Donal was restless. Maybe the island touched

something in his blood that Haakon, half-Irish but all Norse by nature, couldn't feel. The harper wasn't sure, but more and more the pleasant fields seemed to him darkened by something evil.

"Come on," Donal said abruptly. "I want to see that church again."

"Why?" Haakon said. He was reluctant to turn his back on his men.

"I don't know." Donal looked flighty, Haakon thought, like a horse that's going to bolt. "Something's going to happen. You can feel it." Donal set off into the wood, and Haakon followed him, unsure why, but suddenly as willing to explore with Donal as to meet with Maeve again.

The roof of the church had fallen in, leaving a tumble of stone that was lair to the wild things of the wood now. There was a sharp bark of fear, and a vixen dived through a hole in the stone, almost over Donal's feet. "She'll have kits in there somewhere." Donal said shakily. He backed away, careful not to disturb the tumbled stone.

"Donal! Come and see!" Haakon called to him from a little way in the wood. Half-hidden in the trees was a round, stone, beehive like shape, an ancient monk's cell. The ruins of others could be seen under the tangle of some red-leaved creeper, but this one had been repaired and last swept out no more than a month or two ago. It was small: Haakon and Donal together nearly filled the space. The only light came from the smoke hole in the roof, but someone had left a tallow dip, carefully trimmed, in a cracked plate on the floor.

They began to investigate the dimness. Haakon barked his shins on a wooden chest against the far wall and sat down beside it, swearing. He opened it, half expecting the lid to crumble with age in his hands, but it swung up easily. Inside was a leather-bound manuscript, full of careful writing and elaborate painted borders such as Haakon had seen in English monasteries. A cake of dry ink and a quill pen rattled into the corner of the chest as he lifted it. Donal bent over, whistled softly between his teeth, and sat down beside Haakon. "This is Christian monks' writing," Haakon said irritably. "I can't read this."

"I can," Donal said. He took the painted pages carefully from Haakon and laid them in his lap so that the light from the smoke hole fell on them. "My father had some notion I might make a priest once. I studied with the monks." Haakon raised his eyebrows at this unexpected revelation as Donal touched the first page lightly with his fingers. The twelve apostles, still glowing brightly in red and blue and gold, marched up the borders among a scrollwork of green leaves. The green stems interlaced like braiding. "This is very beautiful work."

Haakon lost interest. "I've no need for Christian prayers."

"It isn't prayers," Donal said. He began to read under his breath. The Latin words came back to him slowly at first and then with an old familiarity. "It's the records of the monastery."

Haakon had small interest in that either, but when Donal leafed through to the last page of writing and said that that was recent, the jarl paid more attention. He sat cross-legged on the floor with the ax in his lap as if to ward off anything that might come from the women *or* from the monks' books and listened while Donal read, putting the painted pages' story into Norse.

It was monks who had come to the island first, sailing in frail leather boats from Ireland, willing to live a holy hermit's life wherever God should see fit to send them. Not being experienced sailors, the monks had barely managed to land on the island in a storm, but all their craft had been wrecked. There were twenty monks and six thralls—servingwomen—to look after them and let the monks give all their thoughts to God.

"Our boats being taken by the storm," the first abbot wrote in his careful hand, *"it must be this place that God intends for us."*

They built their church and small stone cells there, with huts some distance away for the servingwomen, and began to plant the land with seed brought from Ireland and to tend the few animals saved from the storm. They called it Bridget's Isle then.

Bridget's Isle offered a harsh life, but that was what the monks sought. All went well for a few years, but gradually they found that their faith was not enough to sustain them. Donal could see growing unease and finally desperation in the abbot's hand. The hardships increased, and as they did, the men's faith began to leave them. And there was no way to go home.

Sadly, the old abbot wrote, his flock began to abandon their vows and to quarrel with each other and to lie with the thrall-women, so that babies were born on the island. *"My fault,"* he wrote. *"My fault to have brought women. So foolish and prideful to have thought to give God a greater glory by facing down temptation than by running from it."* The letters in their neat lines shook a little, but the painted borders were as beautiful as ever. The old abbot kept to his discipline in his misery. *"I have told myself that a man who wishes to fornicate will do so with his own sex if there is none other available, but that does not take the blame from my head. I am well served now for my foolish pride."*

Within ten years the whole community degenerated. After the old abbot died, his records were kept up sporadically by his successor, the youngest of the monks, who had been only fifteen when he had landed on Bridget's Isle. His neat round letters were as carefully wrought as the old man's, but he abandoned the pretense of haloed figures and holy symbols. The margins were blank save for a few desperate scribbles that Donal thought must have come from the young abbot's nightmares: twining serpents and children with the heads of beasts. For besides the loss of faith and the strength that faith had lent them, another trial had been sent to them, which the young abbot knew for a curse from God—an inherited disease. Three of the six thrall-women had been sisters, and it was through them, he thought, that the disease had passed. It afflicted only the male children, as was fitting for their fathers' sins. Most didn't live past infancy, and all but a few of the survivors were weak and bled continuously from the slightest scratch. Although the island itself had become gradually fruitful over the years, the human population was cursed.

Here the record broke off again. *"We are cursed before God,"* the young abbot wrote, *"and no more shall I set our shame on parchment."*

Donal looked up at Haakon uncertainly.

"There is more," Haakon said. "I saw it."

"I know," Donal said. "But it is giving me an ill feeling in my stomach to read it."

"Don't play the fainting maid with me, Donal. I am liking this less and less, and that means I want to know the whole of it."

"Very well." Donal turned the parchment page slowly and looked with unhappiness at the straggling letters that sloped across it. No educated abbot this. The writer was a child sired on Bridget's Isle, one of the few healthy males born there. Donal wondered fleetingly if it was the old man who kept the bees, and why he should come here in secret to set down the horrors of their life. He began to read almost reluctantly, pausing to decipher the garbled Latin words.

In three generations the disease spread throughout the entire community. As it spread, the people, mostly women now, mourning their lost babes, began to fall further from God, back to the old religion of their ancestors, handed down in folktales since the ancient days. They believed that these gods would come to their aid where the Christian god had not, would send them men and babies who lived.

Men! There were no men gone sealing, Haakon thought, no men but themselves. "I am no god's gift to an island of madwomen," he said grimly. "Finish reading."

The women's worship was a strange amalgam now of things half remembered from legend and things that were a product of their own desperation and the island itself. The Christian name was long forgotten and they called it Bee Isle now, for the swarms of wild bees they had found there. And if it was the old mother goddesses of the Irish to whom the lonely women turned, surely that was not to be wondered at. The Old One, who spoke for the goddess, had promised them that men would come. But Earth Mother had her dark and bloody side, and in their desperation to propitiate her, the women committed some act so unspeakable that the old man writing by candlelight would not set it down. *"And now they will come from the sea, and the king among them will be the seal on it, so that we may live. I am afraid but too old to fight, lest they give me to the goddess instead."*

Donal choked and looked up at Haakon. The harper's face had gone chalky white in the gloom.

"I don't understand that," Haakon said. He stood up and dusted his hands on the seat of his breeches. "He makes riddles."

"Not entirely," Donal said. "The Old One is mad. Have you thought of that?"

"Certainly," Haakon said. "They all are. It is the inbreeding, I expect. Bad for stock, bad for men."

"That and the disease," Donal said slowly. "To watch their babes die—I suppose there is some excuse for them. But they don't understand. It's in their blood—no man could sire a healthy child on them. And they are going to do a great evil."

"Now *you* are talking in riddles," Haakon said, impatient. "Spit it out."

Donal put the beautiful painted parchment manuscript away in the chest. He looked as if he didn't wish to touch it. "They have killed a man, or maybe only one of their own," he said. "To bring us here. It is the price that the old gods always asked. But Earth Mother will want more, jarl, to give them back fertility. She will want a king."

"We haven't one. And I've no mind to stay and be these madwomen's tame stallion. We sail now!"

"If we can," Donal said.

"What in Thor's name are you *getting at*?"

Donal rose, his dark eyes unnaturally bright. Haakon thought that for all Donal's professed Christianity, the harper was closer to the old gods of his people than he would admit. "For the fertility of the land, there is only one sacrifice—the blood of the king after he has lain with the queen. If you had gone into Maeve's bed, Haakon, you'd be dead already. As it is, they will try to force it. I told you something was going to happen."

Haakon laughed, but the skin crawled on the back of his neck. "I am no maid to be raped," he said gruffly. "Force it *how*, you fool?"

Donal shrugged unhappily. "I don't know. A drug maybe. They may have given you something in your food already."

Haakon thought of the unwilling desire that the woman

had stirred in him, and the fear of an old and evil magic began to turn into a knot in his stomach. It would not be denied. The Norse themselves practiced human sacrifice when the need was great but only when the sacrifice himself chose that death for an assured place in Valhalla. But to die on this island... He wondered if his coupling with Maeve and his life's blood would indeed take the disease away. The cold fear gripped him that it might and that somehow she would call him to her in spite of himself. He would not shame himself in front of Donal by retching, but he felt like it. "We will sail," he said steadily. "Now. Today."

"They will fight you," Donal said. "The men, too, maybe. The hold of this place is very strong." Haakon thought that Donal was fighting the same fear he felt himself.

"They will come," Haakon said. "I will not leave any man here to die in my place."

"They will try to keep us," Donal said stubbornly. "I don't know how, but—Christ Jesus!"

The thought came into Haakon's mind in the same moment as into Donal's—the ship! It was lack of ships that had stranded the first monks on Bee Isle. Unlike the monks, Haakon's folk could both build a ship and navigate the fearsome reefs that guarded Bee Isle, but he knew with certainty that they would not be granted that much time. Without *Raven*, they would stay forever. Maeve and the Old One would know that, too. Haakon pushed his way through the creepers that straggled about the narrow door and began to run.

"There is but one choice." Rosamund paced wearily before the men and women gathered in the great hall three days after her father had sailed for home. Her husband's warriors lounged on their benches and seemed more pleased than not at the prospect of another fight. Cormac's monks clutched the crosses that hung from their girdles, and the little cluster of holy women kept to themselves at the opposite end of the hall from the Norsemen. Cormac stood beside them, large, benign, protective, with the mace that seemed to serve him as an abbot's staff stuck through his belt.

Rosamund stopped her pacing and faced them all. "We must make alliance with my husband's kin here."

Leif gave his Norsemen a look that said that this was his idea as much as the lady's. They had thrashed it out between them, Leif Hildisson, Lady Rosamund, and the Irish abbot, but Leif and the abbot both knew that Lady Rosamund was the only one who could speak to them all, monks and Norsemen both, with any hope of being listened to. The monks thought that Leif was unholy, while the Norse had scant regard for Christians, although Cormac's mace commanded at least an outward respect.

"I know my father," Rosamund said grimly. She was beginning to feel her pregnancy and wanted nothing so much as to go somewhere and sleep. "He will be back next season with an army. I don't think he can gather the men before winter, and in that we are lucky. But it will take the Dal Crimthann to hold him off, and we had best start now."

"There are men in the Trondelag," someone growled. "No need to bow and scrape to the Irish."

"*If* they can sail in time," Rosamund said crisply. "Do we ask them to sail this fall and leave Haakonstead bare over the winter for some other jarl to scoop into his hand or sail in spring and hope they get here before my father. *You* tell me which."

"Neither, lady," Leif said. He looked at his men. "Even with King Harald's peace, a hold bared of fighting men is too much temptation. I've no mind to trade the jarl's land in Norway for this one."

"The Dal Crimthann have no love for Norse," Brother Kevin said. Norse and Irish had lived together long enough at Ole's Hold to have developed a rough speech of common words understandable to both. All the Norse turned and glared at him. Brother Kevin glared back. "Lucky you were to make peace with the Dal Crimthann at all."

"Certainly there will be no alliance if we cannot even make peace with each other!" Rosamund said, goaded. "I am telling you, Kevin, you will like my father somewhat less than you like us. For a Christian, he has scant respect for priests."

One of the nuns began to weep softly, caught between the devil on her porch and the devil overseas. "There's no need for that," Rosamund said, exasperated, then narrowed her eyes suddenly at Fann, standing beside the weeping woman. She was nearly swallowed up in a brown nun's gown obviously cut with no regard for the wearer's figure. A knotted rope girdled her small waist, with a dark cross pendant from the ends. In the last weeks, Rosamund had had scant attention to spare for Fann. A mistake, it would seem. *Oh, dear ...* Ruthlessly, Rosamund pushed Fann out of her mind. She didn't have time for Fann just now. But Donal wasn't going to like this. . . .

Rosamund dragged her attention back to the matter at hand while Fann eyed her with self-conscious defiance. "Better an ally close to hand than a ship sailing from Norway in bad weather," Rosamund said. It was nearly fall. The seasons seemed to have turned without her knowing it. "I will not sit here and count the days and wait, and then find that no help comes." These were dangerous times: Nothing was a certainty. "Our best prospect is Fergus MacAidan and the Dal Crimthann, so to the Dal Crimthann we go." She eyes her husband's fighting men. "Like bridegrooms," she added firmly. "Bearing posies and remembering to keep a civil tongue in one's head. The man who does not will answer to me and then to Leif and then to Abbot Cormac if there is aught left of him."

They began to laugh at that, Norse and Christians alike. There was a hoot and a cheer from the Norse that was more respectful than not, so she let it go by. Lady Rosamund's father was going to be sorry he had made war on his daughter, Leif thought, if she could pull the Dal Crimthann to her as she had the folk of Ole's Hold. *If.* There was always an 'if.' Leif looked his Norsemen over, mentally selecting the best-mannered of them to ride to Dunnaill.

"Norsemen? And an Englishwoman?" King Dungal jerked his gray head out of the doze into which he had let his harper lull him. It was pleasantly warm by the hearth, and he had no mind to speak with Norsemen.

"*And* that saintly old soldier Cormac," Fergus MacAidan said, chuckling.

"*Hmmmph!*" Dungal gave him a baleful glare. "You're drunk. Where would Cormac get an Englishwoman?"

"She's the wife of the Norse jarl—Deirdre's son—at Haroldsson's Hold," Fergus said. "And he didn't get her, she got him. She seems to be in charge. They are carrying peace flags. There are only ten of them," he added soothingly.

"*You* brought them here!" Conor MacLorne burst into the hall in a visible aura of fury. "You and your *peace*! Now this Norseman insults us by sending his *woman* to speak for him!"

"Deirdre's son?" Dungal grasped at this piece of information. "I've a mind to see him then." He grinned evilly at Conor and Fergus. "If he's Deirdre's son, he has prince's rank in the *fine*. It may be I'll acknowledge *him*." He cackled and kicked at the small boy who was tending the fire. "Go and get me a better shirt than this to wear!"

"Thinking to overset us, Uncle?" Fergus inquired genially. Conor looked as if he would catch fire. "The jarl's gone raiding somewhere, I'm told, so you'll have to content you with the wife. But you should let her in, faith, you should. I saw them ride up. You could warm your hands at that one!"

"A beauty, eh?" Dungal said. He considered. "You'd best not be trying to take a Norseman's wife, Fergus. They're touchy about that." He peered at Conor MacLorne, who was grinding his teeth. He had a mind to annoy Conor, Dungal thought. He had not the power to do aught else than to take small stabs at the pair of them, when he could think clearly enough to do so. Sadly, the old king knew, there were days when he could not. But he felt well tonight. And if Fergus should make trouble, maybe the Norseman would rid him of Fergus.

The page boy came back with a fine red woolen shirt embroidered with gold. Dungal put it on over his other one. The page rebuckled his belt and wiped the leaping gold horse on the buckle with his sleeve. A gold fillet lay fallen in the straw on the floor. The page sat the king down again, rearranged the woolen robe across his knees, and set the fillet on his gray hair.

"There, Sire, ye look fine." The boy thought it shame that Conor MacLorne and Fergus MacAidan should come and tease the old man with Norsemen and strange women when he needed to be left quiet.

"All right, lad, go and bid them in. Just the woman and Cormac, mind you. I've no wish to stare at Norsemen."

When the unbidden guests appeared, however, they were three. Over protests, Rosamund had brought Leif Hildisson with her. Her glance swept over Conor's fuming stare and Fergus's amused one and came to rest on the king. "This is Leif Hildisson, Sire, who is my husband's steward," she said firmly. "I do not go anywhere without him."

Leif bowed gravely. He was young, no more than three-and-twenty, and his round, red-cheeked face and sunny hair gave him the deceptive look of a farmboy. He was nearly as good with an ax as Haakon.

Dungal inspected him thoroughly while Rosamund in turn tried to take the king's measure. And, more important, that of Fergus MacAidan and Conor MacLorne. Dungal was old; it was a wonder he was aboveground, she thought. Fergus and Conor were the power. They stood one on either side of the king's chair, with the confidence of youth. Conor MacLorne's flaming hair clashed gaudily with his saffron-colored shirt. He wore a gold collar at his throat and a gold band pushed halfway up his arm. His skin was pale and freckled, and he had the lean look of a wolf in a bad temper. Fergus stood on the other side of the king's chair, equally lean and hungry looking, but his blue eyes were fixed on Rosamund in such apparent appreciation that she almost laughed. *I mustn't underestimate him,* she thought. His face was fine boned, with winging dark brows, but there was an uncanny look of Haakon about him. He stepped down from the king's dais, lordlywise, and bowed over her hand.

"Bid you welcome, lady." He eyed Leif, apparently amused. "*And* your Norse watchdog."

"I thought I might have need of one," Rosamund said with some asperity. Besides the page, the only other person on the dais was a man of perhaps forty, whose hair appeared to have gone white in his youth. The king's harper, to judge by the instrument cradled in his lap. Rosamund looked around the hall in a quick glance for Father Kilian and breathed a sign of relief when she didn't see him. If she could put Fergus and Conor on her side before Kilian got wind of matters, it might make the going easier.

"It may be you will have need of your watchdog!" Conor snapped, lowering this hope considerably. "For a Norseman's woman to come to Dunnaill is ill advised!"

"For a son of the Ui Neill to refuse hospitality ill becomes him," Cormac said.

"And when have the Céli Dé given orders to the Ui Neill?"

The Céli Dé, the companions of God, were radical monks whose simple way of life protested the growing worldliness of the great monasteries. Cormac grinned at Conor. "Since the Ui Neill first founded the Céli Dé, Conor. My line is older than yours. Ask Fingal before you put insult on me."

The white-haired harper looked uncomfortable. It was the business of a harper, as it had been since the days of the Druids, to know by heart the line and ancestry of his king's house and all its branches. Cormac was right, but Conor did not look in a mood to be instructed.

Dungal roused himself. "Enough! Conor, you are not king in Dunnaill just yet." He fixed Rosamund with a watery eye that had some shrewdness in it. "What do you want, woman?"

"Alliance," she said before anyone could speak again. "Armed men to fight for my husband's hold in his absence."

"Oho! And why should the king of the Dal Crimthann send armed men to a Norseman?"

"Because he is kin to you," Rosamund said, and added, before Dungal could tell her that he had more kin than he wanted as matters stood, "and because my father, who is an English earl, will come in spring to try to take it, and you will be sorry if he succeeds. My father is not a neighbor a sane man would wish for."

Fergus MacAidan looked interested. "Say *you* so, Cormac?"

"I have fought him," Cormac said. "Not a month since. He was ally to Olaf Haraldsson. Lady Rosamund bears little love for her father and with good reason."

Dungal appeared to have retreated into his chair, and his old eyes were unhappy. This was complicated and would take much thought. If he weren't careful, Conor and Fergus would ride him down and go their own way. If they could find common ground between them. "I am tired," he said petulantly. "The lady will be tired, from the ride." He looked between Conor and Fergus and settled his eyes on Fergus. "Take them to the guesthouse and have food sent. Likely we will talk in a day or so."

"A day or—!" Rosamund began to protest, but Fergus took her by the arm.

"Matters do not move so fast in Ireland. There is the council to consult and hospitality to be shown. And tomorrow is the Feast of the Assumption. If you have no suitable gown for the king's court, I will have one sent to you."

"Thank you, I have sufficient clothing with me," Rosamund said. Somehow she found that she was at the door, with Leif and Cormac trailing behind her. Fergus kept up an amiable chat as they led their horses across the great open court of Dunnaill to the cluster of stone and timber houses beyond. Dunnaill was old, as old as Niall of the Nine Hostages, the first in the ancient line of the Ui Neill. It was built on a hill, ringed by both earthen walls and a water-filled ditch within them. Rosamund and her escort had felt every eye in Dunnaill on them when they had first ridden through the massive gates and across the bridge that spanned the murky water in the ditch. All around the hill of Dunnaill stretched a boggy flower-strewn valley. The only good ground was the raised road leading to the fortress. Earl Edmund would have a bad time with Dunnaill, Rosamund thought; she hoped that King Dungal would not decide to sit in his hill fort and let Earl Edmund have Ole's Hold if he wanted it. The raths, the walled farms of the other Dal Crimthann folk, would be scattered widely about Dunnaill, and Edmund could take those with little trouble if he had a mind to. Maybe that would give King Dungal cause to think.

"I do not see what is so difficult about a decision such as this—" Rosamund cut Fergus's pleasantries short as they came to the door of the guesthouse, which proved to be a large, rambling hall of several chambers, built partly of stone, partly of interwoven wood plastered over with clay, which was common here.

"To give hospitality to the lady of Haraldsson's Hold—" Fergus said.

"Ole's Hold," Rosamund said.

"Ole's Hold. That is a simple matter. Even to wish that she may win her battle. But armed men—that is a question of more weight."

"Debate too long, and you will find that my father's men loose in your land is a matter of weight!"

"There is also Holy Church to consult," Fergus said, continuing his list of obstacles unchecked.

Rosamund gritted her teeth. "Father Kilian would happily see my folk in hell. But there is a Christian monastery on my land, and my father is no respecter of priests. You may tell Kilian that."

"Assuredly," Fergus said. "When it is time." He considered her, and his winging brows rose a little higher. "It seems pity that so beautiful a lady should be left to take these matters in her own hands."

"If the jarl had known what my father had in mind, the jarl would not have left Ireland," Rosamund said firmly.

Fergus seemed to find it no great sorrow that he had. He leaned on his hand by the doorpost and bent his head to hers. "Faith, a maid of as much courage as beauty. Fingal shall make a verse for you at dinner."

"I am no maid," Rosamund snapped.

"No." Fergus's blue eyes caught hers, and he smiled at her. "Maids are callow and foolish. The lady of . . . Ole's Hold is neither."

"Go away," Rosamund said under her breath, "before my escort cut you into small chips and spoil my chances for the king's aid."

Fergus let out a breath of startled laughter, kissed her hand, and was gone. Rosamund looked after him thoughtfully. What Fergus wanted was plain enough. She hoped he wasn't going to demand it as the price of his support. She didn't trust him at all.

Nor, it appeared, did Abbot Cormac. "That one blows three ways at once like a summer wind," Cormac said scornfully. "He may appear to come tame to your hand, but Fergus MacAidan has never done anything that didn't serve *him* first and the man needing the favor *after*."

Rosamund nodded wearily and went to let Tordis dress her hair. Tordis, who had come with the delegation to serve her lady, looked around the room as she did Rosamund's hair, half-curious, half-fearful. The chamber allotted to Rosamund was a pleasant one, with clean lime-washed walls and a feather bed, spread with rugs of finely embroidered deerskin. The floor was paved with flagstones and covered with wool rags. A new-laid fire of peat blocks was ready on the hearth. Rosamund set Tordis to kindling it from the pot of coals beside it while two of her men brought her chests in from the wagon. She shook out her best gown and laid it across the bed, goaded by Fergus's offer of clothes if hers should not be sufficient for the king's court.

"Did you see the fine gold collar the Irish lord was wearing?" Tordis said, awed. "Not even the jarl has a better."

"The jarl has no need to strut like a gamecock, weighed down with more gold than our women wear," Rosamund said. "Norse are practical: They put their wealth in chain mail and a good ax blade." It did not occur to her, as she tipped the contents of her jewel casket out on the bed, that she sounded singularly like her father. Nevertheless, she picked her best brooches and necklace. She could stand up better to Fergus, she thought, if she outshone him. As for standing up to Kilian—her stomach knotted violently, and she prayed that she wouldn't have to, but she doubted that that was a prayer that even God could grant. Kilian would hear of their presence in Dunnaill and come like an avenging angel to drive them out again.

Fergus came by torchlight to fetch the lady of Ole's Hold and her retinue, and Rosamund blinked at the number of people streaming into the king's hall. It was the Eve of the Assumption, and every lord of the Dal Crimthánn seemed to have ridden into Dunnaill to hear mass and to stare at the Norse jarl's Englishwoman. How word had spread that fast, she didn't know, but they all seemed to know she was there and why she had come.

Rosamund tried to take their measure at dinner, sitting at the king's high table between Dungal and Fergus MacAidan. Since Fergus and Conor MacLorne were both unwed and there was no princess of rank in the king's family, Rosamund was the only woman at the high table. She found herself sharing a platter with Fergus MacAidan, with trenchers of coarse bread as side plates for the sauced dishes. When the lords had dined, the side bread would go to the common folk.

Abbot Cormac sat on Dungal's other side, with Leif Hildisson beyond him, which Rosamund recognized as a considerable courtesy from Dungal. The other Norse had had to be content with the astonishing quantity of food that had been sent to the guesthouse. Rosamund thought that that was very likely just as well; most of the Irish seemed to have brought their wives with them, and the Norse had a reputation, not entirely undeserved, for making woman trouble. A Norseman in a chieftain's service left his wife behind and expected to take his pleasure where he found it. It was a complication Rosamund felt herself well able to do without in Dunnaill.

She looked at the Irish lords and counted up those who could make or break her mission. Conor MacLorne, across the high table from her, looked as friendly as a snake and was head-to-head with Father Kilian, who regarded Rosamund with a dark, implacable stare. Dungal had begun the evening with a shrewd interest, watching all the factions, but now he only stared at the bread and venison on his silver plate while his page hovered over him solicitously. She could have been sympathetic, Rosamund thought, were it not so aggravating to have the old man's mind slip through her fingers just when she had hopes of using this evening to push him to a promise. She concentrated instead on using her time to charm Fergus MacAidan, although warily.

Fergus seemed to have abandoned his blatant gallantry, at least for the moment, and asked instead several questions about the defenses of Ole's Hold, which gave her a better opinion of his good sense than she had had previously.

"It held against *us*, you know," he said with a rueful smile.

"We had twice the men then," Rosamund said honestly. She gave him a thoughtful look, as if to decide if he would take offense. "And my father allows no quarreling with his command."

"That may be a question that won't be arising again," Fergus said. "Conor is less inclined to be sending his men back to your hold again. At least not to fight the earl for you," he added. "Conor would welcome the devil if he drove Norse away."

"And you?" Rosamund said bluntly.

"Are you wanting an honest answer to that?"

Rosamund chewed a mouthful of venison and swallowed. "Would I get one?"

"Faith, as honest a one as I can give," Fergus said. "I've a respect for your husband." He leaned his head a little closer. "And a great liking for his wife."

"And a good mind to do anything that Conor goes against," Rosamund said tartly.

Fergus laughed. "Aye, that too. But I've a longing for yourself, Rose of the World, and that's not a lie."

She gave him an exasperated look at the play on her name, which was close to being disrespectful. He seemed not to notice. His fine, long-fingered hands were peeling an apple for her, and he presented it to her with a little bow as she tried to slide away from him. He slid too, and she stopped trying when their communal platter was nearly out of her reach. If she wished to eat, it seemed she must do so with Fergus in her pocket. She studied him out of the corner of her eye. The resemblance to Haakon was marked but superficial. There was a wild, flyaway quality to Fergus that was none of Haakon's. She thought of what Cormac had said. Fergus might be a chancy ally to have, but so far he was her only one.

"Rose of the World, you are well named," Fergus whispered in her ear.

"Lord Fergus, you do not know me so well," Rosamund said reprovingly.

"But I will." Fergus took her hand to lead her from the table as the servants began to clear the silver plate and collect the bread for the lower tables. Everyone in the hall stared at her as she rose, as if she were a cow with two heads, Rosamund thought.

"They've all come to look you over," Fergus whispered, amused. And then they would all argue the matter of allying themselves with her backward and forward and from all sides, for weeks. He watched Rosamund stalking away from him in icy dignity to pay her respects to King Dungal. The lady would be a long time in Dunnaill if she truly intended to wring an alliance from the Dal Crimthann.

IX

A Fearful Magic

"*Odiiiiiin!*" Haakon screamed the war cry of the Norse as he ran. The streets of Bee Isle were empty, but not, he thought, uninhabited. In the round and secretive huts there was a stirring at his voice, and men began to poke their heads out. When they saw the jarl, they tried to follow, half-naked some of them, shaking their heads as if to shake off sleep. Haakon saw Thórfinn Solvisson fighting for his ax with a naked woman who clung fiercely to his arm. Her hair flew in a wild tangle about her face. She screamed and bit him as he jerked the ax away.

"*Raven!*" Haakon shouted. "To *Raven*, or we'll none of us go home!" He didn't wait to see if they followed him but ran, heart pounding, down the track to the beach. He could hear Donal gasping for breath beside him, and the sound of running feet behind them. He clawed his way up the dunes, and even the sour salt-marsh grass seemed to cling at his ankles and pull him back. At the top he stopped, gasping, eyes sweeping the beach.

"Thor's hammer, *no!*"

All around the ship, a sea of brushwood had been piled, leaving only a space for the boarding plank by which Haakon's men had earlier driven the animals back on board. The women on *Raven*'s deck were unrecognizable, monstrous things set free from Hel. The sealskin hoods that masked their faces showed only bright seal eyes. The women moved, not of their own volition, but to the wild piping that seemed to come out of the very air. All around the mast they danced, lighted torches in their hands, behind a dancer taller than the rest. Her corn-colored hair flowed under the trailing ends of her hood like the fire.

138

The ancient crone, seated cross-legged on the up-turned ship's boat, stretched out her hand toward Haakon. There was a bronze knife in it: The blade glittered whitely in the sun. "He comes! The chosen man!"

Maeve stopped her dance, turned, seal's face watching him. Even at this distance Haakon felt her presence like a drug. Or an ancient magic, old and terrible and undenia-ble. He shook it away from him. He had no time to fear Maeve, with a dozen torches burning on his ship's deck.

"Hel take you, not my ship!" Maeve forgotten, Haakon slid and stumbled down the dunes. Ax in hand he ran with a growing company of the ship's crew about him, roused from their stupor by the horror of those torches.

The women fought wildly, using the torches as weap-ons. One man screamed and fell over the side into the brushwood, his hair on fire. Another dived on top of him and enveloped his head in a cloak before the brushwood could ignite. Yazid clambered up the ramp beside Haakon, cursing shrilly in Arabic, his curved sword slashing at the women. One woman shrieked as it bit through her hand, and Yazid stamped out her torch as it fell. But there were too many of them. It would be only a moment before some woman sacrificed her own defense to fling a torch into the dry wood below.

"The net!" Haakon yelled at Yazid. Three women clung to the jarl, clawing and biting. Haakon flung them away, yelping because one of them had a knife as well as a torch, and cleared a path to the mast. Yazid stuck his sword through his sash and began to climb. Haakon could feel his hair singeing. He swung his ax at another woman while Maeve's voice dinned in his ears: "He be chosen! Must not be marked!"

Haakon swung the ax again, and the women backed away. Through the milling chaos and the blaze of fire he saw Maeve, standing beside the Old One on the boat's keel. The sun was behind her back, and it outlined them both in a golden nimbus brighter than the torch fire.

"I am no stallion for your slaughter, Maeve!" he shouted to her.

"Thee *must!*" Her voice was desperate, compelling, over the shrieking of the women. "Thee must, or we *die!*"

Even then something in him whispered, *Go to her.*
"Die then!" he screamed and turned his back on her, fighting
his way to *Raven's* bow as the net came down out of the sky.

In the next moment the deck was a writhing horror of
fire and bodies. Haakon and the men who had managed to
fight their way on board threw their cloaks over the
flames, not greatly caring how many of the women they
trampled in doing it. Someone unstoppered a cask of
water from the hold, and the men fought the flames with
that too until they were out. The Old One had risen from
her perch and stood on the upturned boat in the stern like
a gaunt bird of prey, calling down Earth Mother's wrath
upon them, curse after curse to blast and wither them
black where they stood. Donal, Yazid, and a horror-struck
Thorfinn Solvisson were trying to tip the net-entangled
women over the side. Haakon pushed his way through
them to Raven's stern, his eyes blazing.

"This is *my* ship! Thor Odinsson's ship!" He picked
the old woman up and threw her, as she raked at him with
the bronze knife. She fell shrieking over the side, and he
turned to face Maeve.

"No," Maeve whispered. The seal mask was askew,
and he could see her eyes pleading with him. "No . . ."

"Jump," Haakon said. "Jump or I'll kill you." He
raised the ax, and she knew that the spell had lost its hold.
He would kill her. She gave a little moan and backed away.
Haakon came at her, his face dark with anger. With a sob,
she jumped.

The dry brush raked at her face. She crouched on
hands and knees, looking up at him. The seal mask had
fallen away, and her eyes were forlorn. Haakon wrenched
himself away and looked out to the water. The tide was on
the turn. *"Launch her!"*

The last of Haakon's men had begun to pour over the
lip of the dunes, weapons in hand. The women who had
been with them ran behind, wailing. The sight of the ship
with dry tinder packed around her shook them from their
stupor. Hagar the Simple, Hjalmar Sitricsson, and ten
others of the heaviest put their shoulders to *Raven's* stern
and heaved while the rest tried to hold the women off.
The men were still loath to kill them, Haakon saw—Thor's

hammer, most of his crew had come half-naked from their beds!—and Haakon hadn't the heart to order it. But the women fought like demons, driven from the last corner of their sanity by desperation. They clawed at Haakon's men with knives, scratched and bit, and above it all rose a dreadful wailing howl that was the Old One calling her gods down to aid her. She broke off suddenly in a shrill shriek, and Haakon caught Thorfinn Solvisson's eye for just a moment, standing above her in the trampled brushwood. Thorfinn's face was grim and a little pale, and he held a dripping ax in his hand.

Raven's keel was sliding down the sand into the foam of the turning tide. Haakon leaped over the side and threw himself into the battle that raged around *Raven*'s stern. Two of his men were down, and nearly a dozen of the women. The tide was pink where it crept over bloodstained sand. An unfamiliar presence at his elbow made him turn, and he recognized with a shock the old beekeeper who had tried to warn him days ago. The old man's gray hair flew wildly about his head, and he had a scythe in his hand. He slashed at the advancing women with it, and two of them leaped on him. Their hands were red to the wrist. The old man stumbled, and Donal MacRae caught him under the arm and pulled him back.

"She's afloat!" someone yelled from *Raven*'s deck.

"Board!" Haakon screamed. He swung his ax in a wide arc and backed toward the ship. All around him men were scrambling over the side. Haakon saw Donal half carrying the old man and then boosting him up as hands reached down to help. On deck, Hagar the Simple was shooting any woman who tried to follow. Donal blanched as the girl Morna dropped with an arrow in her shoulder. Haakon didn't look for Maeve. A high keening that rose from beside the Old One's body told him where she was.

"Out oars!" *Raven* settled in the water and came about as the red oars swung. One glance back was all that Haakon allowed himself. Maeve stood on the shore, the red tide lapping at her feet. She held her arms outstretched, and the voice of her keening for the Old One rose hopelessly over the surf. Haakon took the helm from a shaken Knut One-Eye so that he wouldn't have to look again.

It was easier to skirt the reefs in a daylight calm, but it was wearisome all the same. By the time they had *Raven* into open sea and her red sail raised, Haakon found that the old man, the last male descendant of St. Bridget's monks, was dead.

Haakon looked down at the frail body and thought that he could still hear the voices of the women beyond the reefs. No wonder the old man had been too fearful to speak plainly. But he had fought them in the end, fought with whatever strength was left in him.

Haakon turned to Knut. "Take the little boat and send him with honor to Father Odin."

They wrestled the smaller of the ship's boats out from under the larger and laid the old man in its curve, with dried meat and a handful of meal for his journey. They spread caulking pitch over all, and when the little craft had been carefully lowered to the waves, they set it afire, a proper home-going for a warrior.

Donal MacRae watched the flames blaze up and began a low, solemn chant just under his breath: *"Requiem aeternam dona ei, Domine: et lux perpetua luceat ei."* Eternal rest grant unto him, O Lord: and let perpetual light shine upon him. Donal was no priest, and it had been years since he had committed those words to heart. But it seemed to him that the old beekeeper should have them at his leave-taking. There had been something of the Christians' god left in the old man after all.

When the boat was well afire, Haakon grunted his satisfaction and went away into the hold to see that the animals had taken no hurt. He was in a foul temper and in a mood to be by himself. A red cow nuzzled him curiously. He batted her head away and sat down on a sack of meal. The golden ax was foul with blood, so he found an empty sack and began to clean it.

A gash across the knuckles of his right hand still oozed blood and pained him every time he flexed his fingers. Haakon braced the ax in the crook of his arm and tried, awkwardly, to clean it left-handed. *You might have warned me*, he thought at it, not really expecting any reply. But it seemed that Thor Odinsson was in a mood to converse with him after all. The golden blade began to glow more brightly, and a voice in Haakon's head said distinctly, *Have I not kept my bargain well enough, Haakon Olesson? You are yet alive, are you not?*

Haakon jumped, then doggedly resumed cleaning the ax. "Two of my men are not," he said in a low growl. He didn't like voices in his head, he liked the idea of his crew overhearing him speaking to an ax and a red cow in the hold even less.

The god seemed unconcerned. *I promised to aid you, Haakon Olesson, not to be your nursemaid.*

Haakon gritted his teeth and tried to swallow his temper. The gods were not always entirely fair, but it was not for men to point that out. Thor Odinsson was a chancy partner to go adventuring with. Haakon had known that from the start. He looked up, past the awning that was stretched partway over the hold, to the scudding clouds that ran across a bright sky. He was undeniably alive. And *Raven* was whole and running before a fair wind. Haakon knew that to Thor Odinsson's mind he could ask for little more than that. Haakon lifted his hand to brush the sweat-dampened hair back from his eyes and yelped as the pain of his gashed knuckles brought him abruptly back to earth. He wouldn't be able to hold an ax for a week or more.

A faint chuckle rang in his ears. Thor would have little sympathy for so light a wound. *And when were you promised invulnerability? Not by me. That is for you to devise.*

With that enigmatic comment, the god appeared to take his departure back to the halls of Asgard, or wherever it was he went when he was not mixing in the affairs of men.

Raven sailed on, with a crew more than somewhat shaken by their escape. Resigned to a week of going weaponless by the fact that there would very likely be no one to fight anyway, Haakon bandaged his wounded hand and decided that he had learned one thing at least: When he left a settlement in the new land, he would allow no siblings, and there would be an unbreakable rule that the second generation born in the settlement must go home to Norway or to Iceland to choose their mates. The effects of in-breeding could be too terrible. Haakon shuddered. He wondered how many nights it would be before he no longer heard Maeve's voice in his sleep. The ring-shaped

scars that the *kraken* had left still itched and plagued him
as they healed, but there were worse things than sea
monsters to meet on a voyage, and the worst was humans
when a madness struck them.

Haakon looked at his crew, backs bent to their oars
and singularly well behaved since their perilous escape
from Bee Isle. They had nearly succumbed to the madness
themselves. The two who had died had been the ones who
had paid most heed to Eilaf Eiriksson when Eilaf had
busied himself arguing with the jarl against leaving Bee
Isle. Late to realize the peril they were in, they had been
caught by the women before they ever reached the ship.
Eilaf himself, however, was very much alive and seemed
to find no fault with himself for his ill judgment.

"That was the jarl's fault," Eilaf said briskly, in a
confidential undertone to Hjalmar. "Although likely he will
blame *you* for it."

Hjalmar growled at him and stalked off, but he gave
Haakon a wary look across the deck. Donal MacRae, who
had been eavesdropping, stormed off to Haakon in a
blazing rage.

"You should drop that one overside, so you should,
and I'll be doing it for you if he opens his mouth in my
hearing again!"

"Be *quiet*! Another killing to your score, Donal, and
you won't get back into Norway until you're as old as
Father Ask." Father Ask was the first man, created from an
ash tree by Odin. Haakon pointed a finger at Donal. "Also
Eilaf is a helmsman, which you are not, and I need him!"
They were truly in midocean now, farther west than man
had ever gone. All around them there was only gray sea.
Not even birds flecked the sky above. They took direction
from the stars and sun, and when the sky was overcast,
from a sunstone, a translucent piece of Iceland spar that
darkened when turned sunward. A notched bearing dial,
aligned with the noon sun, gave a rough calculation of
latitude to the experienced mariners of *Raven*'s crew, of
which Donal was not one. Haakon carefully noted wind,
current, and sea marks such as water color and schooling
fish, lest they not be able to go home again. "Unless

you've magicked yourself into a helmsman, Donal, do not be yammering at me about Eilaf!"

"I wouldn't be knowing if we were on the sea bottom, except for being wet!" Donal snapped. "But that one will make you more trouble than he will give aid!"

A hand on his arm pulled him away before the jarl lost his temper, and Donal found himself glaring into Yazid's dark face instead.

"Undoubtedly that Eilaf had a mother who spread herself for caravans," Yazid said, "and his loss a thing for which to bless Allah, but the jarl cannot have quarrels on a ship this size. I doubt he is best pleased with Eilaf himself, but if you make a fight, there will be bad trouble. We are too much in each other's way. Start blood-feud, and you'll find there is no room to stop it."

"Haakon is going to be sorry he didn't put him overboard," Donal muttered.

"Then when he is, he will do it himself," Yazid said. "Not you."

Donal grudgingly subsided, with many black looks at Eilaf's back. The helmsman was perched jauntily on an oar bench and telling lies to someone, no doubt.

The Scotsman was in the right of it, Yazid thought, but it would do no good to be telling the jarl that now.

Haakon, ignoring them, went back to making his map, painstakingly drawing it on parchment, which was too costly to make errors on. Eilaf's presence, no doubt, was the price of bad judgment, and he was a braggart, but not so dangerous as Donal seemed to think. Braced against the rolling of the ship, Haakon drew a careful oval and marked it Bee Isle. More important than Eilaf Eiriksson was that no ship should go again to Bee Isle, lest the horrors that *Raven* had met there should still survive. He hoped violently that no man of his had left his seed to breed another generation of dying men and twisted women. Maybe he should have taken Rosamund, he thought wistfully, missing her. She might have seen the women there for what they were. Haakon put his map away in a sea chest and looked at the gray, endless ocean. No, better she should bide in Ireland where he could know her safe.

*   *   *

Rosamund's most immediate concern for safety was from Fergus MacAidan, who courted her relentlessly. He showered her with bunches of posies by morning and the choicest tidbits from the table by evening. Rosamund thought she was in no immediate danger of rape, but Fergus's intentions were obvious. As a further indignity Rosamund's maid Tordis had so far succumbed to Fergus's charm as to forget her dislike of foreigners, and Wulf had taken to him as well.

Rosamund had little time to spare to hunt for brides for a dog, but she had brought Wulf with her for companionship. Now she thought with disgust that she was likely to have more than enough leisure to choose a suitable bitch while she stayed talking in Dunnaill. The Irish seemed to do nothing but talk and fight, but Rosamund had yet to convince them to fight Earl Edmund.

Still, Wulf's approval brought Fergus an unexpected boon. Rosamund had never known Wulf to be wrong in his judgment yet, and when Wulf made his liking for Fergus plain, she drew in her defenses a little and consented to ride with him one autumn afternoon.

"You look worn down, Rose of the World," Fergus said. "If there's aught I can send to make your chambers more to your liking—"

"If I am worn down, it is from talking to the Dal Crimthann!" Rosamund said tartly. She clucked to her mount, and the mare ambled sedately along a green path under overhanging trees turning golden with the first frost. Fergus drew his horse up beside hers. "You must consult with your lords," Rosamund enumerated, "who all conveniently go home to their own raths before you can talk to them. Then you must consult with King Dungal, and he must consult with *his* council, and Conor MacLorne consults with Father Kilian, who thinks I am going to fry in hell for wedding a Norseman! And after everyone in Dunnaill has consulted with everyone else, I have nothing— *nothing*, Fergus!—to tell my people!"

"Ah, and I told you how it would be, Rose of the World, did I not?"

"Fergus, you mustn't call me that. It isn't seemly."

Fergus gave her a smile, full of flyaway charm, and

took her hand off the mare's reins and into his own. "Faith, I have no intent to be seemly." He leaned over and kissed her ear, quickly, before she could move.

Rosamund giggled in spite of herself. She couldn't help liking Fergus even though she suspected it might be dangerous to. "Fergus, surely you can see by now that I am with child."

"What difference does that make?" Fergus inquired, undaunted. "Thus there will be no accidents that your lord might not be liking."

She ought to kick up her mare and leave him there, she thought. Haakon would tear him limb from limb, cousin or no.

"Ah, but you need me, Rose of the World," Fergus said, apparently reading her thoughts. "You will be grateful when I have brought the Dal Crimthann around to your way of thinking."

"Not that grateful," Rosamund said automatically, then narrowed her eyes at him. "Fergus, do you think you can? Surely *you* can see the need for it."

"Aye, I can see the need," Fergus said, serious now. "I will be king one day, Rose of the World, whatever Conor thinks, and don't think I am a fool. But it will take time. And it will take the bishops to make Father Kilian bend. It may be that Conor will come round to us without Kilian behind him."

Rosamund said something under her breath, crossed herself, and added a hasty "Father forgive me," to ask pardon for the sin of wishing ill to a priest of God. "Abbot Cormac has gone to Armagh to speak with the bishops of Ulster," she said grimly.

"May he prosper," Fergus said, but he looked doubtful. The Céli Dé and the abbots of the great monasteries such as Armagh had been at drawn swords not so long ago, each desirous to convince the other of the rightness of their cause. The bishops of Ulster, most of them *tuath*-chieftains in their own right, were about evenly divided in their sympathies between the ascetic Céli Dé and the older and more worldy ecclesiastical centers, of which Armagh was the greatest. The bishops would vote for the course that would most directly benefit them, and it was to the bishop of Armagh that Father Kilian answered.

*   *   *

Kilian, knowing Cormac's errand, set out no more than
a half day behind him, to give the bishops his own opinion
on the matter. Thus they came together to argue it out
between them before the six assembled bishops of Ulster in
the high-ceilinged audience chamber at Armagh, and they
glared at each other with un-Christian dislike as they met.

"It is no business of ours if an English earl chooses to
squabble with a Norseman over land and marriage rights,"
Kilian said. His dark cassock was sleek and neatly draped.
His dark tonsured head was held high, as befitted a lord of
the Ui Neill.

The bishop of Armagh in his gilded chair regarded
him thoughtfully. He had no great love for Abbot Cormac,
but he could not help but think that to let an English earl
loose in the land was perhaps a worse thing than one more
Norseman. The Norse were there already.

Cormac fingered the plain wooden cross that hung
from his girdle. He leaned on the spear that served him for
a walking staff and pointed the cross at the bishops. "*This* is
our affair. The Norse jarl allows the Holy Church to serve
God on his land. The English earl will not be so kind."

The bishop of Armagh sniffed. "Have you no better
staff of your office, Cormac, than that spear?"

"No," Cormac said shortly. He towered over them all,
a mountainous figure in unkempt robes. The bishop of
Armagh smoothed his purple gown and considered.

"Better a Christian lord to have the land than pagan
Norse!" Kilian said acidly. "I have spoken to the woman
there, and she will not bow to the Church's will."

"You bade her to leave her husband," Cormac said,
"with one child on her hip and another in her belly. Small
wonder she was less than grateful for your advice."

Kilian's face was bitter, raw with an old hurt. "A
Christian woman who sullies herself in a pagan's bed
deserves to be cast off from all help of Holy Church!"

"You let pride and hatred for your sister overset your
judgment, Kilian," Cormac said, not unkindly. "Let God
condemn, if He will."

The bishops looked from one face to the other, conscious that his brangling did not accord with their dignity.
Two of the younger monks of Armagh peered interestedly

through the little door that led to the vesting room until their bishop shot them a steely glance. Armagh, founded by holy Patrick himself, laid claim, much disputed, to being the chief see of all Ireland. The support of secular kings in that struggle must be taken into account. The bishop of Armagh knew that, when it came to the Dal Crimthann, that meant Conor MacLorne or Fergus MacAidan, not old Dungal. In the present dispute Fergus had ranged himself on Abbot Cormac's side, and Conor, more likely to spite Fergus than aught else, on Kilian's. But the bishop thought that it would be Fergus who would be king in the end. The bishop sighed. Also there was the matter of pride, which Kilian owned in too great an amount, and the honor of God, which did not permit that an English earl should be allowed to slaughter a community of holy monks. The primate of Armagh eyed his brother bishops, saw that their thoughts lay in the same line, and extended his hand in regal dignity to Abbot Cormac. "You may leave us. We will send to you with our decision."

Cormac bowed, kissed the episcopal ring, and took his departure. The bishop would be unwilling to shame Kilian in front of him, but Cormac knew that he had won. The bishop of Armagh had a good grasp of the political realities in a troubled time.

"God works in many ways, Father Kilian. We must humble ourselves to them." Cormac heard the bishop's voice, solemnly reproving, as the carved doors swung shut behind him. And Kilian's voice, low with anger but obedient: "Yes, my Father."

"So he has set the bishops against you." Conor leaned back in his chair and eyed Kilian, seated across the table in the library of Dunnaill.

"The bishop of Armagh is my spiritual father. I cannot go against his express command," Kilian said. His mouth was set in a bitter line. He carefully completed the block of graceful letters in the half-copied gospel that lay open before him and sprinkled blotting sand across the page before he looked up. "Never will I support that woman in my heart, but I can do no more for you in Dunnaill. I am forbidden."

"Then likely I will have to mend fences with Fergus this once," Conor said. "I warned you I would if this happened, Kilian."

Kilian thought that Conor's green eyes looked sardonically amused. Kilian had no love to spare, save for God. He would have been better suited as a cloistered monk, but his bishop had refused it because old Dungal had had a mind to have a kinsman for his personal priest. Unable to change his nature, Kilian was bitterly aware that no man loved him, although they gave him the respect that was owed to the Church. "Then why did you trouble yourself to support me in this?" Kilian asked, knowing the answer.

"To trouble Fergus," Conor said truthfully. "And because I don't like Norse, half-blood or no. But this Rosamund has old Dungal near wrapped around her finger, so mayhap I will change my mind this time."

Kilian stared at him coldly. The candles on the table set his face into high relief—sharp bones and hollows around the eyes. He was an ice-block of a man, Conor thought, cold through and through.

The chapel bells began to peal, a sweet, mellow sound lifting joyously to heaven. Kilian put away his pens and poured the blotting sand back into the shaker. His hands shook. "I must prepare for vespers."

Conor thought that he was eager to be gone, to hide himself in the Church, where his office was a shield against human contact and he need speak to no one save God.

"*Praecinge me, Domine, cingulo puritatis...*" Gird me, O Lord, with the cincture of purity. Kilian knotted the green silk girdle about his waist. Green for hope, for the days between Pentecost and Advent. Green for the hope of heaven.

"*Redde mihi, Domine, stolam immortalitatis...*" Restore to me, O Lord, the stole of immortality...

"*Domine, qui dixisti: Jugum meum suave est, et onus meum leve: fac, ut isted portare sic valeam, quod consequar tuam gratiam.*" O Lord, who hast said: My yoke is easy, and My Burden is light: make me so able to bear it, that I

may obtain Thy favor. Kilian bowed his head as the
young monk slipped the chasuble over it. He clenched his
hands, lest his acolyte should see them tremble. Even
here the memory of the Englishwoman's victory pursued
him.

When the vesting was done, he knelt before the little
altar in the corner of the sacristy, to speak in his own
tongue the prayer of holy Patrick, a corselet against the
heathen:

> "I bind to myself today—
> The Power of God to guide me,
> The Might of God to uphold me . . .
> The Hand of God to protect me,
> The Way of God to go before me,
> The Shield of God to shelter me,
> The Host of God to defend me . . .
> Against the black laws of heathenism,
> Against the false laws of heresy,
> Against the deceits of idolatry,
> Against the spells of women, and smiths,
>   and Druids,
> Against all knowledge which blinds the soul
>   of man."

The chanting of the monks who served the Chapel of
St. Columba under Kilian's thumb rose with an unearthly
beauty, as if borne on the peat smoke that drifted upward
over Dunnaill until it vanished into the gray vault of the
heavens. Rosamund and Fergus heard it and guiltily turned
their horses homeward. They had ridden far longer than
they should, and it would behoove them to show their
faces at vespers with proper piety. As Rosamund alit in the
courtyard, a tall familiar figure strode toward her.

"Cormac!"

"You may thank God, child, for the practical nature of
the bishop of Armagh," Cormac said, smiling. "He has
taken a stand for our side. And I have been to Ole's Hold
on the way back, and all is well there."

Rosamund gave the mare's reins to the groom who

came running. "I will thank Him thrice over, I promise you!"

"I am grateful as well," Fergus said with such obvious sincerity that Cormac, who had been composing a lecture on the double sin of frivolity and coveting another's wife, merely raised his eyebrows and recommended him to say his thanks to God in chapel if he could remember how to find his way there. Together the three strolled across the court and up the stone flight of stairs that led to the upper level of Dunnaill and the Chapel of St. Columba, founded by King Dungal's grandsire in a timely burst of deathbed piety.

The present king was just going in to vespers, leaning on his page's arm, a heavy robe wrapped around him to give warmth to his legs. He patted Rosamund's arm in friendly fashion and told her she should sit next to him at table tonight. "A better thing to look at than my nephews, so you are." He made his way with painful steps into the chapel, and Rosamund let her hopes soar a little higher, carried on the beauty of the music.

The chapel had a corbeled roof, supported by a semicircular vault, which gave the chanting voices their unearthly quality. She could see Kilian, robed in green, moving before the altar while his deacons swung their silver fans, edged in bells, to keep the insects that zoomed and buzzed in the last autumn warmth from falling into the chalice. On the Lord's Day, Father Kilian held mass at vespers. He would think, no doubt, that she should not have been riding on the Sabbath, much less riding with Fergus.

> "*Kyrie eleison.*
> *Christe eleison.*
> *Kyrie eleison.*
> *Gloria in excelsis Deo.*"

As always in his church, Kilian's face had a look that Rosamund could only describe as a peaceful intensity. He seemed far different from the harsh, ascetic man who, for the three months she had been in Dunnaill, had refused to speak to her. But Rosamund knew that Kilian wore that look only when he served God. There was no peace in him for her. He had never barred her from the mass, but she knew that he would have liked to.

"Et in terra pax hominibus, bonae voluntatis."

On the end of the bench just across the aisle from her, Fergus made his responses in a dutiful voice while Cormac spoke his with the quiet sincerity of one who has never found any reason great enough to question his faith. Rosamund could see Conor MacLorne's bowed red head three rows away, beside the king. Fergus, she suspected, was thinking of how best to turn Abbot Cormac's victory to use, and Conor, no doubt, was debating the same thing. Rosamund, seated among the women of the king's house, tried to turn her mind properly to God, but it was hard. She missed Asa, she was beginning to be heavy with the new child, and she wanted to go home. With Kilian ordered into silence by his bishop . . .

"Dominus vobiscum."

"Et cum spiritu tuo."

Kilian turned to face the worshipers, and Rosamund's weary, hopeful face seemed to leap out at him from the women's side. When she saw his eyes on her, she lowered her own, but not before he saw the gleam of triumph in them. *She knows,* he thought savagely, and felt his hands begin to shake again. He turned away abruptly, stumbling through the proper words, trying to regain the sheltering peace of his closeness to God, furious with her for having intruded on his only haven.

"Now tell me, Rose of the World, just *why* you must be going?" Fergus took her hand, kissed it, and gave her a wistful look. For half a second, she almost kissed him back. *I must be mad.* Cormac was in the next chamber, seeing their trunks packed, and Tordis bustled in and out, her arms overloaded with her lady's gowns.

"Because I'm grateful enough for your alliance that I've no wish for my husband to cut your heart out when he comes home," Rosamund said frankly.

Fergus crossed his arms and leaned against the white lime-washed wall. "He may try." That had pricked his pride. "I am accounted the best champion among the Dal Crimthann, and I do not run like a rabbit from injured husbands."

"Oh, do you make it a habit to seduce other men's wives?" Rosamund inquired sweetly.

Fergus put his hands on her shoulders. "No," he said. His face was serious now.

"Then stop before you get in the way of it," Rosamund said. She drew his hands away. If she had never known Haakon... But no man could compare to Haakon, not even Fergus. "I am not faithless, Fergus. Don't tempt me to it." She giggled suddenly, unable to stay solemn for long in his company. "And I should look so silly." She put her hands across her heavy belly. "A fine romance!"

"I shouldn't be caring," Fergus whispered.

She turned away suddenly. "That is why I am leaving. Oh, and a thousand other reasons—I want my babe born at home, I have my own folk to look to, I want to strengthen the defenses at Ole's Hold, Leif is needed there to see it done right.... And I am lonely!" she said, her voice sharp. "If I grow lonelier still through the winter, I do not want you there, quite so close to hand!"

Fergus put his hands on her shoulders again and turned her to him gently. "One kiss, Rose of the World—"

"No! Go away. I won't kiss you, Fergus."

He laughed, half-sad, half-amused, and bowed himself out of her chamber. Rosamund sat down heavily on the bed. It was past time she left. Fergus had wrung a commitment for an alliance out of old Dungal, with Conor's grudging acceptance. Now there was nothing to do but go back to Ole's Hold and hope that the alliance held till spring when her father came back. There was no doubt in her mind that he *would* be back. Rosamund was not Earl Edmund's daughter for nothing. But the Holy Mother be thanked that they were going. Less and less she trusted herself to be alone with Fergus. Rosamund hadn't lied when she said that she was lonely—achingly lonely. Why didn't Haakon come *home*?

"His luck has left him, that is what it will be!" Eilaf Eiriksson perched importantly on a sea chest between

Thorfinn Solvisson, who was doing his best to ignore him, and two of Haakon's more impressionable men, who were beginning to look uneasy. A chieftain's luck was important; men who were thought to have lost theirs had found themselves deserted by their warriors or the object of a mutiny designed to set another leader, more favored by the gods, in their place. For three weeks *Raven* had floated becalmed, her sail hanging limp, without a breath of wind to stretch it.

Eilaf bit into a dried fish and spat a bite of it out on the deck. "Aye, the food is going foul. That is the first sign, when even salt fish rots. It is because of that sorcerer's weapon he carries, mind you. The gods will turn their backs on a man who practices an evil craft!"

Thorfinn had had enough. "Shut your mouth," he said, and stalked away. If he stayed, he would put Eilaf overside as Donal had been loudly recommending, and the jarl had forbidden it. Thorfinn tilted his head back and stared at the sky. There were clouds coming, and the stillness of the air was unnatural. A storm brewing, he thought. Thorfinn shrugged, weary with boredom. At least they would have wind. A shadow fell on the deck beside him, and he turned to find Yazid, who moved as quietly as a cat. The Arab stood thoughtfully, cleaning his knife.

Behind them, Eilaf's voice said with satisfaction, "When *I* was captain, in Frisia that was, we never put out oars but to make extra speed for a raid. And fine raiding that was! We swept the coast of Frisia bare, with a fair wind the whole way, and there was a chest of silver and two women for every man."

Yazid looked at his knife. He wasn't wishful to make an open quarrel, for the reasons he had given Donal, but many things could happen to a man after dark.

"If you are thinking I cannot see what Eilaf is doing" —the jarl's voice made them both jump—"you must credit me with being a greater fool than he. But you will not kill him, because I have said not. Also," he growled, looking at the credulous faces turned toward Eilaf, "I want no man on my ship who cannot see through such a one as that."

Thorfinn looked dubious, and Yazid said, "Men who

are frightened, jarl, do not see anything very clearly, and these men are beginning to be."

Haakon looked at the still sea, boundless in all directions, a terrifying emptiness. "There will be no murder done on my ship," he said distinctly, but he turned on his heel, went to Eilaf, and picked him off the oar bench by his collar. Eilaf yelped, and Haakon held him with one hand, just to prove he could do it. "If you wish to be a captain, Eilaf, I will give you a little raft," he suggested.

Eilaf made an inarticulate noise in his throat, and Haakon set him down again. A hoot of laughter from the men nearby told him that, for the moment, Eilaf had lost his credit. But if they stayed becalmed much longer, they would be listening to him again by nightfall.

I am as stubborn as Donal maybe, Haakon thought dubiously. He had hesitated to ask Thor Odinsson's aid because he never knew in what form that capricious deity might see fit to send it—but anything would be better than this. If Eilaf weren't murdered, someone else would be. The men were stretched taut with fear and the boredom that gave them little to do but think on the fear. Haakon took the ax from its sheath on his back where it always rode, and stretched it out over the gray water. The blade glowed golden as the sun struck it, with a light that seemed to come from within as much as without. *I will give Eilaf Eiriksson something to think on, at any rate*, Haakon thought triumphantly.

"Thor Odinsson, Thunderer, god of sailors, give us luck and fair wind!" Haakon's voice boomed across the water, and a living presence seemed to brush past them with the wind on its tail. Above them in the east the rolling crash of thunder had begun.

"By the Hammer!" Thorfinn shouted gleefully. "Wind!"

With a dark amusement in his eyes Haakon turned on Eilaf. The ax still glowed in his hand. "Shall I call up something else, Eilaf, or will that suffice?"

Eilaf jabbed a finger fearfully at the ax and backed away. "A sorcerer's weapon! Did I not say it?"

Nearly the full ship's crew had gathered around Haakon now. "No," Hjalmar Sitricsson said, awestruck. "A god answered. I saw his face—in the wind."

"Make sail!" Haakon yelled. They left off staring and ran. The intrusion of a god's hand into their lives would be something about which to tell tales around a winter fire for years to come, but not if they drowned. The Thunderer would not make his wind cease to blow while they fumbled with the rigging.

It might have been that the god was angered by his servant's stubbornness in delaying to ask his aid, or only that the Thunderer wished to amuse himself. Or maybe, Haakon thought grimly, grasping *Raven*'s side, that having lost three weeks in delay, the god now wished to blow them to wherever he wished to have them in three days. The wind, when it came, was a storm such as none of them had ever seen. It blew out of the northeast with a howling fury that sent sheets of water over the side and heeled the ship halfway over with every roll. They ran before it with full sail only briefly and then were forced to reef in the billowing scarlet cloth before the gale rolled them mast over keel.

Haakon, struggling with the lines, saw the tacking boom break loose and sweep three men backward over the oar ports. He lunged and caught the last of them by the knee, falling backward onto the deck as a great wave sheeted over them.

Donal MacRae sat up, gasping and white faced, spewing water. He looked around him and saw that the other two had vanished entirely in the raging sea. "Oh, Jesu, they're gone—" He struggled to his feet and vomited more water.

Haakon pushed his way to the tiller to add his strength to Knut's to keep the ship from turning broadside to the wind. He would mourn his lost men later. There was no time now for anything but the howling storm that was all around them. The sky was black with it. A water cask in the hold broke loose, and before it was tied down again, it killed the luckless soul whose body had kept it from crashing through the hull. Above the boom of the storm the terrified screaming of horses and cattle rose unendingly.

Haakon leaned on the tiller, and it fought him like a live thing. The rain beat at his face, and a jagged bolt of lightning illuminated a Hel-world of foam and roiling water. The oars were useless. They would break to kindling seconds after they were run out. But Yazid had built a ship meant for open ocean. *Raven* writhed under the pounding waves and wind, easing out from under the hammer blows of the storm and skimming the surface like some great seafowl. Buffeted but seemingly unsinkable, *Raven* flew before the storm.

For how many days they fought Thor Hammerer's gift wind, none of them was ever sure, but when the storm died at last, the fading stars of a dawn sky were set in patterns that showed they were far to the south, and on the western horizon a low irregular shape rose green above the water.

"*Land!*" Knut One-Eye shrieked. He bounced up and down beside the tiller, trying for a better look, until Haakon thought he would go overboard. Haakon grinned. Knut was ordinarily the most stolid of men, but their voyage into the unknown had strained everyone's nerves to the breaking point. The land—if indeed it *was* land and not some sea-trick—was proof that they were not to sail on endlessly until the water should swallow them. Haakon watched the land rise higher above the horizon. No, it was real enough. He ran to the prow and stared at it. It was *his* land, even if King Harald would have some of the glory.

"You have done it, jarl!" Knut shouted gleefully. "That Scotsman shall make a song of it, and we will have word-fame to last ten generations!"

"Tir-na-nOg," Donal whispered. The legendary land in the west. He laughed at Knut. "Aye, I will tell how Knut One-Eye the helmsman fell overside and drowned tryin' to walk across the water to it."

Knut stopped jumping up and down lest he look foolish and gave Donal a black look. Every man in the crew was leaning over the side to watch the land draw near. Haakon let out a sigh of relief as a sandy beach backed by green forest showed clearly in the sun. It had been a near thing: They were low on water, low on food, low on fodder for the animals, and more than somewhat low on patience.

As they drew nearer, Haakon saw that the beach broke into a series of bays and inlets that were part of a greater bay sheltered by a long arm of land reaching down from the north. They ran *Raven* ashore in a likely spot, and the men were over the side while the water was still waist deep, laughing and throwing handfuls of wet sand in the air. Even Eilaf the troublemaker had nothing to say and looked more relieved than any of them to have his feet on the ground again.

Beyond the sand, rough grassland made a little meadow, and beyond that the forest rose up, darkly mysterious, inhabited no doubt with unknown animals. Thinking of the salt fish, Haakon hoped fervently that some of the animals would prove edible. A cold wind swooped along the meadow, almost playfully, but there was a bite in it all the same. Haakon pulled his cloak around him. He had been cold and wet for days until he almost didn't notice it, but the wind told him what had been in the back of his mind since before they had sighted land—it was late in the year, and the gale that had blown them here had been only the first of the bad weather. As he opened his mouth to say so, Eilaf Eiriksson appeared to find his voice.

"The jarl won't have noticed," Eilaf said importantly, "but *I* know the signs. We will have to winter here. There'll be no going back this year."

X

Newfound Land

Haakon stood, hands on hips, his face stretched into a broad grin, and looked down the meadow, where their animals—a half-dozen sheep, cattle, and four shaggy-coated ponies—which a week ago had emerged from the hold on wobbly legs, now sank their noses greedily into the grass. Haakon rocked back and forth on his heels a little. *We found it,* he thought. *I wonder how far it goes.*

It was a new land—not an island, he was sure of that; the coast seemed to stretch endlessly north and south. And a rich land... Here was timber for the taking; a profitable venture might be made of shipping it back to treeless Iceland.

The first thing that Yazid and Snorri Longfoot had done was use the wood to build a little boat to replace the one in which they had sent the old man of Bee Isle to his gods. The rest of *Raven*'s crew, meanwhile, had built shelters for themselves and a byre for the animals out of timber cut from the forest's edge and sapling trees woven together, with the interstices packed with mud; already it was growing cold enough to make a winter spent in tents on *Raven*'s deck an unpleasant prospect, and a fair-sized village had sprung up in the meadow. Haakon regarded it with proprietary pride.

There was game in the forest: deer and several kinds of wildfowl, fish in the streams that emptied into the bay, and in the bay itself, uncounted sea life. For a week now the men had gorged themselves on lobster, crab, and oysters from a bed, which, Snorri maintained, Hagar the Simple had found with his nose, like a hound tracking rabbits. As Haakon watched, Hagar and Donal came wading out of the surf, dragging the boat and a wooden lobster trap behind them. Scalding steam boiled up from an iron pot on the communal hearth, and Donal was whistling—a rolling tune like waves; it was the beginning of his *Song of the Voyage of Haakon Olesson*. Already Haakon was beginning to feel that the price Thor Hammerer had asked for his gift-wind had not been too great. *No man before me has done anything like this*.

There was only one uneasy thought in his mind, and the longer they stayed, the more certain he grew that he was right. Something made the skin on his neck prickle, but when he snapped his head around, there was nothing in the forest behind him except the green darkness. But something was there; more and more he felt certain of it. For three days now he had felt watched, and Haakon had never known that feeling to lie.

Haakon strode back down the meadow to tell Thorfinn that no man was to go out alone from the camp—not until whatever it was should choose to come out of the forest and be seen. If there was game in the forest, there could easily be men—a foreign race of trolls or giants or something utterly unknown. Something with the patience to watch him.

The next morning they were there. They came silently

out of a gray fog and stopped not fifty feet from Haakon's camp. They stood staring while the Norsemen stared back. No one moved. The men of the forest were dressed in skins—shoes, leggings, and shirt. Their hair was black, dark as Yazid's, and sprouted wildly from their heads like a cock's comb, and there were pictures painted on their skin. But the thing that made the Norsemen stare open-mouthed was the skin beneath the paint. It was red, red as a chestnut horse.

"Goblins," Eilaf Eiriksson said, with much of his bluster gone.

"I doubt it," Haakon said dryly. "Goblins do not watch you for three days trying to gather their courage. They are afraid of us. Nearly as afraid as you are, Eilaf." Haakon put out his hand to them to show that it was weaponless. The red-skinned men looked as if they would vanish into the forest again, but the leader of them straightened himself proudly as if to show that he scorned to run from these white-skinned strangers. He stared at Haakon and then, yet more curiously, at the fair-haired men behind him. Haakon motioned with his hand at his men to keep still. He felt as if he were trying to tame a wild thing out of the woods. The red-skinned men were armed, but he saw, startled, that their spear points and arrowheads were of stone. Their deerskin shirts were pinned with bone pins. *Wild things indeed,* he thought. *I am looking at the morning of man.*

Like most Norse, Haakon wore a silver Thor's Hammer on a thong around his throat, for guidance and good luck, much as his wife wore a Christian cross. Carefully he pulled it over his head. He held it out on an open palm with a gesture that said the red-skinned chieftain should take it. The chieftain regarded him warily, but slowly his hand came out, touched Haakon's briefly, and closed around the silver hammer.

Neither having burst into flames at the other's touch, Haakon and the red-skinned man each let out a slow breath and inspected each other cautiously. He looked like a wild bird, Haakon thought, staring in fascination at the other's beaked nose and upflung crest of hair. After a moment the other reached up and pulled off the leather band that circled his forehead. It was embroidered in some kind of stiff red fiber, in which a crest of feathers had been sewn. The chieftain held it out to Haakon with much the same gesture that Haakon had used.

Haakon took it. He smiled, a universal indication of good intentions. The chieftain smiled back in a brief flash of white teeth. Then the men were gone, as suddenly as they had come, back into the shadows of the forest.

"Freya! Did you see?"

"Red they were, like a roan pony! Likely they're not human."

"Then what would they be?"

"Spirits. Elfin-folk maybe."

"Nah, only wood *skraelings*. They had stone spears."

A babble of Norse voices erupted around Haakon. He scratched his head. There were black men, and once he had seen a yellow man. Why not red? There had been no feel of magic about them.

"*Skraelings*," Knut said contemptuously, the Norse word for uncivilized savages.

Haakon stopped pondering and decided he had best lay down the law. "They will be back," he said. He wanted them to come back. Like the new land, he felt that the red-skinned men were his, his personal discovery. A race that hadn't found the use of metal yet, or even a loom for cloth. "When they come, be careful. We are better armed, but Thor knows how many they are. And they looked like they can fight."

"How can you be so sure they'll come?" Donal looked at the still forest.

Haakon smiled. "We are too great a curiosity to them. I do not think they have ever seen anything like us. They will try to decide what we are, and then they'll come back." He turned into the mud-and-withy-walled house they had built to sleep in and emerged again after some minutes with an armload of carefully collected plunder: a blue wool shirt with fine red and silver tablet braiding on the sleeves, a gold arm ring, a soapstone pot full of meal and salt fish, a pony bridle made of carved plaques of walrus ivory, a red-fox hat, and a piece of soft red-and-white checked cloth. Yazid protested indignantly when he saw the cloth, and Donal MacRae at the fox hat, which happened to be his, but Haakon just grinned and trotted to the forest's edge with his loot. He spread it all out on a flat rock under a birch tree near where the red-skinned men had disappeared, squatting down in the dry leaves to arrange his choices.

Donal regarded him balefully. The jarl was laying out bait for the forest men like a man luring wildfowl, but it seemed unnecessary that Haakon had chosen *his* hat with which to tempt them.

When Haakon had his offerings displayed to his satisfaction, he came back to the camp, informed his companions that they, like himself, had contributed to the common good (after all, the blue shirt had been his second best), and went off to inspect the pot that Hagar the Simple was tending on the open fire. A heavy porridge of meal and milk bubbled on it, and Hagar had added a bucket of oysters for good measure. Haakon scooped up a bowlful and sat cross-legged by the rear of the cow byre, where he would have an unobstructed view. The morning mist had faded. As he ate, he watched the birch trees with bright, inquisitive eyes.

There was no sign of the forest dwellers for the rest of the day, and Haakon finally gave up his vigil and went about his business. But the next morning the things on the rock were gone. In their place were a deerskin shirt sewn with bits of shell and feathers, and a pile of furs. The shirt was a curiosity, but the furs spoke with another voice. There were four of them: otter, beaver, bear, and the thick pelt of some sort of spotted cat. Haakon, who like all of his kind was endowed with the natural Norse acquisitiveness, scooped these up and bore them triumphantly back to the camp. He hung the spotted cat hide around Donal's shoulders and gave the otter skin to his aggrieved shipwright. The beaver pelt and the bearskin he kept for himself. The rest of the jarl's crew, inspecting this return on the jarl's investment, began to rummage through their own belongings like a dog after rats, with greed writ large on their faces. Haakon stopped Eilaf Eiriksson as he pulled a dagger out of a boot sheath and prepared to add it to his pile.

"No iron. Not so much as a cookpot, much less a knife." He pushed it, hilt first, back at Eilaf.

Eilaf shrugged, refusing to take back the dagger.

"What matter? I can get good furs for it, and it's not so good a knife anyway."

"And no doubt these goblins of yours have magicked what little sense you have out through the holes in your ears," Haakon said acidly. "Or were you not noticing, just yesterday, that these men have no metal? Not even copper or bronze. But I do expect there are a lot of them, and if it comes to fighting, I expect it will be better if someone hasn't given them iron knives in the meantime." He stuck the dagger in his own belt and stalked off to see that no one else was inclined to be such a fool. Eilaf glowered after him. He pulled a hat down over his thinning, unkempt hair and went to lay out his goods in what he thought would be the most likely spot.

All along the meadow edge, *Raven*'s crew were doing the same. Haakon inspected them all, lest anyone else's good sense should desert him. He pulled a pair of breeches out of a pile and handed them back to Hjalmar Sitricsson. "You only own two pairs, and there is winter coming. Or do you have a mind to go about in your shirt like an Irishman?"

"I can buy ten pairs of breeches with good furs," Hjalmar protested.

"Not here," Haakon said.

"Then I will bargain for the leather ones the *skraelings* wear," Hjalmar said. He put the breeches back in the pile.

This time the *skraelings* reappeared from the woods almost as soon as the Norsemen had spread their wares out in the meadow, giving weight to Haakon's suspicion that the actions of the interlopers on their shore were being carefully tracked. They came in force, some twenty or thirty men striding along behind their chieftain. Haakon saw a few women, in long deerskin skirts and very little else, peeping from the trees, but they came no closer. With the *skraeling* chieftain was an old man to whom the chieftain appeared to give much honor. The old man's hair was gone nearly white and was crowned with a coif of feathers and scarlet bristles like the plumage of an exotic bird. He stared long and hard at the carved figurehead on *Raven*'s prow and at the pale skin and yellow hair of the Norse, then broke suddenly into a solemn chant that startled Haakon nearly out of his skin.

But whatever it was the old man said—he must be a priest, Haakon thought—it proved a boon to the Norsemen. The *skraelings* treated the Norse with some trepidation and great respect, and unloaded an astonishing variety of furs as trade for the Norse goods: marten and otter and more of the spotted cat hides, and something with a bushy tail ringed in black and silver. The *skraelings* were eager for the loomed cloth. As Haakon had suspected, they had none of their own, although a few of their narrow pack-straps appeared to have been roughly woven. They stared openmouthed as Donal rode up on one of the ponies and burst into such an agitated chatter when he dismounted that Haakon decided they must have thought at first that Donal was part of the horse. Anything made of gold or silver was equally admired, and Haakon saw that the chieftain now wore the walrus-ivory pony bridle around his neck. But they were not a people to be laughed at—primitive, a dawn people still working with stone tools, but not to be underestimated. The red-skinned men had no metal of their own, but they were not slow in grasping what it could do; they had seen the stumps of ax-felled trees in the forest. They bargained persuasively and persistently, and with sign language indicated a fortune in furs for even the smallest knife of the Norsemen. Haakon remained obdurate as his men came protesting to him that with fortune so close at hand, one knife, one iron arrowhead, would make no difference.

"And it would not be one, would it then? It would be one from each of you, until you had loaded my ship with a cargo that no one still had a sword to defend. Or are you thinking to find iron ore on the ground like hailstones? There may be a good reason why these *skraelings* have none. They may also slit our throats and take back their furs if we give them the knives to do it with. No."

They departed, grumbling, and found other things to trade.

The coming of these pale-skinned men had given Swift Hawk, who had been chieftain of the People of the Deer since his eighteenth year, much to think on. Even Elder Wolf, whose age and wisdom were greater than any other man of the People, had, after he had heard of the white men and the bird-ship they had come in, gone away inside himself to think for three days. When Elder Wolf had come out of his wigwam again, he had said nothing except that he must see the pale men for himself, but he had not looked happy. He still did not.

Swift Hawk ran a thoughtful finger over the strange necklace that the pale men's chieftain had offered them. They were artisans of much skill; the smooth white links were carved with magic beasts that seemed to leap under his fingers. Swift Hawk folded his arms across his chest and tried to open his mind so that his guardian spirit could speak to him, but no word came. It might be that these strangers were Corn Mother's children; their yellow hair seemed to proclaim them as such. Again, perhaps the bird-ship meant that they were the thunder god's, who often took that form. Many of them, seen close, also proved to have blue eyes, like apertures from the sky. They had hair on their faces where the People had none, and they carried magical weapons, which, Swift Hawk knew by the marks they left, would break stone axes as easily as stone broke wood. But were they spirit men or true men? The thunder god had spoken through his sky-fire the day before the bird ship's arrival, but no one was certain what had been meant by it. Even Elder Wolf, after three days alone with his pipe and his trance, and then the long wearisome trudge to the shore, could still say only that for now the pale men should be given the respect that was due to spirits. Manabus, who had made the People and shown them how to live, would send a further sign when it was needful.

Swift Hawk uncrossed his arms, a decision reached. If Manabus would say no more, it might be that this was a test of Swift Hawk's fitness and his place among the People of the Deer. Nothing was ever without meaning.

The red men moved with the silent agility of deer through the forest. Haakon, following behind them, felt clumsy—loud and large footed—and stumbled over tree roots that the soft deer-hide shoes of the red men passed across like ghosts. Beside him Knut swiveled his one good eye left and right like an owl and kept up a commentary of suspicion. Knut was shorter than most Norse and nearly fifty, but he was tough and wiry and had attained this advanced age by trusting nothing. Just now he did not trust the red-skinned men, or the forest, or the jarl's sanity in acquiescing when the red-skinned chieftain had insisted, by sign language, that they should follow him. Haakon had called up Knut, Donal, and Hagar to go with him. The *skraeling* chieftain had agreed to that but put out a peremptory hand as if to say, *No more*. Now they were going Odin knew where, and not even Knut's iron ax and belt knife made him feel better about it. You could beat anything to death with stone clubs if you had enough of them.

Certainly there were more *skraelings* than anyone had seen before. The women had come out of whatever hiding place they had occupied while their men were trading with the strangers, and now, as curious as a gaggle of children, they stared openly at the Norsemen. The women wore knee-length skirts of deer hide, wrapped and belted above the hips, leggings and shoes like the men, and nothing else above. Their glossy black hair hung loose down their backs or was gathered into thick knots like beavers' tails. The younger ones were very comely indeed.

"Are you supposing they *all* go about without their shifts?" Donal MacRae inquired appreciatively. Haakon gave him a look that said if Donal valued his health, he would take less notice, shift or no.

The trail they followed seemed plain enough to the *skraelings*, but it was crossed and recrossed with deer tracks and rabbit trails that all looked much the same to the Norse. The *skraeling* village was closer than Haakon had thought, disguised only by the lack of a clear path to it. The Norse must have come very close in their hunting and never seen it. *They have been looking over our shoulders since we landed*, Haakon thought.

The *skraeling* village, if it could be called that, lay along a riverbank, a string of round huts covered with slabs of bark or mats of cattail stalks. Haakon could see no pigs or cattle, but there seemed to be dogs and children everywhere. The littlest babes were swaddled in pouches that could be strapped to their mothers' backs or hung up on a branch to be rocked by the wind. The older ones, who mostly went naked, stopped their play by the river's edge and stared with wide black eyes at the newcomers. The dogs barked, and adult faces popped out of huts and babbled in the *skraelings'* tongue. The chieftain ignored them. He motioned to one of the huts, stepped inside, and turned, waiting for Haakon to follow him.

There was more room inside than there had appeared to be. The smoke hole in the roof, and the open doorway, let in the light, although the air was smoky. The floor was of packed earth, swept clean. Around the sides were low wooden hurdles overlaid with reed mats. The chieftain settled himself on one of these, with the aged priest beside him. Haakon sat also. A conference was plainly intended, and Haakon wondered how on earth he was going to talk to them.

One of the women came in and laid a deer-hide pouch beside the chieftain. She stared at the Norsemen in fascination and seemed inclined to linger until the chieftain glared at her. She departed reluctantly. With great solemnity the chieftain took from his pouch a small bowl of red stone, with a wooden stem fixed into its side, and a smaller pouch of dried leaves. He tamped the leaves into the stone bowl with one finger. Haakon watched, perplexed, as the chieftain now took out a pair of wooden tongs and with them lifted a small coal from the fire that burned at the center of the hut. He put the stem to his mouth, touched the coal to the leaves, and sucked hard on the stem to set them burning. A curious odor rose up with the smoke, and as the chieftain exhaled, smoke came from his mouth. He passed the bowl and stem to the priest, who also drew in a mouthful of smoke. The stem was painted with wavy lines of red and tied near the end with a bunch of feathers. From the solemn expressions on the faces of the *skraelings*, Haakon decided that this was a ceremony of much importance, but what its purpose might be, he couldn't fathom.

The chieftain passed the bowl to Haakon, and he took it gingerly. He sucked experimentally on the stem, choked, and nearly dropped it in an explosion of coughing. The chieftain's eyes narrowed suspiciously, and Haakon realized he had given offense. He tried again, even more cautiously, and managed to expel a mouthful of smoke without suffocating. The chieftain smiled solemnly, and Haakon wondered if he would ever breathe freely again. With an evil grin, he passed the bowl to Donal.

Donal took it with the air of a man who has been handed a snake. The red-skinned chieftain and the old priest watched him expectantly. The tobacco pipe was great magic, a gift of the manitous, the spirits. If these pale-skinned strangers would not smoke it, it was an evil sign. Donal put a stem to his mouth, drew in a puff of the acrid smoke, and blew it out again almost immediately, clenching the muscles in his throat as they fought violently with the innate desire of the human body not to be asphyxiated. He handed the pipe on to Knut, who, forewarned, managed creditably, and to Hagar, who seemed not to notice the smoke at all. Hagar puffed at the pipe, gave a grunt indicative of surprise and satisfaction, and handed it back to the chief again.

This ritual completed, the chieftain shouted something in his alien tongue, and the woman who had brought the pipe reappeared with two more women behind her. This time they bore bark bowls full of hot mush, which they handed, apparently stifling giggles of curiosity, to the chieftain and his peculiar visitors. The chieftain dipped his fingers in his bowl, and Haakon, prepared for the worst, did likewise. To his surprise, it was good—some unfamiliar grain with pieces of yellowish fruit mixed in. He smacked his lips appreciatively, smiled at the *skraeling* chieftain, and the chieftain smiled back, less solemnly this time. Hagar the Simple was eating steadily—Hagar ate anything— and even Knut and Donal seemed to find the mush an improvement on the burning leaves.

They wish to be friendly, Swift Hawk thought. *Or to appear so.* He studied the white-skinned chief to see if his spirits would tell him if the friendliness was false. The white chief had brown eyes and hair, the color of brown clay, not black like the People or the blue-eyed man beside him, or corn-colored like the others of his kind. He was broad shouldered, heavily muscled, not quite so tall as the rest. But there was an air of power about him; Elder

Wolf said that it came from the tomahawk he carried—a weapon even more menacing than the others, with a pale blade like the dawn sun. But he was not false, no. Swift Hawk did not think so, and it was this wisdom as well as his hunting skill that had made Swift Hawk leader of the People of the Deer.

But how to speak to the pale-skinned chief? If these were spirit men, they must be from some far realm, for they had no understanding of the People's speech. Swift Hawk thumped his knuckles against his chest and spoke his own name. The white chief tried to imitate him, failed utterly, and spread his hands, fingers opened, to show that the word fell through them. Swift Hawk took a stick and scratched a diving hawk in the earthen floor. He spoke again, more slowly this time, tapped first the hawk and then his chest, and the white chief repeated the name after him with more success. Then the white chief pointed at the hawk and said a word in his own tongue, pointing a finger afterward at Swift Hawk, to make his meaning clear. Swift Hawk laughed, pleased with the exchange. Now he had a name in the spirit men's tongue, which was a thing to give him much honor.

In this fashion they managed to introduce themselves, but it was too cumbersome a manner of speech for the negotiations that Haakon and Swift Hawk had in mind. In the end they resorted instead to the stick and the earthen floor. Swift Hawk drew a man with a bird's crest of hair along his head, which Haakon took to be one of Swift Hawk's own kind, and then flung wide his hands to encompass the hut and the whole village without. Haakon nodded. Swift Hawk drew more men, many of them, armed with spears and bows. More tribes of *skraelings*, at war perhaps with Swift Hawk's people. Swift Hawk drew a map. He circled Haakon's camp and drew a figure to indicate the bearded Norsemen in their iron hats upon it. He drew a line from the Norsemen to his own people, smiled and nodded, throwing wide his hands in hospitality. Drawing another line from the Norse to the rival tribes, he frowned solemnly. Then he returned to Haakon's camp and drew a field beside it, neatly planted. He was offering them land, Haakon decided, and in return they

were to make no alliance with Swift Hawk's enemies.
Haakon nodded, hoping he understood to what he was
agreeing.

A bargain such as this would take a great gift to seal
it, Haakon thought. Surely that was a universal custom of
mankind. He drew his dagger, conscious of a collective
scowl of outrage from Hagar, Knut, and Donal, and presented
it, hilt first, to the *skraeling* chief.

Not even Swift Hawk's most solemn expression could
conceal the eagerness in his eyes. He tested the blade with
his thumb while Haakon prayed to all the gods he could
think of that the chieftain wouldn't have the ill luck to cut
himself on it. Haakon undid the sheath from his belt and
presented Swift Hawk with that as well, for safety's sake.
Even Elder Wolf, whose seamed face had been hitherto as
expressionless as cedarwood, looked impressed. The spirit
dagger was great medicine. Elder Wolf closed his eyes and
went away inside himself again so that the manitous might
tell him whether it was for good or ill, but no word came.

Swift Hawk called again to the *skraelings,* who were
no doubt gathered thirty deep around the hut by this
time. The woman who had brought the pipe came in,
carrying in her delicate hands a necklace of blue and white
beads cut from shells. It was very beautiful, as fine as
anything turned out by the bead makers of Hedeby. Swift
Hawk pointed at Haakon, and she put it carefully about
his neck. She seemed greatly in awe of him, and Haakon,
not immune to flattery, took a closer look at her. He could
hardly help it, with a pair of breasts the color of dark
copper nearly under his nose. She was beautiful, as a wild
thing of the forest is beautiful, lithe and long legged, with
reddened cheeks, white, even teeth, and a waterfall of
thick black hair. She wore an embroidered deerskin skirt,
whose side opening showed a graceful curve of copper skin
nearly to her waist. Her hands were graceful, long-fingered
with neatly trimmed nails, but Haakon felt the calluses on
palm and fingertips as they brushed his neck. In the harsh
life that this forest village accorded, there would be none
who did not work.

The woman smiled at him, with her dark eyes as well as
her lips, and again Haakon thought of a forest creature, a

deer. Indeed he would learn later that her name was Doe Leaping. For now he strove to put his eyes elsewhere lest he offend Swift Hawk. Out of the corner of his eye he saw Donal, much amused. The woman smoothed the dangling strings of beads and stepped back. Feeling like a maid at a market fair, Haakon bowed his thanks to the chieftain.

"'No iron,'" Knut grumbled as they left the hut and made their way through the village with a curious band of *skraelings* traveling after. "'Not so much as an iron nail,' so said the jarl. Bah!"

"*One* iron dagger, to seal the bargain," Haakon said soothingly. "I am the jarl and may do so. If I let you, old friend, I will have to let the rest."

"*I* am chief helmsman," Knut said truculently, "and may have a privilege the jarl does not give the rest."

"Tell that to the rest," Haakon chuckled, as Donal opened his mouth to object.

Knut relapsed into a morose silence, ignoring a woman who trotted at his side, peering in apparent fascination at the patch over his missing eye. Donal, easily diverted, began to whistle, pondering a new verse to his song and attracting an enthralled band of *skraeling* children with the tune, while Hagar the Simple concentrated on accepting anything remotely edible from the elm bark bowls and dishes that were pressed on them by their growing escort. They arrived at their meadow in triumph with nine-tenths of the *skraeling* village on their heels. Plainly Swift Hawk's people now felt themselves in no danger from the Norse. They had made none so bad a start, Haakon thought.

"Look at old One-Eye," Donal chuckled. "He flees like a reluctant bride."

Haakon gave a thoughtful eye to Knut, diving round the corner of the cattle byre to skulk in its shadow, while the *skraeling* woman looked about her in puzzlement. After a moment, seeing a flicker of movement from the byre, she pattered after him. "And I would not be displeased if you were doing the same," Haakon said. In the weeks that they had been in the *skraelings'* land, a rough language, half-Norse and half-*skraeling*, had sprung up

between them. And indeed in the matter of a man and a
maid, very little talk was needed.

"Ah, now, and you can't expect us to be ignoring
what's given so willing," Donal said.

"As you did on Bee Isle," Haakon said sourly.

" 'Tis not the same."

"No, and it may make more trouble." The *skraeling*
women felt that there was much status gained from con-
gress with the spirit men, and the Norse, long womanless
and womanizers by nature, were only too happy to bestow
their favors. Haakon had the feeling that the *skraeling*
men might well take a dim view of this, and lately it had
begun to seem that the other, less favored, women among
the *skraelings* were growing jealous. Those adopted by the
Norse were the youngest and the prettiest, and they gave
themselves airs about it. Woman trouble, whatever form it
took, was always major trouble, Haakon had found. He
would have greatly preferred that his men leave the
women alone entirely, but chastity was an unenforceable
order, and he hadn't even tried.

The only one who preferred a solitary bed was old
Knut, who had always claimed that a ship made a better
mistress than a woman and was greatly more to be trusted.
But it seemed that Wren Singing had discovered that the
great god of the Norsemen, Father Odin, had but one eye.
If Knut were not the god himself in human form, then
certainly he was a man of strong magic, and Wren Singing
had marked him inexorably as the father of her sons.
Knut's discomfiture had given his shipmates unending
amusement, and there were even bets on the outcome.
The odds were running heavily in favor of Wren Singing.

It was common knowledge that Haakon also found
himself pursued by a pair of willing arms, but no one, not
even Eilaf, had the nerve to bet on the jarl. Doe Leaping,
who proved to be Swift Hawk's unmarried sister, had come
into the camp on the day after the treaty meeting with a
rush basket of squash and beans and the foreign ears of
grain from which the *skraelings* ground their meal. She had
set it on the longhouse floor and set herself down opposite
Haakon. Mindful of her relationship to Swift Hawk, and
what Rosamund would think of the matter, Haakon had got

a grip on himself and sent her home with a pat on the head.
His men plainly felt that he was being unnecessarily faithful
to his wife and felt no inclination to follow the example.

As the trees turned bare and autumn wore on into
winter, Doe Leaping continued to make her affection for
the white-skinned chieftain plain, but she was a prideful
woman and would not pursue him in the manner of Wren
Singing and Knut. But she was always there when Haakon
came to the forest village to smoke a pipe with Swift Hawk
(he was learning not to choke on it) and talk, after their
fashion, of hunting and old battles. The People of the
Deer were at war, in some way or another, with most of
the other peoples around them, but that was the way it
had always been, and it was more a matter of stealthy
midnight raids and crop stealing than of pitched battles.
Between Swift Hawk and Haakon there had grown up an
odd comradeship, less the brotherly bond he felt with
Donal than the natural affinity and respect of one leader
for another. While they talked, Doe Leaping brought
them food and drink—a mixture of green beans and *skraeling*
corn, berries, shellfish, deer meat, nuts, and drinks brewed
from berries or from boiled roots—some familiar, some
not, until Haakon began to realize that unlike Iceland or
Bee Isle whose fruits were laboriously wrested from a
miserly land, this newfound land that his god had showed
him was one of almost unending plenty.

Perhaps he regarded it with too acquisitive an eye.
Whenever he was in the *skraeling* village—and sometimes
alone on the forest trails or in his own camp—he felt Elder
Wolf's meditative gaze upon him. *The old wolf doesn't
trust us*, Haakon thought. Maybe he was in the right of it.
What would happen when the Norse came in force, with
iron axes to break the *skraelings'* stone ones? Was there
land enough for all of them?

Lately Haakon had begun to feel that others of the
skraelings shared Elder Wolf's suspicions, although they
seemed for the moment more angry over their women
than aught else, and Swift Hawk held them in check. The
red-skinned men still traded with the Norse and made
free of their camp, but the last time Haakon had gone to

talk with Swift Hawk, a faint muttering had followed him
on his way to the chief's hut.

Still, matters went well enough until the first of the
bitter winter winds came blowing down the meadow and
blew with it two stumbling figures, beaten black and blue
under their deer-hide robes.

Haakon met them at the gate of the timber palisade
with which, more from force of habit than from real fear,
he had ringed his camp.

He took in Doe Leaping's battered face. "Who has
done this? Not your brother?" Surely Swift Hawk was
incapable of beating a woman that savagely.

"No, it was the other women. My brother the chieftain has had *them* beaten," Doe Leaping said with some
satisfaction.

"Then why?"

"They are jealous. We were prideful, they said, for
lying with the white spirit men."

Haakon recognized the second woman as one who
had been much in the Norse camp. He looked at Doc
Leaping. "But *you* have not."

She straightened her back, wincing. Her lovely dark
face was marred by a puffy eye and a split lip. "I did not
tell them so."

She *was* prideful, he thought. Too prideful to tell a
crowd of jealous women that although she had offered
herself to the white-skinned chief, he would not have her.

"Did none of the men stop them?"

"Not until my brother came. Not even Young Elm,
who asked for me to wife. We will stay here," Doe
Leaping said. "We will go no more home again."

Haakon looked at the sky, leaden with the wind pushing
snow before it. Behind him the sea was angry, topped with
sullen whitecaps even in the inlet. If he took the women in,
it would make worse trouble, a war maybe. Haakon had
learned that a *skraeling* chieftain, like a Norse one, once
made, could be unmade again if his tribesmen found his rule
not to their liking. Swift Hawk might not be able to hold
them. And the Norse had nowhere to go until spring.

"I cannot," he said, trying not to look at Doe Leaping's eyes. She was the chieftain's sister; she would be
safe. The *skraeling* men had obeyed Swift Hawk well

enough to thrash the culprits at his order. "It will make an
ill between your people and mine."

   She didn't answer him, as she hadn't answered the
women who had beaten her, only turned away into the first
flurry of snow. The feathers in her hair were a bright splotch,
like red berries against the black. From somewhere a bright
red bird alit to peck for a moment in the grass at Haakon's
feet, and then it too vanished in a whirring of wings.

XI

The Fires of Thor

"With a crew of fifty was Raven flown,
   Thor of the Thunders give us luck!
And I sing of a voyage to seas unknown,
When we and *Raven* fared forth alone."

   The harp song rose above the crash of surf and the
whistling of a winter wind. They gathered about Donal in
the fire-lit longhouse, knowing the great thing they had
done and not reluctant to hear it praised. The music
glittered around the singer like the firelight. He sang in the
Norse tongue but with a Scots bard's way of making a verse
and with a certain ruthless honesty. Haakon, nursing a horn
from their rationed store of ale, thought that it was a tribute
to the harper's skill that he could make them chuckle at
their doubts and never think of breaking his head.

"The jarl with his eyes on the beckoning west,
   Thor of the Thunders go with us!
Called his helmsmen out to him from the rest,
Laughed and said, not quite in jest,

"Now what man thinks us bound for Hel,
   Thor of the Thunders give us wind!

And hears in the storm the sea-wife's spell?
And what other tales do the doubtful tell?'

One man looked at the *Raven's* head,
    Thor of the Thunders keep us safe!
And her frothing tail where the ship's wake sped,
And, 'We sail for the edge and death,' he said.

'The earth is round, who tells you? I!
    Thor of the Thunders, we shall know!
Do you fear on the edge of the world to die?'
Asks the jarl, and half his men say, 'Aye.'

The sea grows black, and the gale wind cries,
    Thor of the Thunders let us live!
But the jarl still looks where the low sun lies,
And like an arrow the *Raven* flies.

Storm-hurled far from Norsemen's home,
    Thor of the Thunders remember us!
Till we see no sight but the gray sea foam.
We and the *Raven* fare forth alone."

They grew closer still, caught in the telling, the old
fear of the unknown and the unknowable crowding around
them again as it had on the breast of the limitless sea.
Donal laughed, made the music laugh with him, and
finished his song triumphantly.

"While skalds yet live, our voyaging tell,
    Thor of the Thunders give us luck!
How the jarl held the helm till the storm winds fell,
And we came to land from the mouth of Hel,
    By Thor of the Thunders who gave us our luck!"

As if in answer, a bright crack of lightning split the
sky above them, sending through the smoke hole a ghostly
flare that vanished as soon as it had come. A rolling boom
of thunder answered almost on the heels of the lightning.
The gold ax at Haakon's feet—it was never far from

him—gave off an unearthly glow and then faded to still-ness again. Haakon chuckled. The god had acknowledged his praise-song, he thought.

"That was close," Thorfinn said. "The *skraelings*'ll be running like rabbits." The day before *Raven* had come, a bolt of lightning had split a *skraeling* wigwam in two and killed the man and woman in it. The red-skinned men's fear of their own thunder god was great, and the Norse had learned that they fled in terror now from his storms. Haakon had stored away this information as being possibly useful and made it a point to let the *skraelings* see his ax close to when storm weather was brewing. If the storm was near enough, Thor Odinsson's ax glowed as if it were the living heart of it.

"If it comes any closer," Yazid said as another deafen-ing crack snapped above them, "I shall call to Allah for a hole to hide in myself."

Haakon grinned. "Give us another song, Donal, some-thing less to Thor Hammerer's liking. Mayhap he will turn his attention elsewhere. And give me something to eat. I am hungry."

"There is lobster in the pot," Hagar said. "A fine country this, and very full of lobster. And butter, churned yesterday."

"You become a housewife," Donal said. "Some man will marry you."

Hagar ignored him. If there were no women and a man wished to eat butter, then he churned it. The *skraeling* women would have been willing to come and cook for them, but the jarl had forbidden it.

Haakon fished a cooked lobster from the hot water in the pot. Ignoring what seemed to him a reproachful look from the creature, he pulled a long, thin-bladed dagger from its sheath in his boot and began to wiggle the tip through the plates. The scarlet tail was curled around itself like a closed fist. Haakon stopped prying at it, with an arrested look in his eyes. He uncurled the tail in the firelight, curled it back again, and watched the plates move against each other.

"A fine piece of engineering, a lobster," Yazid said idly. "Allah is the greatest builder of them all."

Haakon flexed his hand (nearly healed now but still painful and with a red ridge of scar across the knuckles) in imitation of the lobster tail. "Get me a piece of hide," he said to no one in particular. When they had found him a deer hide and dragged it in, he thanked them abstractedly and began to saw at it with his dagger. Thor Hammerer never promised to make him invulnerable, so said Thor himself. So. Here was invulnerability in a lobster pot. Haakon laid the scraps of deer hide across the knuckles of his sword hand, pinning them down with his chin, and adding more strips with his left. His men lost interest and went back to prod Donal into more songs, but Haakon wouldn't have noticed if they had all filed out the door and disappeared into the next world. Yazid watched him, amused. The jarl in pursuit of a problem was always very single-minded. But it was a fine idea. A man with the eyes to see a handguard in a lobster tail would have made an engineer if someone had given him the training.

In the morning Haakon had Snorri Longfoot, who was smith as well as carpenter, building a forge fire just inside the open door of the cattle byre, with Haakon's deer-hide pattern and a broken helm on the ground beside him. Snorri, inspecting the jarl's pattern, decided that there was something in it. And it was midwinter, with very little else to do. Even Haakon's land-bound sailors, driven by cold and boredom, came to watch and lay bets on whether the jarl's invention would work or no.

Haakon stood with his thumbs hooked into his belt, wrapped in a beaver cloak, and watched the sparks fly up from Snorri's hammer. It wasn't until three *skraeling* men, and then six, and then two dozen, appeared that it occurred to him that it might not have been so fine an idea to let the red-skinned men watch the Norsemen working metal. Swift Hawk, solemnly courteous as always, stood beside his friend the white-skinned chieftain and watched Snorri cut and shape the pieces of the broken helm against the red heart of the fire. It took three others to work the heavy forge bellows and bring the water for the quenching, and Snorri ordered them about peremptorily as befitted the master of the forge. Surely Snorri, who could shape the magic iron to a new form with fire and water, was a being second in greatness only to his chief. Swift Hawk touched a hand to the iron dagger in his belt—a spirit gift to be passed on to his children and their children's children.

Behind him the men of the People of the Deer stared with open greed at Snorri's blackened hands and the swing of his hammer against the anvil. It was not right that the spirit men should show them how this great medicine was made and then refuse to let them have a piece of it. Surely that much was owed to the men of the People of the Deer, Young Elm thought—thinking viciously of Doe Leaping—in exchange for the women who had grown so fine and lordly in their ways that they would have none of their own kind now.

Young Elm scowled at the back of the white-skinned chief of the spirit men—and saw that not ten paces away, one of the spirit men also scowled at his own chief. This man's white face was flushed, sullen, and angry; Young Elm, with a growing look of cunning in his eyes and seeing that Swift Hawk was head to head with the spirit chief, slipped away from his place, toward the angry man. In their hatred, they might find a common ground.

When Eilaf crept through the doorway for the last time, the fire in the longhouse hearth was only a red streak of embers overlaid with the ashes of the log that had burned there all night. The others were all asleep, huddled deep in their furs and sleeping bags against the winter chill. Eilaf slipped catfooted past the snoring men. He had already taken the weapons he wanted from the storehouse: spare spearheads and arrowheads, and extra sword blades. The *skraeling* folk could haft them. It was the metal they were interested in, and it was easier to carry loose blades. But there was one more thing that Eilaf wanted. With the jarl's golden ax and Young Elm's warriors to back him up, there would be no question as to who should be chief over the Norsemen. And with the price in furs that Young Elm had offered for the blades, Eilaf would be very rich indeed.

Eilaf slipped through the chill dark to the jarl's sleeping place at the end of the hall. Most men wore only a dagger in the camp and left their fighting weapons with the common store or decently hung on the wall. It was a pity that the jarl should choose to keep his golden ax by him always, from jealousy that some other man might touch it, Eilaf thought, but the jarl and Donal MacRae, who shared the other half of the jarl's sleeping bag, were snoring like pigs. And after he had taken the chieftainship from the jarl, Eilaf thought savagely, he would give the jarl's harper to Father Odin for a thanks-gift. Donal had named no names when he had sung of a helmsman who had feared to go on with the journey, but who he meant had been plain enough to set the others laughing.

The jarl's ax lay on the sleeping bench just beyond the jarl's head. Eilaf's night-accustomed eyes found it easily in the faint moon-wash that came through the smoke hole in the roof. He held his breath and reached across the jarl for it.

Young Elm crouched beyond the gate at the forest's edge, waiting. There had been no snow since morning, and the full moon that rode over the inlet turned the white meadow to silver, with the dark bulk of the spirit men's fenced camp rising from it like a black rock. Two others crouched with him, squatting on their haunches, silently patient. Between them were the stacked furs that were payment for the promised weapons.

Dog Smiling looked at the trail of stars across the sky. "He is late."

"He will come. He is angry at his chieftain. And when such a one as that grows angry, it does not leave him."

"Take care it does not spill onto us," Winter Goose said. If these were indeed spirit men—and Elder Wolf still said that they must be treated as such—Young Elm and his brothers might stir up a battle they would wish they had had no part in.

"I do not care," Young Elm said. He waited, watching the silent palisade.

A shriek split the winter air, a horrible tearing sound that rose and fell. Torchlight flared up, casting its glow into the sky above the fence. The sound of running feet and voices followed it, and still that terrible howl of pain reeled through the camp, endlessly on and on.

The timber gate swung open—Eilaf had left it unbarred—and Eilaf stumbled through, with his left hand clutching the elbow of his right, and that fearful, agonized

howling filled the air around him. At first Young Elm
thought that Eilaf carried a torch, and then he saw that it
was the Norseman's hand itself that was burning.

An instant later Haakon came through the gate. The
ax was in his hand, a savage golden blade like a fire in the
moonlight.

"How do you like my ax, Eilaf?" Haakon shouted.

Eilaf screamed and plunged his hand into a snowbank.
A cloud of steam rose up from it, and Eilaf bent sobbing
over the blackened thing that had been his hand.

Haakon advanced on him. He was shaking with rage,
but he nearly choked when he saw Eilaf's hand. There were
no fingers at all, only a blackened stump and the horrible
smell of burned flesh. Thor Hammerer had guarded his own.

At the edge of the trees even Young Elm drew back
from the sight of the spirit chief with that fearful ax in his
hands. The glow from the blade cast a yellow ghost-light
on the snow and the writhing figure in the snowbank.

"I do not want those weapons badly enough to fight—
that—for them," Dog Smiling said flatly. Winter Goose
was putting his hand through the carrying strap on the
baled furs.

Young Elm ground his teeth at them and called them
evil names, but they did not listen. Tomorrow, maybe, by
daylight, they would listen. But not now, not in the face of
that ax and the man who wielded it.

The thunder god's fire could blacken a whole village
with one bolt. Dog Smiling had no mind to call it on
himself, and he ran.

In the meadow, Eilaf Eiriksson lifted a contorted face
to Haakon. His thinning pale hair was burned clear across
his forehead, and his face was ashen. The jarl's eyes
showed as yellow in the light from the axhead as did the
blade itself. Haakon raised the ax, and the last thing that
Eilaf saw was a face, red bearded, ancient, and terrible,
above the jarl's left shoulder. Its eyes glowed red, and it
reached out both hands for him as the ax came down.

"What—do you want done with him?" Donal bit back
the rising in his throat because it was beneath his dignity
to vomit in front of his shipmates. The smell of burned

flesh was a cloud over the meadow, and to the day he died, Donal would hear the howling that had begun when Eilaf had touched the ax.

Haakon looked for a moment at Eilaf. The ax was still, lifeless now, avenged. The blood made a black pool in the snow. "Put him up in a tree for Thor Odinsson," Haakon said shortly. "He belongs to him."

Donal nodded, grateful that as a Christian it would be an offense to the god for *him* to do it. He shouted for Thorfinn and Hjalmar Sitricsson.

"We found the other weapons," Donal said, as Hjalmar and Thorfinn lifted what was left of Eilaf Eiriksson. Thorfinn had a coil of rope over his shoulder. "The spare blades from the storehouse. They were in a sack by the gate."

"And the *skraelings?*" Haakon said. Surely not Swift Hawk, his friend. He was beginning to feel a little sick too.

"They took to their heels when the commotion started," Donal said. "But you can see where they were waiting yonder. Three of them, by their tracks."

Not Swift Hawk then. If there were only three, it had been a secret matter. But it might mean trouble all the same. And the more fool he for signing on Eilaf Eiriksson in the first place. Haakon looked down the meadow, where a lone beech stood out from the rest. Thorfinn and Hjalmar had raised their grim burden into its branches.

They left him there, as a blood-price for Thor Odinsson, until the bare limbs of the beech tree were black with carrion birds. None of the Norse seemed to feel that the death of Eilaf Eiriksson was aught but long overdue, and the *skraelings* still came and went about the camp, although they skirted in a wide, respectful circle the thing in the beech tree. Swift Hawk made an apology for the unknown culprits (he said they were unknown; Haakon wasn't sure), and Haakon asked an equally solemn pardon for one of his own having led Swift Hawk's young men into evil. But things were not the same. There was constraint between the red-skinned chieftain and the white one that neither could put entirely from his mind.

Lately Haakon had begun to know that again the Norse were silently followed wherever they went in the slushy, thawing snow. The unseen eyes were like an itch between his shoulder blades, although Swift Hawk was as courteous as ever. What would happen to the People of the Deer, with only their stone clubs, when the next shipload of Norse—with women and more livestock—came to make a city here? And what might Swift Hawk feel that he must do to stop it?

The next day one of the crew, Bjarni Hauksson, was killed, and Haakon felt his vision of peace between Norse and *skraeling* slipping into the grave with Bjarni.

It happened so quickly that no one could stop it. They were felling trees for a brewery in the slushy snow, and maybe Bjarni, also conscious that they were watched, had his mind on the unseen eyes and not his tree. It came down the wrong way, across his chest, and he was dead before anyone got to him.

No one saw the *skraelings*, but no one doubted that the *skraelings* had seen them. They were there in force before the Norse had laid Bjarni in his howe, standing a little back from the rest, their black eyes watchful and knowing. Haakon, sorrowing over Bjarni, still found it in him to curse the dead man for his carelessness. If anything had been needed to show the *skraelings* that the white-skinned interlopers were no gods—and thus, very likely, fair game—it was this. Gods did not die of accidents. They might kill each other in their rage, as Haakon had killed Eilaf, but they were not crushed by falling trees. Haakon, heaving rocks onto Bjarni's howe to keep the wolves away, wondered how soon Swift Hawk's people might put that theory to the test. He looked over his shoulder at the grisly thing still hanging in the beech tree. "Bury him too!" he snapped. He had enough of corpses.

In the morning there were two more good Norse oarsmen and fighters dead. Hagar the Simple found them lying across a deer trail, with flint-tipped arrows in their backs. Haakon watched Hagar's burly form lumbering down the meadow with its double burden and felt his beautiful newfound land retreating from him like a tide going out. He grasped, and there was nothing left in his hands but foam and sand.

"They fell like birds to our arrows," Young Elm said. He gave Swift Hawk a stubborn look.

"You shot for sport? And left them lying on the trail? Is this the way Manabus has taught us to live?" Swift Hawk's eyes were dark. The People of the Deer killed nothing for amusement. From skin to teeth, every piece of every dead thing was put to use, and the few bones left over were given back to their own kind, for respect— beaver to the water and red deer to the forest.

"These were men," Dog Smiling said, standing at Young Elm's shoulder. "And not for sport, no?"

"For knowledge," Winter Goose said. And for hatred he thought, looking at Young Elm, but that was Young Elm's affair. "Our arrows have killed the pale men, and the pale men are no spirits."

Young Elm nodded in satisfaction. It had taken much to change his brothers' minds after they had seen the magic in the white chief's ax, but now they had seen the pale men die with their own eyes. Now they saw the truth. "They are only another tribe of men, who will take *our* corn land, and *our* deer runs—" he gritted his teeth and looked straight ahead at Doe Leaping, who was serving food to Elder Wolf "—and *our* women, if we do not fight them!"

Doe Leaping looked back at him as if she would not care greatly to see him drowned in the beaver lake. She had never forgiven him for letting the other women beat her. Nor he her.

Swift Hawk stared into the fire as if the answer lay in the heart of it. All along the riverbank the snow was melting into soft patches, with the green grass growing up between. The trees were thick with swollen buds, and the early flowering ones made a smoky drift of petals against the new green. Always new life came again. Swift Hawk had no wish to greet it with the white chieftain's blood. Elder Wolf stirred in his place by the fire and handed the empty bowl to Doe Leaping. Regretfully, Swift Hawk said, "We will hear what the wisest of us says."

Elder Wolf put his gnarled hands to the fire. He was old, and each spring it took him longer to grow warm. But in return for age the manitous gave wisdom, and at last they had spoken to him. "All winter have I watched the signs and the lights of the northern sky, and always they have said the same thing. Now the manitous have spoken, and their words are the same as those of the sky, and thus I know what must be."

"Then speak, old father," Swift Hawk said. Young Elm's eyes glittered brightly.

"If the white-skinned men gain a foothold here, it will be the end of the People. More and more white skins will come after them across the water, with beasts to carry them on their backs and iron weapons to slay us. And soon the People will be no more. This is what the manitous have said."

"Kill," Young Elm said softly between his teeth. "Kill them and hang their yellow hair over our fires that they may never come back."

"Kill!" The heretofore silent young men crowded outside the chieftain's wigwam took up the chant.

Swift Hawk looked at the fire, but there was no other answer in it. The manitous had given the People of the Deer to his leadership. They were his to guard. He took the iron knife that the white chief had given him and held it, blade up, to the unseen sky. "We do not allow the white skins to live here longer. Neither to depart, lest they bring back more of their kind."

The chanting grew clamorous and savage: "Kill! Kill! Kill!"

XII

A Birth and a Death

"I am stifling! Open you the window!" Rosamund rolled in the down mattress—it seemed to cling to her sides—and her long legs thrashed at the fur coverlets.

"It is only the child coming." Tordis was wiping her face with a cool cloth when Rosamund kept still long enough. "You will take a chill else."

Bergthora was humming to herself by the fire, hanging swaddling clothes and a little fur wrap near it to warm. The fire seemed to fill the room. Rosamund's night shift clung to her stickily, and there were feathers, worked loose from the ticking, plastered with sweat to her legs. Another wave of pain clamped down across her belly and then settled like a hot fire in the small of her back. "Very good," Bergthora said complacently. "Always it is—"

Rosamund's eyes gleamed balefully at them in the firelight. "And the next one of you who tells me it is always easier the second time—" She gasped and howled as the next pain bore down.

"Do you think we should?" Thirteen-year-old Freydis glanced doubtfully at the hall. She could hear the lady yelling, even in the courtyard. If it was a bad birthing, it would be an ungrateful thing to slip away in the midst of it. Lady Rosamund had never been anything but kind.

"Nah," Njal said scornfully, with the assurance of one who would never have to do it, "I heard old Granny Bergthora say that it was going well enough when she came out to fetch clean linens. But with all the hustle, they won't look for us."

"Should we leave a message?"

"After *you* asked Lady Rosamund to send you home, and she wouldn't?" Eleven-year-old Svein demanded, "Do you *want* them to stop us? Bide here with the girls if you're afraid."

"I am not!" Freydis said indignantly.

"Then take this and be quiet," Njal said. Freydis put the knife under her cloak. "We are viking folk. We do not need anyone's permission to go home to Norway." He gave a last glance around the courtyard. It was nearly dawn. All the hall folk were waiting for the birth, and the monks were all at matins. No one would miss them until they were well away. He slipped the bar off the gate and set out down the path to the river, a slim, limping figure with a stolen sword in his belt and Svein trotting behind him.

Freydis hovered in the gateway. She knew little of childbirth, except for having seen a mare foal in the field. But the mare had not screamed like that. If Lady Rosamund should die, it would be a great evil to have run away. But Bergthora had said she would not. And if she should—an icy fear gripped Freydis. If Lady Rosamund died, then she would be alone here. She could barely see Njal and Svein in the predawn dark. Frantically, she ran after them.

*   *   *

"Push!"

Rosamund, aware in her lucid moments that she was
not helping greatly, gritted her teeth and pushed. Fann was
praying dolefully in a corner, which was somewhat less than a
help, Rosamund thought savagely, but Fann greeted any
crisis with more prayer than action. There was nothing that
Fann could have done, but Rosamund was angry with the
world just now. The child wanted to be born, and Mother
Mary knew *she* wanted it born, so why didn't it *come*?

"Push," Bergthora said insistently. Privately she thought
that she would rather deliver a she-cat than the lady Rosamund,
but the lady would be herself again when it was born. She
would have to be. Those heathen Irish were due to ride into
Ole's Hold today, and if Lady Rosamund spat at them in a
temper, very likely they would all go home again.

There was one last tearing pain and then a sudden
empty feeling. Bergthora held the baby aloft triumphantly.
It was male, and he screwed up a furious red face and
shrieked. "A fine son for the jarl."

For the jarl, Rosamund thought. *Let the jarl bear the
next one*. The smoldering anger went suddenly from her
eyes, as quickly as the pain had gone. She held her
dripping arms out. "Give him to me."

"Be quiet! You'll wake the whole steading!" Njal
pinched Freydis's arm.

"I'm cold!" she said. Her teeth were chattering. Her
gown and boots were soaked to the skin from helping to
get the boat in the water. She sat shivering while Njal
pushed the little skin-covered curragh out into the river
and Svein struggled with the sail. The burns that fed the
river were swollen with the spring runoff, and the current at
the center was black and swift. The monks in their candle-lit
chapel chanted their lauds to God as the boat stolen from
them vanished in the dark. As the curragh fled away
downriver, the chanting changed to a joyous peal of bells.

Rosamund listened wearily to the bells. Someone must
have taken a message to the chapel. Fann most likely. It
would never have occurred to Tordis to have the bells rung
for her babe. She stroked the pale fuzz of hair on its head.

There was a great deal of bustle in the hall outside her chamber, but she felt too weary to take an interest in it. She was clean and dry now, snuggled with the babe into new linens and grateful now for the fire and the fur coverlet. She admired her son drowsily, with a fleeting prayer for forgiveness for having been such a trouble. One should bear pain gladly, she knew, but she had never been able to. Bergthora hurried in and out on endless errands, frowning blackly when Abbot Cormac pushed his way in past her. This was not man's business, much less monks'. He gave the old woman a genial smile and propelled her gently through the door. Rosamund heard the bolt click behind him.

She opened her eyes. "I picked a most inconvenient time. Have the Irish come yet?"

"Not yet. It's only first light outside." He hesitated. "I thought you might want me for the babe." She saw that he was still vested for mass, in simple robes of Lenten purple, far less fine than Father Kilian's. Ordinarily the abbot did not say mass at matins, but he had said one for her this morning, for the safe delivery of the babe. Now he carried a covered stone font in one hand. She smiled at him, grateful for his worldly good sense. Her Norsemen would riot if she had Haakon's son publicly christened in Christ's church. But christened he would be, for the peace of her mind, and because she could not find it in her to tell Abbot Cormac no.

"What will you call him?" Cormac said.

"Ole." That should please Haakon, who had loved his father so greatly.

Cormac took the infant in his arms and spoke the comforting, familiar words; a shortened service usually reserved for an infant likely to die, but Bergthora would be pounding on the door in a moment, and surely God would understand.

Indeed, the abbot had barely put small Ole back in Rosamund's arms when the old woman returned, with Tordis and Leif Hildisson for reinforcements. Cormac admitted them, and Bergthora glared suspiciously at the font. Tordis shrugged. If Lady Rosamund wished it, what harm? A little Christian water would have small effect on Jarl Haakon's son. Wulf, padding after Tordis, sniffed gravely at the baby and lay down by the bedside, a self-appointed guardian.

The room seemed very full of people, Rosamund thought. She surveyed them with what dignity she could muster.

"The Irish have come," Leif Hildisson said. "Fergus MacAiden and I have been quarreling about the defenses this past half hour." His round, farmboy's face split into a grin. "But I am winning. That is a fine son you have given the jarl."

"He comes somewhat inconvenient," Rosamund said, "but I could do little about that. If you have trouble with Fergus, send him to me when I have dressed."

"You'll never be up so soon!" Tordis said indignantly. "A full week you should keep your bed!"

"If I do, I won't be keeping this hold another week after it," Rosamund said. She looked at Cormac's purple robes and sighed. God forgive her, but she was likely to be at war with her own father by Easter week. She was so tired. It came on her in a sudden wave, and she nearly closed her eyes. "But you may put a robe around me and send him in here. I'll keep my bed for today."

Bergthora looked shocked, but Leif said, relieved, "We will have to. Your father the earl could come any day now. Conor MacLorne has gone north downriver with some of his men to keep a watch for him, but there is more trouble yet. Three of the Rogaland brats have stolen the abbot's curragh and gone."

Dear God, what next? "Gone where?" Rosamund said faintly.

"There's no knowing, but they couldn't go upriver in *this* current. To the sea. And home to Norway, very likely."

"In a curragh?"

"I wouldn't put it past them. It was Njal and Freydis, and that troll's changeling Svein."

Rosamund struggled up onto her elbows, and the baby mewed in protest. "They'll drown! They—Someone must go after them!"

"We haven't a boat," Leif said. "But I've sent one of Fergus's riders to look for them and to tell Conor MacLorne to keep an eye out."

Rosamund sank back onto the pillows and looked

bleakly at her own babe. So much care for this one and not enough time to spare for those three. She should have known when Freydis asked her to send her home again. And Njal—Njal was old enough to be a warrior, but they treated him as a babe, all for a lame leg. When they got them back—*if* they got them back, she thought despondently—she must tell Haakon to take Njal into his own band, lame leg or no, and find a Norse husband for Freydis. They were too old to change their ways and come to live here. She should have known it. As for Svein, there was no knowing what to do with him, but she'd make some decision when she had him safe again.... And had given him the thumping he had coming. *Holy Mother, send them back to me and I'll keep better care of them.* She looked up at Leif. "Saddle a horse and send one of our own men after them too."

"You don't trust Conor?"

"No, I—I don't know. He gave his word, and Fergus says that he always keeps it. But—I don't know. The children are Norse, and it's the Irish they're running from. Send one of their own kind."

Conor wriggled forward on his elbows and belly and peered down through the wet fern at the burnside, where the small stream came splashing down to join the river Bann not far above its mouth. The river was swift and rock strewn at the center, boiling into a white froth where the burn joined it, and just below, on the eastern bank, there was a camp of Englishmen. So far as Conor could tell, Earl Edmund hadn't made his landing yet, but he had sent out his scouts. Conor could see the red-cat standard that Rosamund had told them to look for. There were eight of them, on fast ponies, in a camp that they had been at some pains to conceal.

"The earl's ships will be just offshore and lying low out of sight of the Norse in Larne, I'm thinking," Conor whispered as Kilian wriggled forward to peer down beside him. Kilian rode with him only because he had the bishop's business to see to at a parish church downriver. Conor could have done without his dour presence, riding like a black crow at his elbow.

"At least the English will have a slow time of it, coming up against that current," Conor said with satisfaction.

"They may leave their ships and ride," Kilian said. He was still blackly angry that Conor had turned his tail and given his word to the Englishwoman.

Conor's green eyes gleamed, and he gave the priest a wolfish smile. "Then we will burn their ships at the river mouth."

"He'll not be leaving them unguarded."

"The Holy Mother save me from quarrelsome priests," Conor said rudely. "He'll not be leaving them at all, because he won't be wanting to split his men to guard them. I think we've seen what we want. I'll leave a man to watch, and you may take another with you, to take the bishop's letter, and leave me in peace. I'm going back to Haraldsson's Hold before my cousin Fergus sets himself up to rule the roost there." He grinned again, with the same red-wolf look. "Maybe the English will kill him and do me a kindness."

"That is a sin, Conor," Kilian said.

Conor didn't answer; he had turned back to the river and noticed something unsettling. "Who is fool enough to take a curragh into that spate?"

Kilian looked down. A frail leather boat, with its sail torn loose, spun end around end in the rushing water. As Kilian and Conor watched, it lurched sickeningly into the rocks. Three small figures tumbled from it into the rushing sweep of water.

Njal had known their peril when the mast had snapped, and the children tried frantically to work their way to shore. None of the three had ever sailed a curragh before, and to their dismay it was a far different matter from a Norse ship. Freydis felt as if she clung to a spinning leaf, whirling uncontrollably in the fast current. With the mast gone, they knew they would never reach the river mouth, much less take this frail craft across the Irish Sea to home. They looked at each other, white faced, as Njal struggled with the tiller and the two younger ones frantically bailed. There seemed to be icy water all around them, and a dull roar below them spoke of rapids. The Irish plied up and down this river nearly all year long in these skin boats, but the children knew now, terrified, that they themselves could not. They clung to the sides, unable even to stand, as the curragh slammed broadside into the rapids and upended. With a bone-shaking jolt, Freydis felt the cold water pull her under.

"Those are children!" Conor stared at the small bodies tumbling in the river. Three silvery heads emerged and began to swim. If they made it to shore at all, they would be not ten yards from the English camp. Conor put a hand on his sword, weighing the risk of putting Earl Edmund on the alert by interfering.

"They are Norse!" Kilian hissed. Those silvery pale heads were unmistakable. "They are pagans! Let the English have them."

The cold torrent rolled Svein end over end before Njal grabbed him by the collar. Despite a lame leg, Njal was the strongest swimmer, and he struck out for shore, gasping and cursing himself in his mind for stealing a boat he couldn't sail. It was his fault, all of it, and if he drowned and never saw Valhalla, it was because he was not fit for it. He dropped Svein facedown on the wet sand, saw him choke and start to breathe, and looked around him for Freydis. She clambered over the riverbank like a drowned cat then shrieked in fear, her eyes on the woods beyond.

The English had seen them. Edmund's men-at-arms advanced, grinning broadly at their unexpected luck. Three Norse brats out alone on the river promised an afternoon's amusement and a fat profit later.

There was no doubt in any of the children's minds as to what would happen to them if the English caught them. The miseries of a slave market were the best they could hope for. And Freydis was old enough to be ill used first. They could see it in the Englishmen's eyes as they looked at her in her wet, clinging gown.

Njal tugged at his sword, and it came protestingly out of the wet sheath. He saw that Freydis already had her knife in her hand, her feet planted desperately on the loamy riverbank.

Conor's green eyes widened. "Mother Mary, they're going to fight! They're brave little souls." If there was

aught that impressed Conor MacLorne, beyond a desire to
be king and the fear of hell, it was courage with a knife in
its hand. He turned and half slid, half stumbled, down the
hillside to the horses, whistling up his men as he went.

"You are mad! You will let the English know they're
watched!" Kilian snatched at Conor's cloak. "And very
likely we will all be killed, for the sake of a pack of devil's
brats! I forbid it!"

Conor put a hand out and knocked him flat in the wet
fern. "I won't stand by and see children slaughtered!" His
men were in their saddles, holding Conor's bridle. He
swung up on the horse's back and spat at Kilian, who stood
quivering with fury and rubbing at a bleeding ear. "You're
a poor pretense at a man of God!"

By the time they came round the far side of their hill
into the English camp, the Englishmen had pushed their
quarry back into the river and were finding them no easy
pickings. The smallest boy was hip deep in the fast-running
water, struggling in the grip of a burly man-at-arms. The
sound of hoofbeats and the war cry of the Irish made the
man turn his head, and the boy leaped like a wildcat onto his
back and sank a dagger into his shoulder. The Englishman
pulled the child off and flung him into the water in the
instant before Conor's sword went through his throat.

Freydis, struggling with her captor in the shallows, felt
his grip go suddenly lax and looked up to find a grinning,
bare-legged Irishman wheeling his horse around for another pass through the scattering English men-at-arms.
The English were on foot and much surprised. With the
Irish behind them and Njal and Freydis before, the fight
was brief and savage. Conor had no mind to let any of the
English go free back to their earl, and the eldest Norse
boy seemed bent on hacking to pieces any Englishman in
his sword's reach or else die in the trying. In minutes the
river was red with English blood.

Conor drew rein, panting, and looked about him. The
third child was nowhere to be seen.

"Svein!" Freydis shrieked. "In the water!"

Conor hurled himself out of the saddle, remembering
how the man had flung the boy from him, into the rushing
current where the rocks lay just below the surface. He

snatched his helm off, sent it rolling along the riverbank, and dived.

The river Bann was home ground to the Dal Crimthann, who had grown up along its banks. It was bone-chillingly cold at this time of year, but Conor knew every inch of its placid bends and hidden treacheries. The boy was where he had thought he would be, unconscious, caught in the rocks, one foot wedged between them and his body kept under by the flow of the river. He didn't move as Conor pulled at him. If he wasn't drowned now, he soon would be. Conor fought the current that would pull him away from the boy, his own lungs beginning to ache. It was murderously dark under the surface, but there was a curious white light in his eyes. In desperation, Conor caught the child by the foot, put both his own feet against the rocks and kicked backward. He thought he might have broken the child's ankle, but he was free. They burst through the surface in a dizzying explosion of light just before Conor lost consciousness too.

The Dal Crimthann men waded into the current to pull them out. Conor spat up water while the trees spun around him and the glare faded gradually to daylight. The child was blue, and cold as the grave. Conor desperately rolled him over and pressed his hands into the small back. "Don't you die now!" If there had been time to think, it would have surprised Conor how greatly he wanted this child to live.

Water ran from the boy's mouth, but he didn't twitch. The two older children looked on bleakly. Conor, swearing under his breath, pressed down again. After what seemed an eternity, the boy gave a gasp, vomited up more water and everything he had eaten that morning, twisted like a fish and tried to hit Conor in the eye.

"Bide still, you little hellcat!" Conor said in rough Norse. All the Irish spoke a little Norse; they had lived with the viking folk hammering at their doors for too long not to. "I'm not going to hurt you."

Svein glared at him balefully from red-rimmed blue eyes, and Conor looked back at him. He was dripping wet, and his red hair hung dankly in his face. Freydis, watching, thought that some odd understanding, a grudg-

ing kinship, passed between the two in that moment.
Certainly Svein grew uncharacteristically docile.

"Where do you live?"

"Nor—" Njal stopped. It was no use. "Ole's Hold,"
he said dully.

"Oh ho. Then we'll be taking you back there." Conor
scooped Svein up and dumped him in his saddle. He
swung himself up behind and crooned softly in Gaelic as
the white stallion fidgeted. Two of his men put Njal and
Freydis up before them, and then there was a hurried
sorting out of events as Fergus's courier and Rosamund's
rode up together, somewhat after the fact. Everyone talked
at once until Conor shouted them down. "We'll take them
home. Do you stay and bury these and try to blur over their
camp. We'll leave the English guessing and hope it worries
them." He pointed to the one man without a child in his
saddle. "You bide here and watch for the main army." That
done, he turned his attention to Kilian. "You. I don't care
where *you* go, but I haven't a man to spare now to send
with you about your business. If you are coming with us,
ride behind, where I don't have to be looking at you."

Spring came early to the new land, Haakon discovered,
and came in an almost indescribable flood of beauty.
Flowering trees, of sorts he had never seen before, filled
the air with perfume and the drone of bees. At night,
fireflies made a luminescent cloud above the meadow, and
the *skraeling* children caught them in baskets to play with.
Not even the growing tension between Swift Hawk's people and Haakon's own could tear his mind from the
heart-stopping beauty of his new land. It was Thor's wish
that they stay here, he told himself, postponing their
sailing first one day and then another. He knew that he
would have to take all his men home now and come back
later in greater force if his colony was to have a hope of
enduring, and somehow that seemed an abandonment that
he could not bear to make. He couldn't shake the feeling that
if he left this land, he would not be back, and the longing to
hold it to him for one more day grew greater. In the end he
delayed his leaving one day too long. The People of the Deer
called in every warrior of their tribe to give the weight of

numbers to their fight against the white men's magic. And
then they came howling out of the forest and caught the
white men's chieftain still dreaming in his meadow.

Haakon sat watching a scarlet bird and its pink and
brown mate flickering in a courtship flight above him, and
it was the birds that told him, as swiftly as a thunderclap,
that death was in the air. One moment they swooped and
dived overhead, and in the next they were gone, winging
straight across the meadow, their joyous mating dance
abruptly broken. All around him the forest had the still-
ness of fear.

"*Haakon!*" Hjalmar and Thorfinn came stumbling from
the wood, Hjalmar with an arrow in his arm and Thorfinn
half pulling him along. "The *skraelings!* Near two hundred
of them!"

Haakon ran, cursing himself, and the three of them
dived through the gates as the bars dropped down and a
flood of red-skinned warriors burst from the forest with a
unearthly, undulating howl that sent every Norseman's
hair straight up on his neck. There was no catwalk inside
the wall, and the Norse could see what they were fighting
only when the *skraelings*, armed with rawhide ropes and
hooks of deer antler, dropped down inside. Their faces were
painted garishly, like masks, and their black cock's combs of
hair were stiffened with red war crests. They fought in only
leggings and loincloths, with small bark shields to hide behind, but there were four of them to every Norseman. All
too soon the acrid smell of smoke told the beleaguered Norse
that the *skraelings* meant to burn them out. Or worse yet,
Haakon thought with a gut-wrenching fear, remembering the
women of Bee Isle, to burn their ship.

"Open the gates!" There was little use in hiding
behind their walls if *Raven* went up in flames outside.

They threw up a shield wall as wide as the gateway
and hacked their way through the churning red bodies
around them, like a plated tortoise swarmed with bees.
But how long they could hold the *skraelings* was another
matter, and the incoming tide had not yet begun to turn.
Haakon, in the forefront of the shield wall, saw the
meadow churning with yelling red-skinned men, fighting

to be the first at the kill. Beyond them, women danced and screamed, knives in hand, urging on their warriors.

A red figure, mouth contorted in a feral snarl, danced and shrieked just out of reach of the Norse spears. Haakon recognized Young Elm, teeth bared like an animal and black hatred in his eyes. He thought the man would be at his throat in another moment, spears or no. Young Elm leaped at him, his stone ax splintering a Norse shield. Haakon swung the golden ax, and it cut a gash in Young Elm's arm. He dropped his bark shield, howling, and then he was lost in the swaying mob of *skraelings* that pressed forward. Other warriors took his place, but the shield wall held, and slowly the Norsemen backed toward *Raven*, beached on the sand above the inlet. What they would do when they got there, Haakon had no idea. They couldn't cast off with this mob around them, even if the tide turned. The frantic lowing and neighing of cattle and ponies in the byre echoed the chaos of the battle. And they would be sorely in need of their stock and their stores to make a homeward crossing over those empty, uncharted seas. Haakon could see Swift Hawk, painted like the rest, his hair crowned with a bloody plume of feathers, fighting in the front ranks of his tribe, not ten paces from him.

"Call them off!" he shouted in the few words he had learned to say in the *skraelings'* tongue. "We mean you no harm!"

Swift Hawk only shook his head. His stone ax was bloody to the haft, and it said all that needed to be said. He fought for the life of his people.

In another minute the Norse were ringed around *Raven* in a line of defense that was pitifully thin. Haakon swung the golden ax with the untiring strength that the god's weapon always lent him, but not even Thor's ax was proof against two hundred enemies. The sky above had begun to darken with one of the spring squalls that were common here, and Haakon remembered the *skralings'* fear of lightning. They were all around them. With a bloody sword Donal cut one man down, and two more took his place. Haakon splintered a stone club with the ax and killed the man who had carried it, taking no satisfaction in it. Let the god aid them then, he decided. "I found your new land as you bade me, lord!" he shouted at the darkening sky. "Now send us home safe, with no more blood on our hands!"

The clouds rolled like a serpent above them, and the god's voice spoke in a boom of thunder. Lightening crackled all around until even the Norse looked likely to dive for cover. At the center of the storm the jarl stood, ax upraised, and called it down. The lightning leaped and flashed, and a torrent of water poured from the sky, driven horizontal on a rising wind. He had waked the fires of Thor, Haakon thought. Never yet had the god refused to answer him, but the last time the answer had cost three lives and blown them halfway around the world. Donal MacRae watched openmouthed as the jarl appeared to vanish in a sheet of fire. He thought of Eilaf Eiriksson's blackened hand and crossed himself, while the *skraelings* gazed heavenward and howled in fear. Swift Hawk tried at first to rally them, but the boom of thunder and the blue-white sheets of fire sent them scattering like leaves into the storm.

"Count noses!" Haakon shouted. He wanted to leave no wounded behind by mischance. "And get the animals on board!"

"We canna sail in this!" Donal shouted back over the roar of the storm. The sky was nearly black.

"No, but we can be ready when it clears. They'll be back as soon as the lightning stops." The fire still crackled in the air, and the meadow was empty save for the *skraeling* dead. Haakon walked among them sadly, with the cold rain running down his back. Surely there should be room for white men and red in a land this size, but he thought that Elder Wolf was right, and there was not. At the edge of the meadow, where the women had stood, he stopped and knelt, with a low cry of protest in his throat. One woman lay, arms outspread, with her wet black hair tangled in the grass. The steadily falling rain washed away the blood that had sheeted down her breast from the wound in her throat. It was Doe Leaping. Haakon knew without asking that no Norseman had done this. It had been her own kind, because she had offered herself to him. He looked up to find Knut One-Eye beside him, very bedraggled, like a wet wildcat. "I should have let her come to us last winter when she asked," Haakon said bitterly. "This is on my hands."

"Nah, it would only have made trouble sooner," Knut said. "And if the savages had thought to fight us before sailing weather, what then?" But there was a troubled look on his face. A flurry of movement in the undergrowth caught his eye, and a small, terrified face peered out. He left the jarl mourning the dead woman and dived through the trees after it.

Wren Singing huddled herself into a ball under the thicket and waited for whatever was coming. She wasn't sure whether she was more frightened now of the one-eyed white god or of her own people. It had been Young Elm who had cut Doe Leaping's throat, but it might have been any of them. They were mad with killing fever and with terror, and with a burning shame because they had run. There would be more women who would die for having slept with the white-skinned men. Wren Singing had stolen a sack of food and run, but she didn't think she could run far enough to be safe.

Knut One-Eye stood with his hands on his hips and looked down at her. He could think of no reason why he felt responsible for her—*he* hadn't asked her to run after him like a dog and give his shipmates a fine joke. But he couldn't leave her to be hunted down by her people, not if he hoped to sleep at night afterward. The animals would be all loaded in the hold by now, and in the darkness and the storm he doubted that anyone would notice one more person. He pulled her to her feet. "Come," he said gruffly. "And bide still where I tell you to."

The rain had put out the fire in the camp before the Norsemen could get to it, and the terrified beasts were all on board, with Haakon thanking his gods that he had had at least the sense to keep their extra stores on board *Raven*. The men huddled on the deck, watching the white-lashed water, and waited for the god to call off his wind.

The storm died as suddenly as it had come, and with it the *skraelings* came back anew, carrying bark boats on their shoulders. They must have known that the Norse would run for the sea. Before *Raven* had cleared the inlet, they had launched them on water, still choppy but naviga-

ble and gold flecked with the reappearing sun. A flight of
arrows hummed, a last desperate hope of halting the
white-skinned men before they could escape, back to
whatever land they had come from, to tell others of what
they had found here.

The Norsemen threw up their shields and swore, but
they were nearly out of range. *Raven*'s oars skimmed the
water like a gull's wings, outdistancing the bark boats.
Haakon could see Swift Hawk, standing in the prow. The
skraeling chieftain put away his bow, knowing that he
would only lose his arrows. Haakon wished that there was
some word of farewell to be said, some gesture to make,
but there was none. He leaned against the carved black
feathers of *Raven*'s figurehead, fighting an overwhelming
weariness, the price of the unnatural battle strength that
came from the golden ax. Always there was a price. The
gods gave nothing for free. Beside him, Hagar the Simple
nocked an arrow to his bow—no one could pull it but
Hagar, and it would outdistance the *skraeling* bows easily.
Hagar drew the bow and grinned at Haakon, aiming it
over the widening water at the red-skinned chieftain.
Haakon pushed the arrow down again. "No. I liked him."
He lifted a hand to the wind, steady now and thick with
the inland smell of the white-flowered trees. "Make sail!"

Raven set her course for home—or for where the jarl
thought that home might be. The careful chart of sea
marks and currents had ended with the storm that had
driven them onto this shore. The best that they could do
was sail east and north, trusting in the power that had not
failed them yet. Haakon, still bone tired and possessed of
a ravenous hunger, which he ruthlessly suppressed in
deference to their rationed stores, went at nightfall to sit
in the prow with the golden ax on his lap and ask the god
if he, in turn, had failed *him*.

Thor's voice came softly, a faint unmistakable chuckle
in the moonlight. *I bade you only to find it, Haakon
Olesson, not to raise a city there. You have marked a trail
that others will follow in their time.*

"But I didn't want to leave," Haakon said. Even to
himself his voice sounded a little plaintive, but the god

forebore to mention it. For reasons unclear to his human companion, the Thunderer was in a good mood.

And how long would you have stayed, once you had built your colony? You are not a settler, Haakon Olesson. You are an explorer, who goes before the rest and leaves the settlers to follow after.

The voice sounded very certain of that. But what would happen when they did come? Elder Wolf had been right: The white men would push the red forest-people from their hunting runs until they would be only a small, sad remnant. Maybe if he had stayed . . . Could he have forced his will on the settlers to give Swift Hawk's people some protection?

Everything must have its season of change, Thor Odinsson said almost gently. *Even we of the Aesir will fade before the new ways that are coming. But you have given us a mark to be remembered by. That was all we bade you to do.* The voice seemed to come from a great distance, quiet and almost thoughtful. Then the god was gone, and there was only the small part of him that lived in the golden ax left behind.

Haakon drew his feet up on the sea chest on which he sat and wrapped his arms around his knees, to think. The god was in the right of it, he admitted to himself with a rueful smile skywards. To found a settlement would have been a great thing, but he would not have stayed in it for more than a season. He would have grown bored, restless to go on, to find what lay around the next headland and the next. . . . So then. Better maybe to give in to one's nature than to fight it. He *would* come back, with enough men and women and stores to do the thing properly, and then sail on, to find more wonders. The new land was very full of wonders, of that he was sure. And this time, he thought wistfully, suddenly lonely, he would let Rosamund come if she were still determined. *Raven* had proven herself seaworthy, and Haakon grew tired of being alone. He brightened. This new vision began to look very fine. And in the meantime, he had a richness of furs, plant seedlings, two of the scarlet birds in a twig cage, and even—he had discovered with some amusement—Knut One-Eye's *skraeling* wench, all to show to King Harald Fairhair in Norway, and prove where they had gone.

XIII

"Thou Wilt Stretch Forth Thy Hand...."

"Before God, man, she's your *daughter*!" Athelwulf swung himself into the saddle and stared at Earl Edmund. "Why should she not give you heed?"

For the reason that Earl Edmund's daughter bore too close a resemblance to Earl Edmund, Theofric thought, but he forebore to say so. He patiently sat his horse, with a white truce flag knotted to his spear.

Earl Edmund muttered something unintelligible. If his daughter had been willful last season, it was likely she was willful still, but he had struck a bargain for her with young Athelwulf, and it might be wise not to say so. Athelwulf would have taken anything to wife to get the alliance Earl Edmund proposed—but maybe not if he thought she would murder him in his bed afterward. "If she doesn't heed now, she will heed well enough when we have done," he grunted. He pulled himself into the saddle, swearing at the pains that age plagued him with.

Oswain and Wilfrid drew up their horses and eyed each other malignantly. Oswain had ordered out the scouts, of whom no trace had since been found. Wilfrid had employed the morning profitably by inquiring of his brother at regular intervals where his scouts were, until Oswain had tried to throttle him in a murderous rage. Athelwulf found himself wondering uncomfortably how greatly their sister resembled them. He looked upward across the empty meadow at the barred gates of Ole's Hold. The Norse had known they were coming, which explained the vanished scouts. The church and monastery buildings were deserted but orderly; not a single grain had been left among them to feed the English. Even the gardens had

203

been systematically stripped bare. The only welcome they had found had been a field littered with caltrops, four-pronged spikes made to land points up. Earl Edmund's carls had spent an unpleasant morning trying to pick them up while the Norse shot at them from the walls. They had, however, agreed to talk under the white flag. Athelwulf straightened the silken tunic that covered his mail. He would set himself to woo his recalcitrant bride with somewhat more cajolery than Earl Edmund had used. So fine a marriage would be better coin than she could expect for her rebellion.

Rosamund, peering through the arrow slits that Leif and Fergus MacAidan had drilled in the walls, considered this new turn of events. Athelwulf was only an indistinguishable figure among the crowd of men gathered under the white flag and her father's red-cat banner, but she remembered him: as handsome and egotistical as a jay. No doubt he wouldn't be inclined to beat his wives to death, she thought venomously, but in no other way could she find him an improvement on Harud Olafsson.

"What now, Rose of the World?" Fergus MacAidan said gleefully. "Will you tell your father the earl to go and boil himself, or shall I be doing it for you?" She thought, vexed, that Fergus was enjoying himself.

"Get me a horse," she said.

They brought round a docile mare, considered suitable for a woman two weeks out of childbed, and bedizened as all Irish horses were with more jewelry than Rosamund wore. She winced as she set her foot in the stirrup and swung her right leg over the mare's round back, but she had no intention of walking docilely out to meet her father while he bellowed down at her from the back of his war-horse. A hunting horn sounded stridently, and the gates were swung open, while the Norse archers spread themselves out along the catwalk to see that the English abided by the truce law. A high council indeed, Rosamund thought, inspecting them: Earl Edmund, bellicose and snappish; the tall, graceful figure of Athelwulf; Wilfrid lounging in his saddle and eating apples; and Theofric sitting straight and wary in his and watching the archers on the catwalk.

Rosamund and her mare paced sedately through the gates in the midst of her own retinue: Leif Hildisson,

Fergus MacAidan, Wulf padding at her heel, and Abbot
Cormac with the chapel's altar cross in his hand. Earl
Edmund was unlikely to pay any heed to that, but as
Cormac had said, a heavy cross made a fine weapon with
the power of God behind it. They drew rein while Earl
Edmund huffed his breath out and glared at his daughter.

"What do you want?" Rosamund said flatly.

"God's blood, what do you *think* I want, you whoring,
ungrateful jade?" Earl Edmund bellowed, all tact fleeing
from him. "You have an hour to pack your baggage and
your brat and come out to me, or we'll push the walls in!"

"There are two now," Rosamund snapped, "and their
father will have something to say to that. And their father's
kinsmen," she added, indicating Fergus. "I warned you
not to anger the Irish, but you wouldn't listen."

"Irish!" Earl Edmund yelped. "What do I care for
Irish? These were Harud Olafsson's lands, so now they are
mine! And call off that cur, or I'll ride him down." Wulf
had begun a low, continuous growl at the first scent of Earl
Edmund. Now he raised his head, mouth open in a fanged
grin, and eyed Earl Edmund's throat hopefully.

"I do not think," Rosamund said, repressing the
inclination to scream like a fishwife, "that we have aught
to say to each other."

Athelwulf, feeling that perhaps the earl was taking the
wrong approach, spurred his horse forward and bowed low to
his prospective bride. Rosamund eyed him with distaste.
"Come, lady. Your father wants only a Christian marriage for
you—lawful in God's sight. He fears for your soul. No doubt
you have been sore used here among these Norse, but if you
are wishful to take your babes with you, we can find them
some place at Appleyard." He beamed at her, pleased with
his consideration. She had kept her beauty, he was happy to
see, even after two children. The matter wanted only a less
hasty hand than her father's. "It will be a fine thing to be
mistress of Appleyard, and you shall have all as you like it,
for my sister is married now to your brother Oswain."

"Your sister has my sympathy," Rosamund said. "And I
am wed already."

Athelwulf made a pious gesture, indicative of Christian horror. "Not in God's eyes."

"If you are wishing to speak for God," Abbot Cormac said, "let you go into a monastery, the better to hear His voice."

"You, Priest—who are you?" Earl Edmund peered at him malevolently.

"This is my settlement here." Cormac pointed his cross at the empty village. "My folk are so affrighted of your Christian charity that they have all fled yonder into the hall."

"There is no room for monks on my land," Wilfrid said. He finished his apple and flicked the core at Cormac's feet. Cormac's eyes narrowed dangerously.

"There is no room for *you* on *my* land, Wilfrid!" Rosamund hissed.

"But it's not your land," Wilfrid's voice was an insolent drawl, and he noted with satisfaction that his sister was in a rising fury. He glanced at Athelwulf. "You are in want of a husband, Sister, to teach you manners."

Rosamund fixed a baleful gaze on him, like a snake's. "I would like to kill you, Wilfrid, but I fear someone else will have the pleasure. Besides my Norsemen, there is an army of Irish in Ole's Hold, and another behind you." She gave a tight-lipped smile of satisfaction as Theofric and Earl Edmund stiffened. "You may guess where," she added.

"Come now," Athelwulf said, making a last halfhearted try; the shrew was growing less beautiful by the minute. "Am I so fearful a husband?" He preened himself a little and pulled the helm off his handsome head. Rosamund wished one of her archers would disobey her orders and shoot him. "You will like me well enough when we are wed, I think."

"Get out," Rosamund said between her teeth. "Get *out,* before I set the dog on you." Wulf pricked up his ears hopefully.

Fergus swung down the spear on which his own truce flag was tied and leveled it at Athelwulf. "Be taking the lady's advice, friend, or we'll be showing you where our other army is."

Athelwulf's eyes betrayed a flash of pure dislike as they met Rosamund's blue-violet ones, unpleasantly like her father's. He spun his mount around with a savage jerk on the reins, and Earl Edmund, losing his temper permanently, kicked his own horse back down the track. Wilfrid and

Theofric followed after, Wilfrid polishing another apple to a bright bronze on his sleeve and Theofric, with a troubled gaze, scanning the wooded bank across the river.

"Irish," Wilfrid said as they trotted behind the others, and he studied his apple as if it might suddenly speak Gaelic to him. "My father never thought of the Irish, did he?"

"No," Theofric said sourly. "He did not."

Fergus MacAidan eyed their retreating backs and bowed to Rosamund. "Faith, you told them finely, Rose of the World." A look of blatant disgust followed after Athelwulf. "It would be a shame before God to waste you on that one. Myself it should be, if you are thinking of taking another husband."

"I am not!" Rosamund snapped at him. "Fergus, don't start that now."

Fergus took the opportunity to kiss her hand before she could snatch it away. It might be that her Norseman would not come home at all, he mused. Certainly that was worth hoping for. "Athelwulf is going to get killed," he said with conviction.

Rosamund gave him a look of exasperation and kicked her mare back through the gates before her father should lose his temper enough to break the truce law. She had enough to worry her without Fergus's wooing to add to it—the matter of command, for instance, over which Conor MacLorne and Fergus were already quarreling with each other and with Leif Hildisson. Rosamund had solved that one, with Abbot Cormac's voice behind her, by sending Conor's men out into Dal Crimthann lands until such time as they would do the most good by cutting up Earl Edmund's rear, and by ordering the defenses of Ole's Hold herself. She knew how her father thought, and what he was most likely to do, she said, and no one had been able to dispute *that*. But it weighed heavily on her, with Cormac's people and her own babes and the Norse orphans to keep safe.

The runaways had returned under Conor's wing, somewhat shamefaced, and had shown no signs of further flight. Rosamund had had time for no more than a scolding and assurances that she would find Freydis a husband in Norway in a year if she would bide here and be good for now and that Njal should go into Haakon's band when

Raven came home. How Haakon would care to have Njal foisted on him, she wasn't sure, but certainly the boy could fight, or so said Conor. What to do with Svein, she still didn't know. He remained recalcitrant, other than displaying an odd and unlikely attachment to Conor MacLorne, and Rosamund found herself wishing fervently that if trolls had brought Svein, trolls would take him away again.

And there was the other, more troublesome matter awaiting *Raven's* return: Donal MacRae would not be best pleased to find that his betrothed wife had become a nun in his absence. Rosamund contemplated this thought dismally then put it away from her with an effort. There was the babe to be fed—every hour, it seemed to her. She was drearily aware that the front of her gown was wet with milk again. There was a mass to be said for the Christians among them, and a sacrifice to Odin All-Father for the Norse. If she were wise, she would risk offending Cormac and make an appearance at that too. There was a communal dinner to be cooked, rations and quarrels and lodging to be sorted out. She wished violently as she swung down from her mare that her father would have a fit in the night and die of it.

No such boon was granted them, however, and an hour before sunset Earl Edmund made his first attack on the walls.

While the earl was quarreling with his wayward daughter, *Raven* toiled her way homeward through weather alternately sullen and capricious. Haakon pored over the map he had made on the outward voyage and began a new one for this season's sailing, as he had no way of knowing if they were crossing on the same path or not. He thought not. The weather held cold and clear, and they made fair headway, but toward what, Haakon grew daily more unsure. Although the night sky told them that they were on a northward course, by day they twice sighted land where no land should be—soaring, snow-capped peaks, sun-dazzled—rearing above the horizon only to vanish as *Raven* neared. Once they even hung upside down in the sky like the peaks of Alfheim. And once, another longship crossed their path, sail bellied full in a wind that blew the other way from the wind that *Raven* sailed before. It too was skyborne, and it vanished into the gleaming, ghostly mountains.

"*Hillingar,*" Knut One-Eye said, but he watched these doings unhappily. Every experienced seaman knew of the *hillingar,* the apparitions in the sky that were to be seen near the northern edge of the world, but whether they were malevolent to man or were only some stray bit of magic loosed from Asgard, no one could say. To a restive crew on an uncertain journey, they appeared perilous indeed. If this was a reflection of some Otherworld, might it not reach down a hand and pluck up any who passed too near?

Yazid said calmly that the works of Allah were many and marvelous and studied them with a scientist's eye, making crabbed and mysterious calculations on a slate, but the Norse were more inclined to regard them as the works of Odin, that arcane and secretive god whose path it was wisest not to cross. Haakon kept his thoughts on the subject to himself, but like Knut he eyed these apparitions with uncertainty. He could feel the restlessness of his crew becoming almost tangible, and when they began to look on Knut One-Eye's *skraeling* woman as its cause, Haakon grew worried.

It was Donal MacRae who brought that to a head, unwittingly, striving for some new song to keep the jarl's seamen from thinking on things they shouldn't. It was boredom as much as fear that set men to making trouble. Donal sang all the Norse songs he knew and all the Scots ballads to which he had put Norse words. When he began to dig deeper into his memory for something that they might not have heard before, one morning just at dawn as they sat morosely chewing salt fish and drinking stale water, he pulled forth the tale of a traveler who met a faerie woman in the wood, mounted up behind her on her white horse, and was never seen again by man—for the faerie folk have their own kingdom, far removed from men's, and the hapless stranger who crosses into it may never go home.

He knew as soon as he saw their faces and the odd, dark looks they began to turn on the *skraeling* woman that better he had kept his harp quiet. "That will be where we have been maybe," Hjalmar Sitricsson said slowly, and even Thorfinn Solvisson and others who should have known better grew disquieted. Their eyes went from the eastern horizon to the *skraeling* woman and then back again with growing uncertainty. The light came in a swift flood over the deck. The dawn sun was just beginning to shake itself out of the sea, and as it rose, the sea rose with it.

They spun around, horror stricken, and saw that all around them a towering wall of water was poised like a breaking wave.

In an instant there was pandemonium. Haakon, as fear struck as the rest, came running from the helm to find Knut One-Eye backed against the mast with the *skraeling* woman shivering at his feet, and the others howling around him. Knut had his knife out, and so did they.

"She has done it!" someone screamed. "Give her to Odin before we all are drowned!"

"We'll never go home again else!"

"Give her to Odin!"

"Odin!"

"Stand back!" Someone yelped, and Knut drew his knife back with blood on it, and a gash in his own hand. "Stand away, or I'll kill you! She's *mine!*"

"Give her to us, Knut! Give her to us!"

"The sail!" someone screamed as the water reared higher.

Momentarily distracted, they clawed at the rigging, and the sail came down with a crash. *Raven* slowed and began to drift, and they returned to their prey. Donal and Yazid shoved their way through to Knut's side, Donal horribly aware that it was he who had put this death in their heads. "I'm sorry!" he gasped.

"They want blood," Knut growled. "And maybe we should give it." He glowered at them, as one-eyed as Odin was, and they halted just out of reach of his knife. "So let you choose one of your own to go to Odin!"

They milled around him, frantic with fear and indecision, while the sea fence, that legendary terror, loomed above them. Knut was chief helmsman, second in command to the jarl, and a one-eyed man had a dangerous kinship with the dark, mysterious king of Asgard. No one wanted to attack him, but their fear of the vortex that encircled them was blotting out all other fears as the sea fence had blotted out the sky.

Haakon watched them helplessly, not knowing what

should be done. A life for Father Odin—that was Norse belief and custom and surely the reasonable answer, before the waters sucked them down. And yet, even with his heart hammering between his ribs, he thought that it was not. Knut, Yazid, and Donal were white faced, as frightened as the rest. The woman was curled into a ball behind Knut's legs while *Raven's* crew yelled for her blood and the waters rose. The light was almost unbearably bright and clear so that even distant things came minutely into focus. He could see every feather on the figurehead, every stroke of paint on the gilded beak. The red oars were bars of blood against the sea. Thus clearly men were supposed to see only when death came for them.

All around the captive ship there was a dazzle that was not only the sun's. A voice spoke to him, not inside his head this time, but from somewhere in the white glow, though no one else appeared to hear it.

Haakon Olesson!

Not the Valkyries who take up the dead, but Thor Odinsson. Shivering, Haakon turned his face toward it. "I am here, lord. You promised me Valhalla once. Is this how it is to be?"

Have I ever done you ill, Haakon? Or told you false?

"No."

How great is your faith in me?

"Great enough."

Once it was not so.

"That was once. I have learned, maybe. Also, I swore to serve you, not to be your thrall, and the two are somewhat different." There was small reason for telling lies with death so close at hand.

This is your test then. It comes once to all men who come close to their gods. The waters that you fear are not of this sea. All nature has her dark side and can call up many terrors to frighten men. If your faith in me is strong enough, Haakon Olesson, you may sail through them and come free on the other side.

For just an instant Haakon knew that he looked into the face of the god and would not look there again if he could not summon the strength to obey. He licked at his dry lips. "Make sail!" He spoke as much to Thor Odinsson as to his frightened men.

The shouting on the deck fell away as, the *skraeling* woman forgotten, *Raven*'s crew turned on him instead. Their eyes were wide with fear, driven by their desperation. "We will die!"

"*Make sail!*" He pushed his way among them and began to raise the sail himself, fighting off the hands that pulled at him. "You will die if you do not!"

Yazid and Donal scrambled to aid him, leaving Knut, ragged and bleeding, holding the *skraeling* woman in the crook of his arm. "Odin's curse come on you, you motherless bastards, make sail!" Knut yelled. He pushed the woman down under an oar bench, took the haft of his knife, and laid about him with it.

Haakon, in a fury, had taken his ax out, and he swung the flat of it into someone's head. "Get the sail up and man your oars, or I'll give *you* to the gods!"

The pattern of obedience was strong in them, and the jarl's ax blazed with a light that, remembering Eilaf Eiriksson, they had learned to fear. Thus, mutinously, was *Raven*'s head turned eastward into the fearful water.

"*Out oars!*" As well to be done with it, Haakon thought. The sea boiled around the red oars as they dipped and swung in a ragged line. Haakon took the tiller himself, while Knut stood on the middeck with his knife in his hand, iron hilt outward, and watched them belligerently. The stern oars on the leeward side tangled and almost splintered before Thorfinn Solvisson found his voice to begin the rowing chant. *Raven* settled in her path, and they sailed, praying, straight into the sea fence.

It vanished before them with a rush of wind that shrieked like dead souls. Haakon felt the shirt pulled in tatters from his back and saw nothing for a moment but the swirling gray vortex that clutched them with a furious hand and flung them away. The crewmen howled in terror, oars waving wildly. Three oars rumbled across the deck, sending Knut asprawl on top of them. The sail slackened, spread taut again, and then hung loose as one side of the rigging parted. The wind gave one last groan, and then suddenly it was gone, the sea fence was gone, and there was nothing but clear, still ocean with the calm, unnatural silence of a storm's eye.

Haakon looked about him dubiously, afraid to raise a cheer until he was sure they hadn't sailed into Hel on that wind. There was no wind now, not a breath of it, and on the horizon, lifting green above the water, was the coast of Ireland.

"Mother of God!" Donal MacRae said in an odd voice and sat down suddenly beside Knut on the deck. Knut was swearing and tenderly inspecting his shins. The only other casualty appeared to be Hagar the Simple, who had somehow knocked himself cold with his own oar.

"You should give that oar the champion's place at hearthside," Hjalmar Sitricsson said solemnly. "It's done more than any of us ever could."

Haakon dropped down onto an oar bench to get his breath back, and jerked a thumb at Thorfinn Solvisson to take the tiller. Nature was capricious—someone had told him that once: Thor Odinsson, maybe, or maybe only old Bjorn Karlsson, who had been his first helmsman years ago. Haakon said a silent prayer of thanks to Thor, who truly watched over them, for having forced him to learn that once more. There was a dark side as well as a bountiful one, a force to be mastered but never underestimated. *I have been too blithe about this voyage.* The magnitude of what they had done came home to him suddenly, with a jolt in his stomach. He inspected his men lovingly. They looked as yellow-white as tallow dips, but they had done it. They had set their noses into the sea fence because he had bade them to. That he had the golden ax to back him up didn't matter. Thor's hammer itself wouldn't have forced them if they hadn't trusted him.

A scrambling movement caught his eye: the *skraeling* woman, wriggling out from under the oar bench. She crouched, on hands and feet, eyeing the Norsemen to see if she should go back under or not.

"*Knut!*"

Knut got gingerly to his feet. "Aye, jarl?"

Haakon gave him a solemn law-court look. "Knut Aleksson, I have heard you claim this woman before a gathering of your shipmates. Thus, she is yours. What will you do with her now?"

Wren Singing knew enough Norse to know what the white chieftain asked. She scurried forward then halted respectfully a few paces from Knut, her copper-colored face alight with such obvious expectation that Haakon had to put a hand to his mouth to hide a grin. He tugged gravely at his mustache.

Knut thought it over. Truly she did not look so ill. A man should have sons to come after him. Something in him found that it could not make a thrall of that hopeful face. "Maybe it's time I was wed," he said gloomily.

Haakon abandoned his law-court face and laughed, rocking back and forth on his oar bench, as much in relief at a happy ending come out of the day's voyage as at Knut's morose announcement. "Maybe it is," he said. "Since you've found a woman who's fool enough to want you, you'd best take her. This one thinks you're a god— and that's more respect than a Norsewoman's husband gets!"

He looked eastward to the Irish shore. They would have to row—if they had any oars left unbroken. There was not a breath of wind. But it would be fine to see his own wife again and be peaceful for a while—*Only for a while, mind; I am an explorer,* he thought proudly—to hold his daughter and hear the small domestic news that warmed a man at his fireside.

"When they have done fighting my father, they will all fight each other," Rosamund said dismally. She was huddled by the morning cookfire, under the shadow of the walls, where a chance-shot arrow was less apt to fall. It was raining, and the cowhide awning propped over the cookfire drooped dejectedly. Leif and Fergus had been quarreling with each other all through yesterday, while Earl Edmund hammered at the walls. Conor, who was out there somewhere in the sopping woods waiting until he should see fit to attack the earl's rear, had quarreled with them both before he had left. Abbot Cormac had finally lost his temper and shouted at Conor that he was likely to lose the battle because of his pride. Conor had ridden out tight-lipped but silent finally, and Rosamund had thought that all was well. But if all was well, where was Conor now?

A wet shadow squelched through the rain and dropped down by the fire beside her. It was Svein, his hair plastered over his eyes and his small face more ratlike than usual. "He will come," Svein said defensively. Where Conor was, was the question everybody had been asking all night, Leif Hildisson louder than any. "He is only waiting for the English to get tired."

"I think he's right," Abbot Cormac said through a mouthful of the porridge that was their morning meal. "Not even Fergus will say that Conor ever broke an oath." He looked at Svein. "And what are you doing here, when you are supposed to be in the hall with the rest?"

"I am waiting for Conor," Svein said. "I am going to fight, and I have my knife. Conor *said* I could fight with him."

"Conor said—" Rosamund uttered faintly.

"When I am older," Svein admitted grudgingly. "But I think I will fight today anyway. I don't like the English."

"When I see Conor—"

Cormac put a hand on her arm. "Let be. If Conor MacLorne wants to take the child under his wing, it might be the saving of them both. I am thinking that it is a long time since either of them had anything to love."

"I am going to fight with Conor," Svein said doggedly, and Rosamund burst into a feeble giggle as she saw that the child wore no breeches—only his cloak and a shirt belted around his waist. Conor MacLorne dressed so, and so would his new disciple.

"If he has given up his trousers for him, I suppose it is past hope," Rosamund said as Svein disappeared into the rain again with a bowl of porridge. He had been fed once in the hall, but he was always hungry. She leaned her head against Cormac's shoulder for a moment. "Father, I am so tired."

He tightened his arm around her and spoke softly into the fire. "'If I shall walk in the midst of tribulation, Thou wilt quicken me, O Lord; and Thou wilt stretch forth Thy hand against the wrath of my enemies, and Thy right hand will save me!'"

An hour later, Earl Edmund attacked again.

"Get down from this catwalk before I throw you off!" Fergus grabbed Rosamund's wrists and shoved her toward the ladder. All around them, her father's men, their own ladders pushed against the walls, were swarming over. Below, the gates shook dangerously.

"Conor!" Rosamund gasped. "Can you see him?"

"Not yet. He'll come, I tell you! Now get down!"

She half slid down the ladder, flinching as a body, spraying blood from a severed artery, dropped past her. There was fighting in the central court now. They would have to open the gates and go out to meet the rest, or the English would take the battle too near to the children in the hall. It was almost impossible to set fire to a turf-roofed building in the rain, she thought, grateful for that. "We can't wait!" she yelled up at Fergus. "We have to go out to them!"

"Get inside!" Fergus screamed back, but he gave the signal. The ragtag army in the courtyard massed for the charge through the gates: Norse and Irish, those of Cormac's folk who were willing to fight and capable of it, even the eldest of the children. Rosamund saw Njal with his stolen sword and Brother Gilbert with a bow. Svein darted between them, and Njal made a grab for his collar but missed. Svein disappeared into the press of warriors about the gate. *They shouldn't be here*, Rosamund thought. *Monks and children—it should not have come to this*. That *she* should go back into the hall herself, she didn't stop to think on; Norse and Irish would fight as one only so long as she was there. She was the sole person in Ole's Hold whom both would follow—that was what she had told Fergus, but the truth was that this was *her* hold, *her* folk; she wouldn't take refuge in the hall while Leif and Fergus, or even Cormac, bore the burden of that.

A horn sang out, sharp and clear as the chapel bells—Conor! Rosamund strained to catch the sound again above the shouting and curses of the battle and through the sick smell of blood and vomit, which not even the rain could dampen. She ran, slipping in the mud, to the gates, and Fergus dropped down beside her.

"Did I not tell you?" His blue eyes gleamed under the winging black brows and the shadow of his helm. "The Ui Neill do not break oaths." Rosamund thought that that was less than true, and Fergus and Conor would be at each other's throats as soon as they crossed the bridge into Dunnaill again, but for now their *tuath* honor demanded truce.

"Lady Rosamund!" Tordis appeared at her elbow, her shawl wrapped over her head.

"Mother of God, not you too!" Fergus shouted. There were women underfoot everywhere. "Get *inside*, and take your mistress with you!"

"No!" Rosamund shouted back.

"And what will happen to the babe," Tordis demanded, "if you get your silly self killed? A fine set of wet nurses that abbot's holy ladies will make!"

"Oh!" Rosamund put a hand to her mouth, turned a panicked face toward Tordis, and fled into the hall. Fergus stared after her, bemused.

"Don't fret yourself, Lord Fergus," Tordis said kindly. "It is only knowing the right way to persuade her."

"Clear the gates!" A pot of hot pitch, laboriously hauled to the catwalk, poured down on the Englishmen with the ram. They dropped it, howling, as the gates swung open and the defenders poured out to meet them. Wilfrid, drawn back with the main army while the foot fighters tried to breach the walls, whooped gleefully at the sight. He kicked his mount into a gallop, lance at the ready. Earl Edmund, an older campaigner, spun his horse around to scan the riverbank behind them.

"She wasn't lying," Theofric gasped. All through the trees on the near side of the river, horsemen were pouring, under a white banner splashed with a crimson cross and the blue lion of Dunnaill.

Wilfrid aimed his war-horse at the men who were charging through the gates. His lance drove through a shield and into a Norseman's chest, but he never pulled it out again. An Irish arrow sank into his back, and he toppled onto the dead Norseman, his eyes widened in surprise. His horse, bereft of its master's reassuring weight, wheeled and tried to push its way back through the massed ranks of the English. The earl's men were fighting on both sides now, with the defenders of Ole's Hold on their front and Conor's men driving into their rear.

The Norsemen came through the gates first, armed

with ax and spear and sword, fighting with the savagery
that both English and Irish had learned to fear. Fergus's
riders spread out behind them, wheeling around to come
at the English flanks. In the outer court as the gates
closed, the reserves, monks, and children waited for any
English that might still come over the walls. Most of the
earl's men had dropped their ladders as the Norse came
out, thinking that when they had slaughtered those defenders
who had been so foolish as to abandon their haven, they
could then go in as they chose and deal with what was left
inside. Edmund's men licked their lips and grinned: There
were women in there, and silver. Then slowly those in the
English front lines became aware that they were being
pushed from the rear. In the chaos of the battle, they
could not tell why, but they began to know that something
had gone wrong. In the rear, where Conor's riders fell
upon them, the English knew all too well.

Conor MacLorne, pulling a bloody spear from an
English throat, saw that his men and Fergus's and Leif's
were slowly driving the earl's men into a ball at the base of
the northern wall. He wheeled his horse northward, with
a score of riders behind him before the English could
wrench themselves away from the wall and scatter. Ten
paces away, an English war-horse went down with a shriek,
and Conor saw a small, dim figure flit through the rain,
with a knife in its hand. Another English horse dropped,
hamstrung, but this time the rider threw himself clear.
The Englishman lurched through the mud, sword swinging. The child with the knife dodged, slipped, and went
down. *Svein*. Conor dragged his horse's head around in
midstride as the Englishman and the child rolled together
in mud, which had been churned to swampy muck. Conor
drove his spear throught the Englishman's back, leaned
down, and dragged the child up into the saddle with him.

"I killed him," Svein said with satisfaction.

"You did not. You're lucky I came by."

"I *did*," Svein insisted, tight-lipped. "Roll him over."

Conor wrenched his spear out of the body and flipped
it over with the blade. Svein's knife was hilt-deep in the
throat. "Hah! Maybe you did then." He became aware of
warm blood running down his arm, warmer than the rain.

There was a sword cut over the boy's ribs, and his eyes were beginning to turn up in his white face. "You little fool!" Conor spun his horse wide of the melee and kicked it into a gallop. There was still fighting near the gates, and he circled the hold walls until he came to the narrow gate at the rear, wide enough for no more than two men abreast. It was bolted, and he hammered at it, yelling, until one of the women, recognizing him, came and pulled it open. He kicked his horse past her and through the door of the main hall itself. The holy folk inside looked up and shrieked at this mounted, blood-soaked apparition.

"Here." Conor handed the child down gently, but the wolf-look in his face was more marked than usual. "If he isn't seen to properly, I'll be coming back for the one who let him die."

Slowly the English lines crumbled in on themselves. There was more blood than rain in the air, Cormac thought, and prayed as he fought that the earl would cry for quarter. But he would not. It was beyond him to ask mercy of the Norse or the Irish or, what would be still more bitter, of his daughter. The son for whom he had thought to take this land was dead, but he fought on grimly with Theofric beside him and the red-cat banner, now ragged and bloody, over his head.

Athelwulf lay behind them in the meadow somewhere, with his head split open by a Norse ax and his bright hair turning sodden with blood. Oswain had been wounded, and whether he lived or died, no one knew. Once Theofric had urged the earl to ask quarter, but only once. There would be no place for him at Ram's Head after if he forced Earl Edmund to a peace he didn't choose. This was the earl's war, and Theofric was the earl's man. He fought on wearily while the rain sheeted down around them and the dead of both sides grew.

"There are two choices, Rose of the World. Two only." Fergus knelt by Rosamund's chair in the hall, dripping rain and blood. A piece of rag was tied around his thigh, but the blood kept dripping from under it. "There will be no surrender—we have offered and been spat at. We can try to take your father alive if you wish, but it will cost us men."

More men, Rosamund thought, with so many dead already. And she hiding in the hall here, torn between her babe and her people.

"Or?" She knew the answer already.

"Or we can rush them, with all the men we have. Your father's folk will all be killed, very likely, but there will be more of us left standing at the end." He watched her sympathetically. Not so easy a thing to order your father to death, but the old man hadn't left her a choice.

Rosamund took a deep breath. *No more to die, please God. No more monks and children.* No more of her husband's men or his Irish kin. She would rather have Fergus MacAidan left alive than her father, she acknowledged, and surely that was sinful, but all that had happened Earl Edmund had brought on himself. She steadied her hands, cradling the baby to hide their shaking, and looked Fergus in the eye. "Do what will cost us the least men dead."

The Norse and the Irish hurled themselves into one last charge and battered the English to death under that unyielding wall. When it was over they found the earl with Theofric beside him and the torn red-cat banner fallen across them both.

Only a handful had lived to flee, and Cormac bade the Norse and Irish to let them go. They straggled aboard one of the two ships they had come in, carrying Oswain between them on a litter. He would be lord of the Ram's Head now if he lived. In a final gesture of spite, they sank the second ship behind them.

Rosamund put the baby in Bergthora's lap and went out to look at what her father had left behind him. All dead. So many dead. The Norse were piling the English bodies into a heap, but out of respect for their lady they had laid Earl Edmund and his younger son apart from the rest.

Rosamund stood over them for a long while. Already the birds had begun to circle overhead, drawn like a lodestone by death. She had had no love for her father, ever, for so long as she could remember. Even now she could feel only guilt for having hated him so. She looked at Cormac, standing beside her. "Say a mass for them, Father. They are going to need it." Her voice was strained and

weary. She looked at the piled English dead.* "And find
Theofric. He was my father's man. He should lie with him
now." The smell of death was insistent, everywhere. It closed
around her like a cloud and no longer seemed to be worth
denying. Her knees buckled, and she dropped in the mud.

Cormac bent down to pick her up and bore her into
the hall. She was heavy, he found, surprised. Maybe it was
only his own weariness, or maybe the weight of the guilt
she bore. He laid her down on her bed and sighed. Or
maybe it was only his own guilt, for having killed today.
He drew the furs up over her and went to tell Tordis that
when the wounded had been seen to, she should go and
sit by her mistress.

The hall was nearly as full of folk as it had been before
the battle. The monks and holy women were tending the
wounded, and Leif Hildisson came limping by to give
Cormac a thumbs-up sign. The dead and wounded were
not so great as they had feared at first, far less than the
English dead. Conor MacLorne was talking in a low voice
to little Svein, who looked as if he would live, and Fergus
was gritting his teeth while Fann cleaned out his wound.
In healer's guise, she seemed unconcerned that his man-
hood was practically under her nose. Her nun's robes
were a refuge, a cell in which to hide her mind and set
those matters at a distance. Cormac sighed again. He
wished he knew if that girl's call to the religious life had
been a true one or only bred of her terror of marriage.
Still, it was done now, and *he* had let her do it, so there
was no going back. She had been so frightened that he
hadn't found it in him to turn her away. But she was
certainly devout, and better a nun than an unhappy wife,
for her and her Scotsman both.

Outside the rain had ceased to fall, and the sun
washed palely over the open graves. The Norse dead were
laid together on a pyre, and Leif Hildisson would do
whatever their beliefs demanded. Cormac was left with
the Irish and their English slayers to send to God. And
when he had done, he would say another mass, he thought,
for Lady Rosamund and for the peace of her troubled soul.
If the Norse jarl Haakon didn't know how fine a wife he
was blessed with, Abbot Cormac had it in his mind to tell

him so when he should sail home. He bowed his head
above the earl's cold face. "O God, who alone art ever
merciful and sparing of punishment, humbly we pray Thee
in behalf of the soul of Thy servant Edmund, whom Thou
hast commanded to go forth today from this world. Do not
hand him over to the power of the Enemy and do not
forget him forever. . . ."

Nor the souls of our Irish dead, O Lord. Abbot
Cormac spread his hands to them all and spoke the sure,
familiar words of promise: *"Ego sum resurrectio et vita . . ."*
I am the resurrection and the life; he who believes in
me, even if he die, shall live. . . .

Epilogue: Homing

"By Frigg who blesses marriages, by Frey and Freya
who make them fruitful, and by Thor who has brought us
here in safety, I, Haakon Olesson, master of the *Raven*,
now swear to the marriage of Knut Aleksson and the
woman of the red-skinned folk, whose name among her
own kind means Wren Singing." Haakon beamed at the
bridal couple with the air of a benevolent uncle blessing
the nuptials of a favored niece. Everyone else shouted
loud advice as to what Knut and his bride should do next.
They were all a little drunk, as celebrants at a Norse
wedding tended to be. What might be the bridal customs of
Wren Singing's own people, no one knew, but she seemed
happy enough to be wedded to Knut in any fashion he
should choose. With Ireland's shore in their sight, the men
who yesterday had wanted to give her to Father Odin now
fell over themselves to attest to the validity of the marriage,
and an air of drunken forgiveness prevailed.

In long, rambling speeches, in which the speaker
frequently forgot where he was and had to begin again, they
attested to the sum and kind of the bride-gift and morning-
gift, to Knut's waiver of dowry rights, to his previous free
and unwedded state, and to anything else that might be
called into question later. A Norse widow inherited only
what she had brought to the marriage in the beginning or
been given in formal gift by her husband. If there were no

children, all other property would go to Knut's kin. The bride-gift and morning-gift were provisions for Wren Singing's widowhood and as such were most important.

Knut, having decided to do the thing, had grown protective. "Likely some of our folk won't take to her at the first," he had said, in what Haakon thought was probably an understatement. "Best I not bring her home till we're wed." The Norse were not known for their kindness to strangers. Rosamund had worked the better part of a year for acceptance among her husband's people, and Rosamund was English, closer kin to the Norse than this red-skinned woman with only a deerskin skirt for clothing.

"Best you also give her a shirt to wear," Haakon said mildly.

Now the bridal couple stood before him, Knut looking drunkenly pleased with himself, and Wren Singing somewhat incongrously clad in her deerskin skirt and leggings, with a voluminous woolen shirt of Knut's over all like a tent. Donal MacRae came up, very bright eyed, and danced her around the deck to show his approval of the affair, while Thorfinn Solvisson and Hjalmar Sitricsson began a bawdy song that had to do with the difficulties of an aged groom on his wedding night. They had taken one of the cattle out of the hold for an offering to the gods, and to make a wedding feast, and since it was no easy matter to butcher a cow on a ship's deck, even in calm waters, the desk was now awash in blood and odd, revolting scraps, and full of sea gulls. Hagar the Simple and Snorri Longfoot were attempting to cook the meat, beating the sea gulls away from it, and Haakon hoped they didn't set the ship on fire.

When Donal had set her down again, Wren Singing came to Haakon, out of breath and looking shy, and said, "Wish to...thank...white chief for marry and for—" she gave the remains of the cow a doubtful look "—and for food."

Haakon rocked back a little on his heels, beaming, playing the jarl and enjoying himself. Wren Singing rummaged in the pouch that hung at her waist. She pulled out a cake of some indeterminate composition and gave it to him proudly. Haakon inspected it. It appeared to be composed mainly of brownish fat, with berries in it. It smelled of deer meat.

"Food," Wren Singing said. "Food for journey. Man can eat for—" Forgetting the word, she held up three fingers "—so many days. Keep long time."

Haakon nibbled the edge of it cautiously. It was none so bad. He thought it was mostly dried deer meat.

"Can teach . . . white chief's women to make," Wren Singing said. She looked dubious. "If they . . . will learn from me."

"They had better," Haakon said, impressed. Without a doubt, it was the strangest bride-making he had ever attended.

With Ireland in their sight, *Raven's* crew recklessly squandered the last of everything, gulping down the cow's meat nearly raw and washing it along with the last of the ale. Knut, knowing what was coming, tried to lie low with his bride, but they would have none of it. They found them and bundled them with much suggestive ceremony into the hold, where someone had made up a bed in the stall belonging to the deceased cow. They tactfully pulled the cover over the hold and then sat just above it, singing rude songs until they all went to sleep.

In the morning everyone had a bad head. What had happened in the hold, only the cow in the next stall could say, but Knut looked smug and Wren Singing worshipful enough to set the jokes going round again as *Raven* nosed her way up the mouth of the Bann. They had been womanless too long to suit them, and plainly Knut's wedding night had put an itch in his fellow adventurers. Haakon thought, grinning, that as soon as they could, they would spin fine tales of their bravery, with one hand around an ale horn and the other down some maid's shift. He had some such intention himself.

"The jarl! The jarl has come home!" Tordis picked her skirts up and ran shrieking gleefully through the courtyard. Heads popped through doorways, and in a minute the meadow was full of the folk of Ole's Hold, streaming through the thick grass to the riverside. They waited, pushing and shoving for a better view, as *Raven* came proudly upriver, red oars splashing in the sun and the raven sail spread full. The black head reared gracefully over the water, gold beak gleaming.

Abbot Cormac looked at Fergus MacAidan. "I told you to go home."

"'Tis no sin to hope," Fergus said, but he looked as if he saw small reason to. The faces on *Raven*'s deck were too jovial to be bearing the jarl's dead body among them. He brightened. "There will be a fine feast then, at any rate."

Haakon, shifting from foot to foot impatiently in the prow, inspected his welcoming committee with a growing curiosity overlaid with foreboding. He saw, with a quick catch at his heart, that Rosamund held an infant in her arms, but the unexpected joy of that was tempered by the sensation that he stood just to the left of a volcano, in the form of Donal MacRae, that would suddenly go off with a bang when it saw what Haakon saw: Fann, wearing a drearily pious expression and a shapeless gray gown with a cross that was big enough to sit on at her waist. Rosamund, he noted, when she wasn't watching himself, was also eyeing Donal. Thor blast the woman, he thought explosively. Haakon would as soon have seen Donal wed to a beached fish as that wearisome woman, but Thor blast her anyway for spoiling Donal's homecoming. Another face, unpleasantly like his own, intruded on his gaze. Haakon abandoned the question of Fann to ponder what Fergus MacAidan was doing there, when Raven struck the shallows and beached herself with a jar. The tableau on the riverbank broke up into a milling crowd of welcomers and laughing men splashing their way to shore. Leif Hildisson and his men waded out to help haul *Raven* higher on the bank, and Haakon pulled his wife into his arms, having a care for her unexpected burden.

"What is it?" he demanded when he had kissed her.

"It's a baby," Rosamund giggled. "What does it look like, a pig?"

"Is it a boy or a girl, fool?" He grinned at her.

"It's a boy. Ole Haakonsson." She kissed him again, her arm tight around his neck. "Oh, I am glad to have you home. Pick up Asa," she added. "She's jealous."

Haakon scooped up his daughter, who had been tugging violently at his belt. He and Rosamund beamed at each other for a moment, oblivious to the rest, content in one another's company. A wet nose prodded him in the small of his back, and he turned to find Wulf panting at him happily, tongue lolling.

"He's proud of himself," Rosamund informed him solemnly. "He is a father, too. I got a fine wolfhound bitch from Fergus MacAidan."

"And what is Fergus MacAidan doing—" Haakon began, then stopped, watching uneasily as he saw that Donal had taken note of Fann.

A little circle of emptiness formed around them as Donal's shipmates and the Ole's Hold folk drew back to see what would happen now. "Oh, dear," Rosamund whispered.

Donal and Fann talked inaudibly for a moment, neither one moving, while Haakon wondered if Donal would try to kill Abbot Cormac or Fann or just anyone handy. Then, surprisingly, Donal kissed her on the top of her head and walked away. No one was so lost to good sense as to follow him. In another moment he had disappeared into the wood.

Sure of his refuge, Donal slumped down against a tree and stared at the rotting leaves under his feet. He prodded them moodily with a wet boot. He had never thought *not* to marry Fann. They had been handfasted in childhood. She had been afraid of him since the Danes had captured and molested her, but he had assumed that time would mend it. Wrong, maybe. And himself? He poked at the leaf mold some more, trying to decide if he was grieving or only insulted. If he had wanted to wed her so badly, would he not have stayed in Ireland then, and insisted, and not gone adventuring with Haakon? What kind of wife would Fann have made, afraid of him always? Better she should be Christ's bride, he thought glumly, if she went in such a terror at being his. Christ would have no designs on her body, being content with her soul. There was a touch of blasphemy in that, he thought, and crossed himself. He took his harp out of the bag on his back, with the saints' lives neatly stitched across it. Always the harp had been his solace. More solace than Fann, who had sought relentlessly to make him holy too, which was a thing that doubtless could not be done, not to her standards.

Donal settled himself against his tree and began to play, only a little wistfully.

Haakon and Rosamund looked at each other, and then at the wood from whence issued the harp song. Haakon let out a breath of relief and grinned at her. "A happy ending," he said gleefully, "for all but your Christ god, who has that dreary woman to burden him now."

All around them Haakon's crew were recounting their adventures in high good spirits to anyone who would listen. Knut One-Eye appeared with a woman the color of Rosamund's best copper pot and, while Rosamund stood blinking in disbelief, presented her as his wife.

Rosamund gave Haakon a look of wide-eyed surprise. "It was there—your new land?"

Haakon threw back his head and laughed. "Aye, it was there! Heart of my heart, we have had adventures such as men will sing of when we are a thousand years gone!"

"Your shirt, jarl!" someone yelled. "Take off your shirt!"

"A *kraken,* big as the ship, it was!"

They pulled Haakon's shirt over his head, despite his protests, and exhibited him proudly. Rosamund put a hand over her mouth when she saw the ringed scars that scored his back. Haakon tried to look modest as they told the tale of the battle with the *kraken,* each man trying to outshout the rest, but she could see by the look in his eye that he wished now that he had kept the thing's arm.

But it was when Haakon began to talk of his new land that she saw truly what this voyaging had been. A promise fulfilled, a yearning sated . . . more than that, a necessity like food and drink and air. Never would he have been happy if he had not gone. Now he looked boyishly boastful, but he had a right to it. The last twinge of resentment that he had sailed away and left her alone to fight her father faded and left her lighthearted. He had also a right not to have his homecoming dimmed by an old bitterness. Ole's Hold was in good repair, the marks of battle patched over. She turned to find Fergus MacAidan at her shoulder and hissed at him, "Go away!"

Fergus opened his mouth to protest, but Abbot Cormac pulled him bodily into the crowd. There would be time enough later to explain Fergus's presence, the English grave mounds, and the missing men, whom Haakon would notice soon enough. The women had seen Knut's peculiar bride and were staring at her malevolently, like a ring of cats. Rosamund pulled the woman to her side. "Bid you welcome, Sister," she said, wondering if the woman could understand. She gave her maids a look that *they* could understand.

"Bid them keep their claws sheathed, kind heart," Haakon said, laughing, "or Knut will clip them for them." He sighed, expansively content. Fergus MacAidan seemed to have vanished at Rosamund's behest. Haakon could ask later what his cousin had been doing here. He pulled the blanket back and inspected his son again. The baby had a cap of pale gold hair like wheat straw and his thumb in his mouth. Asa wriggled in her father's arms. Uncle Cormac had told her that God had sent her a little brother as a kindness, but she was inclined to view this favor ungratefully. Haakon chuckled and kissed her. "I am hungry," he announced. "And I wish to eat anything but salt fish." He gave an eye to the neatly tilled fields and the emerald roofs of the buildings beyond the open gate. "It looks fine. You have a housewife's hand. There has been no trouble, I suppose?"

Haakon thought that Rosamund had a choked look, but she said demurely, "No, as you can see, we are very peaceful here."

"Ah? That is good. I will tell you our adventures then, when we have eaten. But I was right, sweet, to have left you safe here."

"Yes, Rosamund said hastily, "there must be a feast— most certainly."

She fled, taking the *skraeling* woman with her, and Haakon saw that Cormac had reappeared. Haakon put a hand on the abbot's shoulder. "I am missing something, Priest," he suggested. "Do you start explaining."

Haakon sat at the high table in the hall that had once been his father's and watched his men feasting with such of Fergus MacAidan's Irish as were still there. Half of the Norse had fought shoulder to shoulder with the Irish, and there was a kinship of sorts between them now. The thin, slightly lame boy Njal was among them, happy now, a warrior among warriors. *I shall have to take him wth me*, Haakon thought. *Cormac is right*. He had wrested the story from Abbot Cormac, having no wish to discomfit his wife. She so plainly wished this night to be his triumph, but he looked at her with a different eye now. Under his love's kind heart was the strength that had been her blackhearted father's. There would be no more talk of leaving her to bide safe somewhere when next he sailed, not if he wasn't wishful to be laughed at from here to Iceland. He leaned over and kissed her ear, and she giggled, a little drunk too, he thought. Everyone was, on the high adventure of the past season as much as the ale. Haakon noted that Fergus MacAidan and Donal, both thwarted in love, were drowning their sorrows together, and he was inclined to be amused. Abbot Cormac had told Haakon about Fergus too, since Fergus had made his attentions to Haakon's wife plain enough for everyone else in Ole's Hold to be aware of them, but Haakon's inclination to tear him limb from limb was fading with the ale and with the fact that Rosamund so obviously preferred his own fine self.

Also, he owed the man a blood-debt. Without Fergus, Haakon would have lost Ole's Hold and Rosamund both. His inconvenient sense of justice made him incapable of denying that. Fergus still bore the mark of a healing thigh wound under the hem of his shirt; the scar glared red and angry in the firelight where Fergus sat with his long legs stretched out from the bench, head to head with Donal MacRae, in whom he appeared to have found a kindred soul. They were singing some mournful dirge in Gaelic, and both looked as if they might fall down. Haakon studied Fergus's face with a brief, unsettling sensation of having caught sight of his own wraith in a mirror. Whether Rosamund would have had Fergus if Haakon had died was a question that Haakon decided was better left unasked. He had not died, so that was that. All the same, he felt himself growing disinclined to leave her in Ireland another season, with himself gone elsewhere. He leaned over and whispered in her ear, growing pleased with the notion that had taken him: "Have you still a taste to go adventuring, Wife?"

Glossary

Aesir: The collective name of the Norse family of male and female gods, some of whose chief figures were fertility dieties

Asgard: Celestial home of the Scandinavian gods

Carl: A commoner

Curragh: A boat peculiar to Ireland, constructed of animal skins attached to a nearly circular wicker frame

Fine: The male members of an Irish princely household

Hel: The underworld home of the spirits of men who had died in their beds, as distinguished from Valhalla, the home of heroes slain in battle

Jarl: Tribal chieftain

Knarr: Broad-beamed ship, deep in the water, with a high freeboard

Norns: Deities who tended men's destinies

Ragnarok In Scandinavian mythology, the day of destruction of the universe

Runes: Characters of the Norse alphabet

Skald: An ancient Scandinavian poet or bard

Spaewife: Female fortune-teller or witch

Thing: Northern assembly of free men for law, debate, and matters of regional importance

Thor: In Norse mythology, the Aesir god of thunder, second in importance to his father, Odin

Thrall: A member of the lowest social class; a slave to a master or lord as a result of capture or an accident of birth

Weregild: A value set by law upon the life of a man, in accordance with a fixed scale. Paid as compensation to kindred or to the lord of a slain person

DON'T MISS
THESE CURRENT
Bantam Bestsellers